THE DEVIL'S PLAYGROUND

Book 2

Deborah Albers

Thrive! Publishing

To Brendan and Keira – in memory of your mom

A portion of the proceeds from this book will be donated to National Domestic Violence Hotline, PO Box 90249, Austin, TX 78709

TRIGGER WARNING

Everyone deserves to read a book safely. This book has brief references to domestic violence, suicide, rape, and murder. Please be emotionally ready before reading this book if these topics make you uncomfortable. If you have thoughts of suicide, please contact the Suicide Hotline in the United States by dialing 988 (like 911 for mental health crises) or your local helpline. If you are the victim of domestic violence, seek help by calling 800-799-7233

PROLOGUE

When I wrote book one, it was partly to honor friends, family, and colleagues who had passed away. It was also helpful for me to process the loss I felt for each of them, and the evolution of the tale was therapy. I could give each of them a story, and in some way, a life.

There was a larger story that I wanted to tell, unrelated to the characters in the first book. A story about good and evil, right and wrong. A question about stepping in or standing by.

This is the second book in the trilogy. It takes some of the characters in Escape from St. David's and puts them into much more uncomfortable situations. The friction forces them to make tough decisions and challenges them to choose a side, where each decision has consequences. Wylder, and those she meets along the way, must recruit other souls for the epic battle that is coming between good and evil, between God and the Devil.

If there is a Heaven, there must be a Hell, right?

BEGINNING

Greg sat in St. David's Cemetery, bound by the stone walls. He was, of course, here because of what he had done not that long ago. If he were faced with the decision again, he would make the same choice today. Sending his wife to Heaven was worth the price of sitting here, alone, for eternity.

Greg found some comfort in knowing that all the souls in St. David's had passed through the gateway and made it to Heaven. All but him. To pass the time, Greg would eavesdrop on the conversations of the living who came to visit their loved ones at St. David's. Of course, they did not know the souls had moved on, so they poured out their hearts to the grave that was once occupied by the soul of someone they loved.

As time passed, the visitors got more desperate. Conversations in the past were joyous baby announcements, upcoming weddings, and family gossip. Now, adults cried and asked their parent's graves for guidance. Others mourned the passing of a child, finding some comfort that the children they loved had not seen what was becoming of the world. Young widows sat and told stories of hunger and poverty to the dirt below, angry to be left alone. The news spoke of slavery, forced sterilization, and mass shootings.

It seemed that in a relatively short time, there had been many unexplained accidents and unspeakable tragedies, each stacking on the one before until the result was that the whole world was falling to pieces. The effect was felt everywhere. The global economy had all but collapsed, the number of people out of work put too much pressure on the governments and social services to support the needs of society, the wealth that people spent their lives collecting was dissolving faster than it could be regained, and there was no leadership. The general feeling of hopelessness was evident in all the visitors to St. David's and probably at all cemeteries. Greg did not know about other cemeteries because he was trapped in St. David's with no way out. No way to help. He could only stand by and listen.

Maybe I am in Hell, after all, thought Greg.

CAN YOU
SEE ME?

When the construction started on New St. David's, a scruffy golden retriever with matted hair and fleas, walked up to the crew looking for food. The foreman shooed her away, but she returned time and time again despite the same response. When he threw a rock at her, she finally got the message, walked over to a rain puddle, and began to drink.

"Don't be a jerk," said one of the workers on the crew. "She's just a dog looking for food; no need to throw things at her."

"Don't be a girl," he said, "she's just a dog. Get back to work," said the foreman.

The woman looked at the dog, and satisfied that she was not hurt, went back to work with the rest of the crew.

Greg looked at the dog with sadness, "I wish I had something to feed you," he said.

The dirty dog walked over and looked at him.

"Can you see me?" Greg asked.

The dog just laid down by his side and fell asleep.

"Well, I'll be a monkey's uncle," Greg said to the dog, but she just slept.

When the construction had finished for the day, Greg noticed a small figure in the setting sun, putting a half-eaten sandwich on the ground. After the young woman had walked away, he went over to the food and tried to pick it up.

Ghosts can't pick up things, he reminded himself.

"Hey girl, hi, can you hear me?" Greg said to the dog.

She lifted her head and looked around. Upon seeing Greg, she stood up and slowly walked towards him.

"Look, here," Greg said to her, pointing to the sandwich. "I think someone left this for you."

The dog walked closer and gently picked up the sandwich, carrying it, like a puppy, back to where she was sitting. She ate the sandwich and fell back to sleep.

When the moon was full, Greg sat on the stone benches and remembered the clash that took place here between Mama and Wylder.

Greg contemplated the slavery that had

gripped the country long ago and the wounds it left that are still felt today. The clash between Mama and Wylder went far beyond what had transpired in their short relationship; it went back before either of them was born and lasted long after they both had died. It took an unexpected act of love to break through the wall that divided them.

"Hey girl," said Greg to the dog, who walked up and then dropped to the ground at his feet.

"Are you okay?" Greg asked, helpless.

The dog just put her chin on her paws and fell asleep.

The next day when the construction crew came back, the sun was shining, and the frame of a building was going up.

"What do you think that will be, girl?" Greg asked the sleeping dog.

He could see the clouds forming on the horizon and was not surprised when the rain started to fall. The crew was more than happy to call the job to a halt due to the weather. When the lightning started, they ran to the work truck. The young woman Greg had seen yesterday walked over to the eight open lunchboxes on the ground and saw the dog behind a headstone. She knelt down and spoke softly to the scruffy dog.

"Are you okay?" she asked, concerned.

The foreman had loaded the truck with the

lumber and was ready to go. Workers, covering their heads from the rain, jumped on the back.

"Get a move on, Summer," yelled the foreman to the young woman.

"I'll be back tomorrow," Summer whispered to the dog, leaving behind all eight lunch boxes. She turned to run for the truck that was driving away.

Greg walked over to the boxes on the ground and called to the dog with excitement. "Hey girl, it's your lucky day!"

The dog just sat there, chin on her paws, eyes droopy.

"Hey girl, come over here and eat. You'll feel better," said Greg as he walked back to the sleeping dog. "Girl? Come on; there is food for you now. Come on, I'll show you."

The dog got up and walked a few steps to Greg, laid back down, and closed her eyes.

"No, no, no," Greg said as he sat beside the dog. "I can't bring the food to you; you have to come get it. Please, come get it," he said, with desperation in his voice.

The dog tried again. She stood, took a few steps, and then sat back down with a little more of a thud this time.

"You're doing great! Try again," said Greg, but she was asleep.

It took most of the night, but as the sun began to rise, Greg had finally coaxed the tired dog over 100 feet to the food, and she was eating a little. The rain had left many puddles, and she could drink without moving very far.

"Ok, girl, we need to move this food to a safe place, so you have it for later." He stood and walked behind a high headstone towards the back of the cemetery shaded by a small tree. "Over here, girl. Bring the food over here."

With a little more strength now, the dog stood and picked up the closest thing she saw, a bag of extra cheddar Doritos, and carried it behind the headstone. Greg encouraged her to make another trip, and she returned with a zip lock bag of beef jerky. Four more trips resulted in a ham sandwich, peanut butter crackers, apple sauce, and four granola bars. The exhausted dog laid down at Greg's feet. "One more trip, girl. Can you make one more trip?" Greg asked.

He walked over and pointed to a peanut butter and jelly sandwich in a soggy plastic bag from the rain. When the dog picked it up, he walked back to the stone benches, and the dog followed. As the construction crew pulled up, she was eating the soggy sandwich.

Greg felt satisfied that the dog had eaten and hoped she would feel better soon. The next day when the crew left the cemetery, the dog got up and sniffed around when the men and women had stopped for lunch. The dog found some jellybeans, the crust of a sandwich, and three oatmeal cookies which she promptly ate.

"You're eating now, girl. Are you feeling better?" Greg asked.

The dog let out a weak bark, which Greg took to mean *yes, I am feeling a little better*.

As the dog slept at Greg's feet, he noticed a daisy by her face and remembered how much Jan had liked daisies. "I think I will call you Daisy," Greg said. The dog opened her eyes just a bit and used her paws to crawl two inches closer to Greg, then replaced her chin on her paws and fell back asleep.

Daisy, it is.

DAISY AND SUMMER

The following day was a Saturday, and the construction crew did not come to St. David's. Greg sat with Daisy and encouraged her to eat and drink and rest, which she did. By Monday morning, she was feeling better and walking around, sniffing the ground, and doing her business which seemed like a good thing to Greg.

When the crew arrived on Monday, they brought a huge metal archway on the back of a flatbed truck. The crew took sledgehammers to a portion of the brick wall that surrounded St. David's and hauled away the broken stones. After resurfacing the broken edges into smooth, flat frames, they erected the archway, and now there was an entrance from Old St. David's to the New St David's.

Over the coming weeks, they poured a cement slab large enough to build a house. Six stone columns supported a steel roof. One of the workers erected a sign near the cemetery entrance that reads OLD ST. DAVID'S, with an arrow to the left. Under that was another sign that read, NEW ST. DAVID's, with an arrow to the right. At the bottom of the marker was a small post that read Committal Service Shelter, also with an arrow to the right. When visitors followed the signs to the shelter, they would see a pavilion set back against the trees and vegetation. The intentional location of this pavilion was in a beautiful and quiet place, sheltered from the elements. It appeared that the space was not intended to be a focal point of the new cemetery. It was isolated and blended in with the background.

As they worked, Daisy began to look forward to the crew coming in the mornings and watching them, from a safe distance. When people would visit their deceased loved ones at Old St. David's, Greg would walk over to listen to the conversations. Over the passing months, the whole crew would throw pieces of their lunch toward Daisy, trying to coax her out, but she would wait until they were at a safe distance to pick up the treasure.

The one exception was the young woman with colorful tattoos down both arms and a short military haircut. She had brought Daisy something special each day. Today she opened a brand-new jar of creamy peanut butter and took out a big scoop, setting it on the green grass. It was the end of the day, and the foreman yelled at the young woman, "Come on, Summer, get a move on. It's time to go."

Summer ignored the man and sat down on the grass near the uneaten peanut and butter and tried to persuade Daisy to come to her. "Hi there pup, are you all alone out here?" she asked Daisy. "Do you want to come home with me?"

Greg was standing by his four-legged friend and said to her, "Daisy, go with her. She will be good to you and give you a home." Daisy looked at Greg and then at Summer.

"I have a little apartment," said Summer, "it's not big, but it's nice. I live there by myself, and you could stay there too. I have lots of peanut butter. I would take you for walks, and you could meet my neighbor, Ms. Miller. She would love you. She loves golden retrievers. She would feed you all kinds of human food."

Daisy stood up, and Summer smiled. Summer scooted a little closer to the dog when she heard her name called loudly, which startled the dog.

"Summer! If you want a ride back, you'd better hurry up!" yelled the foreman from the truck, engine running.

"Come on, girl, do you want to come with me?" she asked again.

Daisy looked at Greg. "Go Daisy, you should go," he said, "She will take good care of you."

Slowly Daisy walked closer to Summer, who held out her hand with chipped black nail polish for Daisy to sniff. When Daisy was satisfied that she was a friend and not foe, she let Summer pet her. Summer stood and called the dog. "Come on, let's go home. I'll think of a name for you." She walked towards the truck with the engine running and opened the tailgate. Daisy jumped in, Summer climbed up next to the dog and pounded her hand on the outside of the truck to indicate she was ready to go. Daisy looked at Greg and barked once. Greg waved. They watched each other until the truck was out of sight.

Greg hoped he would see her on Monday when the crew returned to work, but as he turned around, he realized they had installed a big metal gate and a sign that said New St. David's Cemetery. They were not coming back; the cemetery was finished.

EXPLORING THE NEW CEMETERY

Greg stood in front of the archway that led to the new section of St. David's, struggling with the idea of crossing the threshold.

What if I can't cross into New St. David's? Or what if I can, but I cannot come back? I might not be able to return to where I rest for eternity with my beloved Jan. On the other hand, I know Jan is not there anymore, so why not try to cross into New St. David's and see what happens? If I go, eventually, I will meet some new arrivals, and I will have some company.

After considering the pros and cons, Greg closed his eyes and stepped over the threshold. Nothing happened, no slamming of the gate behind him, no deafening sound, no flash of light, and the ground did not shake. Greg opened his eyes; he was out of the cemetery. Surprised, he looked back into Old St. David's. He took one step, crossing the threshold, and without fanfare, he was back in Old St. David's.

Huh. OK, thought Greg.

With no discernable consequences for crossing over to New St. David's, Greg decided it was time to explore and set out to walk the grounds. It turned out to be a nice place; well designed, simple, and large enough to accommodate the small town for decades to come. The Committal Service Shelter Greg had seen them build from a distance had sharp corners and a cold iron roof, which gave it a bit of a military feel.

As he surveyed the grounds, he found that this was many times larger than the original St. David's. Deep in the back of this nearly four-acre burial site was a patch of shade trees. As he walked under the trees, he felt an unexpected pull that shocked him at first, and then he remembered the Silence that once existed in Old St. David's, that pulled souls to it like a current. If the soul let the pull take control, it would go to a place they named The Beyond. It was here that the soul had to get passed the big mistakes in life to be granted access to Heaven.

Greg gently resisted the pull at first, planting his feet like he did when he was fishing in a stream. After resisting the pull, he started to back up and the grip released with each step.

Greg stopped, *Why not go?* Thought Greg, *Maybe I can find Jan.*

Greg stepped forward again and let the force gently pull him. He saw the familiar blue twinkle, almost unnoticeable in the daylight. He reached for the spark, felt a surge like static electricity, then became the first soul to disappear from the new St. David's Cemetery into the Beyond.

NOBODY'S HOME

As they rode on the horse for the long ride to St. David's, Wylder talked most of the time, catching Jan up on all the ins and outs of the afterlife. She explained the three places a soul could be, starting with where they were laid to rest. This was usually a cemetery. Next was what they called the "Beyond", where souls washed away the mistakes of their life before death. And finally, "Heaven", where the soul was free.

"It's a complicated journey a soul takes after death," said Wylder, "A soul does not know they can go to Heaven when they first arrive, at least I didn't. Come to think of it, no one in St. David's knew. We were all bound to our resting place until we got too close to this thing, like a doorway or a gateway. It pulled the soul towards it. The gateway was in a part of the cemetery no one went to. We called it the "Dark Side" because tall, dense trees hid it while the rest of the cemetery was covered in sunlight and only a few trees lined the boundary walls."

"How did you meet Nala?" asked Jan.

"I would go to the stone benches in the center of St. David's, usually during a full moon. I always liked to ride my horse at night. My dad pretended not to notice when I snuck Blaine back in the barn at dawn," said Wylder, patting Blaine on the neck. "Nala would sneak out of the dark side when her mom wouldn't notice and come sit where she thought I wouldn't notice her. I guess she liked the full moon too. One day I spoke to her without looking at her. I think I surprised her because she ran away. Later, when she was hiding in the shadows, I tried again, and this time she came and sat next to me. She told me she snuck out to ride a horse, and I about fell off the bench. I was so excited."

"How did she find the gateway?" asked Jan.

"I never asked," said Wylder, "but all the people in that part of the cemetery knew about it, they just chose not to go through. We didn't know about it at all. Nala's community never came out to talk to those buried in the main part of the cemetery, and we never went to talk to them there.

"Is this gateway a one-way door?" asked Jan, "or can you go back through the gateway into the cemetery?"

Wylder thought for a moment and then started to explain. "When you go through the gateway, you go to a place created by your imagination. At least, that is what we think happens. You might see a time & place from your life on Earth, or you may not recognize where you are, but it is the place your mind is focused on. For me, I went back to the time of my death. I couldn't stay the first time, so I returned to St. David's until I was ready to try again. Eventually, I went to the Beyond and passed through, I made it to Heaven, the third and final place a soul can be."

"Are there 'real' people in the Beyond?" asked Jan.

"They are real, in the sense that you knew them. But they are a figment of your imagination. They are not actually there with you. That is why you can be with people who have not died yet. It's kind of like a dream," explained Wylder, "but you can come back to the cemetery as many times as you want. "'back' is the keyword. You can only go 'forward' to Heaven once you have come to terms with whatever you have to face in the Beyond."

"What if I like what's in the Beyond? Can I stay there?" asked Jan in a quiet voice. "If my husband and family are there, my grandchild, why would I want to leave?" Jan's voice was different, sad.

"Yes, you could stay there, but you could also go to Heaven and see them for real," said Wylder. "That is the best part. Heaven is a destination for the soul, but it also has a transportation system. Souls can use the gateways and the stars to travel to anywhere they want on Earth, the 'real' world. Time passes differently in these three places, but if you choose not to stay in Heaven and return to Earth, your soul will see your children age and your grandchildren grow up."

"Will they know I am there?" asked Jan, her voice now changing back to the happy tone Wylder had experienced the whole day.

"No. You are there, but you are a ghost. They do not know you are there, but I think they can feel your presence. I don't really know for sure," said Wylder.

"You're telling me that ghosts are real?"

"Yes. I guess that is what I am telling you. I'd love to tell you about my 'grandma experience', but we are here now," said Wylder.

Wylder jumped off the horse and extended her hand to Jan. Jan kicked one leg over the horse and lay across the back of the horse like she was a sack of potatoes.

"How do I get down?" Jan asked, squirming around.

"Jump. What? Are you afraid you're going to hurt yourself?" Wylder asked with a smile.

Jan lifted her head from the horse to give Wylder a look of surprise and excitement as she slid down and landed firmly on the ground.

She slapped her hands together like she was brushing off the dust and put her hands on her hips.

"OK. I think I am catching on. Let's go." Jan said to Wylder, but Wylder was looking past her. Jan turned around to see the tall stone walls, cement drive, and shiny sign that read "New St. David's".

Wylder walked past Jan, "Come on, let's go," she said as she passed.

"What's wrong, Wylder?" asked Jan, jogging a few steps to catch up. "Wylder?"

Wylder turned around and looked at the horse. Blaine walked up and nuzzled Wylder's face, and the three of them started walking. When they reached the gate of New St. David's, Wylder stopped to look at Jan. "Jan, I don't see Greg here. Let's go look around, but I think we would have seen him right away."

"What do you mean, Wylder? Where else would he be?" the panic in Jan's voice was echoed by the look on her face.

"I can think of two possibilities, and I want you to be prepared," said Wylder, walking back to the old section of St. David's, "Follow me."

The two women passed the wrought iron fence, looking inside at the headstones that marked their friends' and family's final resting places. There were no visitors this early in the morning, and the cemetery was eerily quiet, empty, and somehow, lonely.

Wylder walked to the stone benches in the center of St. David's and sat down. "This is where I found my friend Nala," Wylder began, "I feel comfortable here. I hope you do too."

"Where's Greg?" Jan asked, looking at Wylder and holding her gaze.

"He could be in the Beyond," started Wylder.

"How is that possible? The gateway was destroyed," said Jan.

"The gateway in Old St. David's was destroyed. Now there is a New St. David's, and maybe there is a new gateway for all the new arrivals."

Jan's face dropped. She looked again at Wylder and said, "If he is in the Beyond, I may never find him."

"That is the better of the two options," said Wylder. "What I don't know is what kept Greg from coming with you through the portal before it closed."

"Wylder, are you suggesting that whatever it was that Greg held back so I could go through the portal, 'took' him?" asked Jan, eyes wide and head shaking back and forth like she wished that thought away. "No," said Jan. "That's not possible."

"What was that thing?" asked Wylder. "I have never seen it before or since, so I don't know what it can do or what it wants."

"It was not really a 'thing'," said Jan, "it was more of a spirit. A bad, foul entity."

"Let's go walk around the new place and see if we can find any clues about where Greg has gone," said Wylder.

"If he is in the Beyond, could he come back?" asked Jan, "to St. David's?"

"He could if he wanted to, but if he got through the Beyond, he might go to Heaven and try to find you," said Wylder.

"How do we communicate with him?" asked Jan.

"I don't really know how all this works. I am still new to this myself," said Wylder.

"This is heaven, and we can travel all over the world, but we don't have cell phones? Where do I file a complaint?" said Jan with a wink.

Jan stood up and extended a hand to Wylder, who was sitting on the bench with her feet cross-legged beneath her. Wylder took her hand and stood. They walked together towards the New St. David's. "Let's go find my Greg," said Jan, as she picked up the pace so much that this time, Wylder had to jog a few steps to catch up with Jan. Blaine trotted quietly next to the women with an expression that could be mistaken for a smile.

THE BEYOND

The pancakes and eggs were done, and Greg put them on plates for him and his sister. Two fried eggs and four pancakes for him, two fried eggs and three pancakes for Madeline.

Just like every other Saturday morning for the past few years, he set the plates down, and Maddie said, "No. Greggie, did you forget?" she asked with a smile she was trying to hide.

"Oh, my goodness, how did I do that again?" he smiled, stuffed one of her three pancakes into his mouth, and said something with pancake, muffling his words. Once he finally swallowed the pancake he said, with a smile on his face, "There...now it's an even number of eggs and pancakes, two and two."

Madeline smiled and started to eat her eggs first, as was the rule, and then she started on her pancake, but first, they needed to be perfected with strawberry jam and powdered sugar which Greg passed to her. The first bite left a happy little stain of strawberry jam on her pink t-shirt.

As they ate, Greg thought of the new car

his dad had bought. The blue 1966 Mustang convertible was beautiful. When his dad pressed the gas pedal, it sounded like a jet engine about to take off. He couldn't believe that his dad had bought a new car at all, but especially this one. It was not like him to spend money on unnecessary things. His father was very responsible, always putting the family first. His motto was to 'save for a rainy day'. Over the past few years, his health had suffered. Despite giving up smoking and taking daily walks, he had a fatigue that would not go away. He went to many doctors, but no one could find the cause. Last week, he came home with this brand new 1966 Ford Mustang convertible, an 8-Cylinder race car.

Greg grabbed the keys from his dad's briefcase.

"Greggie?" asked Madeline.

"Maddie, don't look at me like that, sis. I'm just checking out dad's new car, want to come?" asked Greg.

"OK, no driving?" Madeline asked.

"No, I'm not going to drive it," said Greg, "but I could. I'm seventeen, and I have my license."

"No," said his sister firmly.

Greg smiled at her, tossed the keys in the air, and caught them again. "Let's go see the car," he said to Madeline, and they walked out the front door together.

There she was, midnight blue and shining in

the early morning sunlight.

Greg unlocked the passenger side door for Madeline. She jumped in, running her hand across the firm leather seat and feeling the cool leather. Greg went to the driver's side, unlocked the door, and sat behind the wheel. Greg put both hands on top of the steering wheel, sliding them apart and together, feeling the cool smooth surface and imagining this was his car.

Greg put the key in the ignition. "No, no," said Madeline, with a motherly tone, and she went back to feeling the soft leather, "Daddy would be maaaaad at you!"

"I just want to hear the engine, relax," said Greg.

He turned the key and the Mustang roared to life.

"What should we name her?" asked Greg.

"Name?" asked Madeline.

"The car, silly," said Greg, "all fast cars need a name. A girl's name."

"Grace?" said Madeline.

"Gracey," repeated Greg, "I like it."

"No. GRACE," said Madeline, matter-of-factly.

"Like Grace Kelly?" he asked.

"Like Princess Grace," replied Maddie.

"Grace, it is," said Greg, and smiled as he

shifted into gear and started down the driveway.

Greg stood behind the car and watched his younger self drive away, knowing what would happen in the next fifteen minutes. He closed his eyes and tried not to remember. When he opened his eyes, he was in the backseat of the Mustang, sitting behind his younger self, and his little sister was rocking back and forth in the passenger seat, laughing that twelve-year-old-girl laugh that he had memorized.

Greg looked at Madeline, no seatbelt he noticed. There were none in the cars in 1966. He leaned, put his hands on the back of the driver's seat, and spoke to himself. "Greg, I don't know if you can hear me, but if you can, please turn around and go back home." Young Greg just smiled brightly in the early morning sun and continued on down the quiet street.

"One more mile, OK, Maddie?" said younger Greg to his sister.

"One more, one more!" Maddie confirmed, and they drove through the intersection.

Greg closed his eyes and felt the impact on the passenger side of the car. He heard the glass breaking, the tires screeching, and felt cold air blow through what was once the windshield. He could not open his eyes.

"This is not real," he told himself. "I am not here. I am in St. David's."

Silence. Greg waited a moment before trying to open one eye, only enough to confirm he was not in the car anymore. He saw the vegetation of new St. David's, felt the sun, and the ocean-like pull back to the gateway. Like walking out of a river, Greg continued further from the portal, and the pull lessened until it had no hold on him. He sat on the dirt, alone. The only company he had was the memory of his little sister before she died.

BACK TO ST. DAVID'S

Greg stood and started walking back to Old St. David's. Cars had begun to pull up, flowers were being brought to grave sites, and tearful loved ones spoke to the departed. There was a time when the residents of Old St. David's heard the stories and looked forward to the visits. Now that all the souls had crossed over, the cemetery was empty and quiet, and there was no one but Greg to hear the conversations of the visitors.

Greg was looking at the ground when he heard her.

"Greg?" Jan yelled and started running towards him.

Greg looked up, confused, to see his wife of over 30 years running towards him. His friend Wylder, and her horse Blaine, were right behind her.

Greg ran, shortening the distance between him and his wife until she collided with him in a warm embrace.

"Oh Greg, you're ok," Jan said, with her eyes closed and her head on his chest.

"Jan?" said Greg, one hand holding her close and one hand on her head. He kissed the top of her head and then put his hands on both her shoulders. "Jan, you're here?" he asked, smiling.

Wylder walked up and smiled, "Wylder?" asked Greg.

"We have a lot to tell you," said Wylder, "and we have a lot to ask."

"Blaine," said Greg as he walked to the horse and put his hand on the horse's face. "Did you bring my Jan back to me?" he asked, smiling.

Blaine snorted, and Greg laughed.

"I am so glad to see you two!" said Greg. He grabbed Jan's hand and held it in his. "Where do you want to start?" asked Greg.

"I want to know what happened the day we left, but first, I want to know why you are back from the Beyond," said Wylder.

"It's a long story, and I think I'd rather start with what happened the day you left."

Wylder nodded and started walking to the path that connected New St. David's to Old St. David's, with Blaine close behind. Still holding Jan's hand, Greg followed the two to the stone benches where all important conversations seemed to take place.

After they all took a seat, Wylder began, "From where Jan and I stood, it looked like you were engulfed in something, like smoke, and then the portal collapsed. Jan was with me, and you were, well, not."

Greg, still holding Jan's hand, looked at Wylder and said, "Smoke is a good way to describe how it looked, but it felt more like a swarm of something. It had mass. It was cold and sharp. I could move it, but it had little effect on the whole. It was angry."

"Angry?" asked Jan.

"I felt it. I felt anger, hatred. Not my own, but the emotion of whatever was around me," explained Greg.

"How did you fight it?" asked Wylder.

"I didn't so much 'fight' it. I think I distracted it," Greg said, "I started waving my arms and yelling. I think it was confused because it could not follow both me and Jan. By the time it decided to follow Jan, she had already made it through, and the portal had collapsed. Once it could no longer follow Jan, it dissipated, and I have not seen it since."

"You said it decided to follow Jan," Wylder said, "what do you mean?"

"I believe it intended to get through the portal. It didn't expect me to stop, so when I did, it hesitated just long enough to miss the opportunity to get in," said Greg.

"You say 'it' like it was a single entity. You also said it felt like a swarm. Was it one thing or many?" asked Jan.

"Both," said Greg. "Like a flock of birds that have one brain but many bodies and can move in a fluid pattern without crashing into one another."

"Whatever it was, I don't want to come across it again," said Jan. She looked at Wylder, "we should get back as soon as we can, right?"

Wylder looked at Greg, who was already looking at her, "We came back for you, but you'll need to go back to the Beyond," she said, "until you are free of the cemetery."

Greg's expression changed. He stood and turned his back to the women.

"What?" asked Jan, looking at Greg's back. "You don't want to go through the Beyond? You want to stay here in the cemetery, is that it?" Jan's eyes dropped to the dirt, and she felt Greg sit beside her and put his hand on her chin, lifting her face gently so her eyes would meet his.

"No, love," began Greg with a combination of a chuckle and disbelief. "I do not want to stay here in the cemetery, but I am not ready to back into the Beyond and deal with that, but that is not why I need to stay here."

Jan tilted her head to one side and looked at

him with a furrowed brow. "Why do you need to stay?" she asked.

"I have not repented for something. That stain is what kept me here in St. David's. That imprint is still on my soul."

Jan sat back down and took Greg's hand. "What have you not repented for?" she asked.

"I have never told you, in all the years we have been married, and I am ashamed," said Greg, looking down at the bench.

This time it was Jan who lifted Greg's chin so he could meet her eyes. "Whatever it is, you can repent, and we can go on together," said Jan.

"I know God will forgive me, but I cannot forgive myself," said Greg.

Jan persisted. "We all have to come to terms with the wrongdoings of our days on Earth. We repent. If you would make a different choice today, then you see the error of your ways, and you will be forgiven and allowed entry into Heaven. I had to deal with my demons too, Greg. Do you remember Rabbi Miller? He used to say, 'Repent one day before you die. If you do not know what day that will be, repent today'. I knew I was going to die. I repented every day. I made amends. "

"I cannot make amends. She is gone." Said Greg.

"She?" repeated Jan.

"My little sister, Maddie," said Greg quietly. "I have not thought about her in so many years. I will not let myself think about her."

"Everyone deserves forgiveness," said Wylder.

"I will not repent because I do not deserve forgiveness," said Greg.

THE SWARM

Silence overtook the cemetery. Wylder was grateful for the sound of the wind, which filled the space between them when there were no words left. The wind was soft, a gentle hum that grew stronger and closer.

Jan looked at Greg in time to see him stand. Abruptly, their eyes locked.

"Is that the same?" asked Jan.

"Same as what?" asked Wylder, in a tone that made it sound more like a statement than a question.

Jan and Wylder stood and turned towards the sound of the wind and followed Greg's stare to the clouds that were approaching.

"What are those?" asked Wylder, "Clouds?"

"No," said Greg, "that's The Swarm. The thing that tried to follow Jan through the portal. Wylder, have you ever seen that before when you were at St. David's?"

"No," replied Wylder, not taking her eyes off the swarm. "I never saw it, and I never heard about it. Not from anyone at St. David's or my grandmother."

"You met someone who was not at St. David's?" asked Jan, curious.

"Yes. I'll tell you about it later." Replied Wylder, "Right now, what do we do about that?" she asked Greg, the only one with any experience with this kind of situation.

The sound got louder, and the swarm got closer. Jan looked around like she was trying to find a place to hide.

As if Greg could read her mind, he said, "You can't hide from it. You can't outrun it."

Within a few minutes, the swarm was all around them, and they could feel anger, hate, and fear crushing them. Wildly, they batted at the parts that made up the whole.

"I got one!" yelled Wylder, looking at the ground where one piece of the swarm bounced and spun like a fly that had been swatted out of the air.

Jan and Greg were still swiping at the air, and Wylder noticed that the swarm did not seem to be surrounding them, but instead, moving as a unit in the same direction, passing through them.

"We are not the target," said Wylder. "Stand still and let them pass."

Greg and Jan stopped moving, and the swarm passed by. As it got further away, the oppressive feeling left as quickly as it had arrived, and the swarm continued on to wherever it was going.

"Are you hurt?" Wylder asked, realizing that they could not be, at least she didn't think they could.

Greg looked over Jan, and Jan looked over Greg. "I'm ok," said Jan, "you?" she asked, looking at Greg.

"Yes, I'm fine," said Greg.

"What was that?" asked Jan.

"I don't know what it was, but I felt it. It gave me the creeps," said Wylder.

Greg walked over and looked down, "You did get one, Wylder. There is a little piece of it on the ground," said Greg.

The three of them stood in a circle, staring intently at the small unfamiliar thing on the ground, vibrating and moving in a circle like a bug that had been squashed. "It has no wings," said Jan, "but it was flying."

"It has no obvious face or head," said Wylder, "and it's solid, like a pebble."

It flickered and flashed then quickly disappeared like it was never there.

"What was that?" asked Jan.

"I'm more interested in where it was going,"

said Wylder.

"We thought it was attacking us, but it wasn't," continued Wylder, "We were just in its way."

Jan began slowly pacing back and forth in front of the stone benches.

Greg chuckled, "You're processing. You're pacing like you used to do, back and forth in front of our bed, when we had a big problem to solve. Should we move to Seattle for the job? Were we ready to start a family? What are you thinking now?"

"When we were all together in Old St. David's, we thought that the residents just needed to face the parts of their life on Earth that they had been denying. We saw evidence that souls could be at St. David's, in the Beyond, or in Heaven. The portal pulled residents gently out of the cemetery, into their regrets, and once they came to terms, they were permitted access to Heaven. It was not based on religion or actions on Earth. Everyone could go. Now, I don't think that is true. If there is a Heaven, there must be a Hell. If there is a God, the must be a Devil."

"Go on," said Wylder.

"Yetzerhara," said Jan, looking at Greg, "The Satan. That is what was around you. It was trying to entrap you into sin."

"Perhaps," said Greg. "But why would it be

going that way," responded Greg, pointing down the road. "You're from around here, Wylder," Greg said. "What's over that way? I can't think of anything except that old quarry."

Wylder looked down like she was thinking and then said, "I have no idea, but I know how to find out." Wylder stood and walked to her horse Blaine.

"Want to go for a ride?" she asked.

Blaine neighed.

Wylder looked at Jan and Greg, "I'll be back," she said as she mounted the horse. "I'll find out where those things were going."

"Jan," said Greg, "go with her."

"I'm not leaving you again," said Jan.

"You know right where to find me," said Greg, "I'm not going anywhere."

"If you go back into the Beyond, I won't know how to find you," said Jan.

"Now that I know what's waiting for me in the Beyond, I'm not going back," said Greg, shaking his head. "I'm not planning on ever going back, so you'll always be able to find me right here. Besides, Wylder needs you. You grew up here. You'll know things that would be helpful."

Jan stood to go. She looked at Greg, "You stay right here," she said with a smile.

"Yes, ma'am," said Greg. "Now, I'll be here

waiting for you. When you get back, you can tell me all about your travels."

"Quite a switch from our lives on Earth," said Jan. "You would call me every night from your business trips. I can't call you."

"More to tell me when you get back," said Greg.

"I hate to break up this reunion, but we really should go," said Wylder.

"Yes, of course. You're right," said Jan.

Wylder extended her hand to Jan, and with a little struggle, she climbed on the horse behind Wylder, who was exchanging friendly smirks with Greg while watching the process of Jan getting on the horse.

"Ok," said Jan. "Ready."

Jan blew a kiss to Greg, and the three of them headed in the direction the Swarm went. Greg waved and sat down on the bench. "So, this is what it's like to be the one left behind with nothing to do," he said to no one but himself. Wylder and Jan were no longer in sight.

LIEUTENANT MASON

"Closing time," said the bartender, "You have to go now, man. We're closed."

"Ok, ok," said Mason, "I'm going."

Mason stood and almost lost his footing. The bartender said, "you look a little wobbly. There is a bench outside. Give me your key. Come back for your motorcycle tomorrow."

Mason handed over his key and stumbled out the door. He sat on the bench until the lights inside went out, and the bartender drove away.

Mason started to walk back to the barracks. He looked at his watch. "Fuck, it'll be dawn by the time I get back."

After an hour of walking, Mason had sobered up and was able to start jogging. When he got to the woods behind the barracks, he stood in the dark for a moment debating his options, then took the shortcut through the trees. He heard voices deep in the trees but slowed down to quiet the sound of his footfalls.

"We can do this the hard way or the easy way," said a voice in a thicket of trees.

The sound of Mason stepping on a branch echoed through the trees, the silence immediately filled the air. No human or animal made a sound for a moment until a young woman's voice broke the spell.

"Help me!" someone cried out, "Is someone there?"

Mason turned from the trail and ran towards the voice in the dense trees. The girl's voice was muffled, but she was still screaming. He broke through the thorns to see a middle-aged man in jogging clothes, holding a young woman by her ponytail. She had a swollen ankle above a bare foot and the other foot still in a running shoe.

"Let her go," said Mason, "Just walk away."

"It's not what you think," said the man.

Mason evaluated the situation; her injury was fresh, her t-shirt torn open, and one breast exposed. She was being held around the waist by the man. The woman cried out in pain, with dirt and tears on her face. Mason could not tell if her pain was from the injury to the ankle or the man holding her, and then he saw the rock in the man's other hand.

Mason did not wait for an explanation; as he ran the short distance to the woman, as the man launched the rock straight at Mason. He ducked and heard the sound of the air as the rock passed his ear. When Mason reached the man, he pulled back his fist and landed a satisfying punch on the chin. The man shook it off and jumped at Mason. "You'll pay for that," he said. Mason grabbed the man's shoulders and put his knee into the man's gut, then wrapped one arm around his neck and held him in a choke hold, "Shut up, asshole," and he squeezed tighter to make his point.

"Run!" Mason yelled to the girl, "GO!"

The girl ran limping barefoot from the trees, stumbling in the dark, towards the road.

"It takes a special kind of ass to attack a girl in the woods," said Mason to the man struggling beneath him, "What do I do with you? If I let you go, and you attack another woman, it would be my fault. If I kill you, not that you'd be missed, that would be on me too. Don't take this the wrong way, but killing you seems like the best option.

When the girl was given enough time to get away, he let go of the man slowly, who dropped to the ground. Keeping a hold of his arm, Mason said, "Get up, asshole," but the man laid motionless on the ground. "I'm not letting go of you, but I'm not going to carry you either. Now get up!"

Mason rolled the man over and looked into his lifeless eyes.

"Oh shit!" said Mason, looking around.

He checked for a pulse, nothing. "Shit, shit, shit."

Mason slapped the cheek of the man on the ground, "Come on, mister, shake it off!" He lifted one arm and dropped it again, seeing it hit the dirt like dead weight, looking for any sign of life. It was still dark, and the girl was long gone. Mason backed away from the body. He saw that the man had a scar on the side of his hand, deep bite marks, clearly human. It was so obvious what it was, that the scar looked more like a tattoo. This girl had left her mark also, two deep fingernail scratches across his cheek, bleeding and angry.

Mason started toward the path he had come from, fighting through the thorns, the tripping vines, and tall weeds. When he reached the dark path back to the road, he sprinted the rest of the way to the barracks, leaving the body behind,

When he arrived at the base, he climbed into his bunk, careful not to wake any of the sleeping soldiers. His heart rate slowed, but he could not sleep. When the sun came up, only a short time later, Mason was the first one dressed and to the mess hall.

"Lieutenant Mason," asked the Sargent, "how is my favorite point guard?"

"Doing well, sir!" said Mason.

"Today is a big day," said the Sargent, "are you ready for the game against the Air Force?"

"Yes, Sir," said Mason, "I couldn't sleep all night."

THE QUARRY

"It seems like we should have been there by now," said Wylder, "Man, I miss my GPS."

"It's actually in the next county over," said Jan, "some people in my family worked there."

"My family had a ranch. We raised our own cattle," said Wylder. "We had a garden where we grew the most beautiful vegetables. My dad ran the farm, and my mom was a Hospice nurse."

"A Hospice nurse?" asked Jan, "What was her name?"

"Mom," replied Wylder with a laugh, "But everyone else called her Sage. I used to smudge my room with smoldering sage to remove negative energy, and she loved the smell. Whenever anyone would come over, the house smelled of sage, and somehow, she got that nickname instead of me."

"Is Wylder your nickname?" asked Jan.

"It's what everyone calls me, even my parents, but my birth name is Falynne," said Wylder.

"That is a beautiful name," said Jan, "I've never

heard it before."

"My mom made it up. She combined two names that she and my dad were considering when I was born," Wylder said with a smile. "I miss them,"

"I understand the feeling of missing those you left behind," said Jan. "Greg and I met our first grandchild just after I passed. We stayed at St. David's for other reasons, but we ended up seeing our family grow. I would not have traded that for the world."

"Once you've gone through the Beyond and made it to Heaven, you can go see them anytime," reminded Wylder.

"Yes, I was wondering about that," said Jan. "Another thing I was thinking about is why I didn't go to the Beyond when I went through the portal."

"I said I would tell you about meeting my grandmother," said Wylder, "now seems like a good time."

"Great," said Jan, "I've been thinking about asking you again."

"After I successfully made it through the Beyond, after many failed attempts," said Wylder, "I went back home. I saw the silhouette of a woman sitting on the hay bales gazing at the embers in the fire pit. I knew it was my grandma, but she had passed away long ago. She hugged me and said she had been coming to the house since she passed. When she knew I had died, she came to the house looking for me, wondering when I would arrive."

"She was waiting for you there?" asked Jan, "so she assumed you would come back home right after you died."

"Yep," said Wylder, "She told me that every cemetery has a portal. All the souls have a choice to stay or pass over. Our portal was hidden deep in the Dark Side of St. David's, so we just didn't know it was there. Well, Nala knew."

"What else did she say?" asked Jan.

"She explained that the place we call the Beyond is the doorway to the mind. In order to rid yourself of the mistakes in life, a soul can take the opportunity to come to terms with their choices and let go of them," said Wylder, smiling. She added, "she also goes there to win at cards when she is bored."

"Really?" asked Jan, "or are you just joking?"

"Since the Beyond is in your mind, she goes there on vacation sometimes," laughed Wylder, "like she used to go to Vegas, but in the Beyond, she always wins."

"Is every soul supposed to go through the Beyond?" asked Jan.

"I've wondered about that too," said Wylder, "my Grandma said that eventually the soul, either through curiosity or boredom, went through the gateway."

"I have never been to the Beyond," said Jan, "it seems odd that I didn't have to go."

"Did you have any regrets in life or a big mistake that you couldn't get over?"

"Yes, I think we all have those. But I was in the hospital for a few months before I passed. I had my Rabbi present, and we went through all my life's regrets. I made amends. I offered and accepted forgiveness. That is what I was going to tell you. Your mother was there with me when I passed. It was her kindness and compassion that made my passing so comfortable. It was the middle of the night; my children and my Rabbi had gone for the day. Greg had long passed, and I was all alone. Your mom came into the room and knew it was my time. I don't know what she had been doing, but she put the clipboard down, sat next to me, and held my hand. She spoke softly, with a smile in her voice. She said I would be surrounded by my loved ones, and I should not be afraid. She even said I should find you. She said her daughter was one of the most amazing people she had ever met. She said that Heaven would be a more exciting place with her daughter there. Wylder, I met your mom. I wouldn't have realized it, but her name was so unique, it stuck with me."

Wylder did not speak; she just nodded her

DEBORAH ALBERS

head, and they kept riding.

After a few moments of silence, they arrived at the quarry. The size of the pit seemed to grow larger as they got closer, although the full size of it was not visible from the road.

"That is one big hole," said Wylder.

"It's an open-pit mine," said Jan, "it's about a mile across and a quarter mile deep. It's nowhere near the biggest in the world. Salt Lake City, Utah has the deepest open pit mine in the world. Bingham Canyon mine is two and three-quarter miles across at the top and three-quarters of a mile deep."

"It looks abandoned," said Wylder.

"Abandoned mines are very dangerous," said Jan, "They attract swimmers, dirt bike riders, and even hikers. A lot of deaths occur in these places. They are a little creepy to me, like something you would see in a horror movie."

"We might just get a firsthand glimpse of a horror movie. Look over there," said Wylder, pointing to the deepest part of the mine, where the swarm surrounded a male body on the ground. "Let's get a closer look," said Wylder. As if Blaine understood what she had said, he started trotting toward the Swarm. The terrain was rocky and steep, and it was slow to circle the huge crater, down to the pit floor.

As they got closer, Jan said to Wylder, "Is that

another body?"

Wylder stopped Blaine from walking and took a closer look, clearing the view blurred by horseback bounce. Behind the male body, which was the focus of the Swarm, was a female body.

"She looks young," said Wylder.

The two women continued down the steep crest and kept their eyes on the Swarm.

"Are you sure this is wise?" asked Jan, "We don't want to get too close."

"We know the Swarm is not interested in us, or they would have taken the opportunity back at St. David's," said Wylder.

"I still get the angry feeling in the pit of my stomach when we are near them," said Jan.

"Me too," said Wylder, "but we came here to investigate, so getting close is kinda the point."

"Ok, said Jan, but let's not overstay our welcome. I think whatever happened, happened recently," said Jan, "They look like they are sleeping."

"They do," agreed Wylder, "except for that." Wylder pointed to the ground beneath the bodies.

As they got closer to the floor of the pit and the scene of the accident, they could hear the buzz of the Swarm and see the blood pooled underneath the two bodies.

"Why is it so interested in that one?" asked Wylder.

"I don't know," replied Jan, keeping her eyes on the Swarm, "Maybe they are focused on him first, and then they will move to the other one, like a pack of lions who have two kills."

The buzzing quieted, and the Swarm slowly began to dissipate until it was gone.

"Where did it go?" asked Jan. "I can feel the difference as soon as they leave. What is that thing?"

Wylder was focused on the picture in front of her. She led Blaine closer to the bodies. When they reached the pit floor, they could see a woman on the ground. Wylder dismounted Blaine and walked towards the body. She was young, tall, and thin. She had blond hair and a strawberry birthmark on her neck.

"I think I know her," said Wylder, "I met her in town at the feed store with her parents. We became friends when we were young, but we lost touch. She's older now, but I remember her birthmark. Her name was Jessica."

"Do you know him too?" asked Jan, still sitting on Blaine.

"No, at least I don't recognize him," said Wylder, turning her focus to the girl.

Jan slid off Blaine and stood next to Wylder.

Wylder bent down next to the young woman and closed her eyes. "She is so young; she had her whole life in front of her. What the hell is going on? Did you notice the size of New St. David's? This is a small town. Why do we need such a big cemetery? Why is this girl, down in the pit of an abandoned mine, getting shot by her boyfriend?"

"He's not my boyfriend," said a voice from behind them.

Wylder and Jan turned around to see Jessica sitting on the pit floor, leaning against the dirt wall, knees bent and her forehead on her knees.

"Jessica?" said Wylder.

"Yes, Wylder, it's me," said Jessica.

"What are you doing here?" asked Wylder, "Jan, why is she here and not in the cemetery?"

Jan shrugged her shoulders in bewilderment.

Wylder looked back at Jessica, "Who is he?" she asked.

"He is my friend," said Jessica, "was, my friend," she corrected herself.

"Your friends don't shoot you," reminded Wylder, with an edge to her voice.

"You haven't been here, Wylder; you don't know what it's like anymore," said Jessica.

"Enlighten me," said Wylder.

"I remember when you died, you know, it

was devastating. The community was shaken by what happened to you. Looking back, it was just the first of many tragedies that hit our town."

Wylder sat next to Jessica; legs crossed. Jan quietly sat next to Wylder.

"Like I said, it started with your car accident, then we had a silver mine collapse trapping 17 miners inside. They couldn't get them out in time, and they all died. Some of them were really young or just married. Some left young widows or children."

"What happened here?" asked Jan. "This quarry was an important part of the town at one point."

"Most of the town's men were working here when it happened. We had a lot of rain one year, and it slowed operations here at the quarry. The rain went on and on until there was a flood that filled the quarry like a lake. This was the only real employer in the town; when it closed temporarily, people couldn't feed their families. Some people, like your family Wylder, had farms and helped feed the town during that time. Some people moved away. When the quarry shut down for good, people were too proud to ask for help Some even took their own lives. It's been bad here for a long time," said Jessica.

"I'm sorry, Jessica. I didn't know it had gotten so bad. That still doesn't explain why you were at the quarry today, or how you ended up dead," said Wylder.

"Last summer, I started getting sick," said Jessica, with a sad, faraway look in her eyes. "I would get really dizzy and would vomit most days. My mom thought I was pregnant, so she took me to the doctor. I was not pregnant. They couldn't figure out what was wrong. This went on through my senior year. I started getting headaches and dropping things. I kept going to the doctor until finally, they did a brain scan. I had a tumor. There was a surgery to remove it, but it was very expensive, risky, and only a 50/50 chance of a normal life. My family could not afford that kind of treatment. My parents told me not to worry about it. They would find a way. I did some research online. The 'normal' life meant that if I was lucky, I could walk and talk. If I was not lucky, I would be eating through a straw and confined to a wheelchair for the rest of my life."

Wylder looked at Jan, who looked like it was her own daughter they had been talking about.

"Why were you here, Jessica?" asked Wylder.

"Jason was my best friend. He saw my health decline. I vomited all the time and lost my balance when I walked. He was caring for me when my parents had to work, so he slept over many times. I'm sure that's why my mom thought I was pregnant, but it was not like that.

He was my friend."

"I had friends like that," said Wylder. "They are the best friends."

"One day, I asked him if he would end this for me," Jessica looked at Wylder, "take me out of this misery. He said 'no,' of course, but over time, I guess I wore him down. He saw me suffering, in pain, not enjoying life. He saw my parents' hearts breaking. One day he said he would do it; he would help me end my life.

Wylder looked at Jessica, "I guess I understand," she said.

Jessica continued, "We planned it all out. This weekend my parents are away. There is a big storm coming in this afternoon. The whole town is worried it will be like the last time the quarry flooded. Jason and I thought this was our chance. We would come down here and take care of business, then Jason would give me a little funeral and a water burial. The floods would come, and no one would ever find my body. My parents would never be hurt knowing I arranged my own death. Jason was not supposed to die. Something must have gone wrong because that was never part of the plan."

Jan said, "Maybe that is why you showed up here instead of in a cemetery. This is where you died and would be buried, even if it was by water."

Ignoring Jan, Jessica's expression changed, "Where is Jason?" asked Jessica, "This might not be so bad if I get to spend eternity with my best friend."

"I'm not sure where he is," said Wylder, "but I think it took him."

"It?" asked Jessica.

"We don't know what it is exactly. It's like a swarm of bees, but it's not alive. I have never seen anything like it," Wylder looked at Jan, "We have never seen it, until today. But we have a friend, Jan's husband, who has some experience with it. He is waiting for us back at St. David's. Do you want to come with us?"

"St. David's, the cemetery?" asked Jessica.

"Yes, back in town," said Jan. "By the way, I am Jan," extending her hand to Jessica. Jessica looked at her hand and smiled, then shook it.

"I'm Jessica," she said smiling, "Such formality, even in death."

"I guess I brought that from my time among the living," said Jan.

"I like it. It reminds me of home," said Jessica. "Is that Blaine?" She did not wait for an answer, "Hi boy! It's so good to see you."

Blaine neighed and nuzzled Jessica's head like they were long-lost friends.

"I don't think we can all fit on him," said

Wylder, "But we have a lot to tell you, so the walk will be nice."

The three of them started up the steep path to the top of the quarry.

"Why are you at the quarry?" asked Jessica.

"We were following the swarm," said Wylder, "it seems to be following some souls and not others, and I want to know why."

"And you came here to see if it took Jason and me?" asked Jessica.

"No, we had no idea you were here. The Swarm went through us on the way here, and we decided to follow it," said Wylder.

"How did you know it would not take you if you caught up with it?" asked Jessica.

"It was all around us, back at St. David's," said Wylder, "it didn't take us then, so we figured it wouldn't take us now."

"How do you know each other?" asked Jessica.

"I knew Greg from my first time back at St. David's," said Wylder, "When I first died. Greg is Jan's husband. Jan was the last one who had a spot in St. David's, so rumor had it, that the portal would close when the last person went through. Jan went through and the portal closed, leaving Greg behind without a way to go forward to Heaven, and he was trapped in the cemetery. Jan and I came back for him."

"From where?" asked Jessica.

"From Heaven," said Wylder.

"Heaven is real?" asked Jessica.

"Yes, it's real and pretty cool," said Wylder.

"It will take a long time to tell you about heaven," said Jan, "but we'll explain the most important things on the way."

As they reached the top of the pit, Wylder asked Jan, "What do you think Greg has been up to today? You'll have a lot to tell him when we get back."

"When we were living, it was him who would leave for business, and I would stay home. He would call me each night and tell me about the events of the day in Beijing, or Tokyo, or New York. Now it is me who is leaving and coming back to tell him about the events of my day. We really need to figure out a communication system here."

Wylder laughed, "Jessica, I am starting a list of things we miss from life on Earth. Top of the list is cell phones, smartphones specifically. Next on the list is a GPS. Anything you miss already?"

Wylder waited for Jessica to respond, but when she didn't, she looked back, "Jessica?"

"I can't get out," said Jessica, a few feet behind them. "Each time I take a step I get pushed back."

Jessica started in a run to break through

whatever was holding her back.

"Wait!" yelled Wylder, but it was too late. Jessica tried to run up the path and a force threw her so hard she flew back and landed with a thud on the stone path.

Wylder and Jan ran to her. Wylder extended a hand, laughing. Jessica took the hand and stood up. "What was that?" asked Jessica, "Am I trapped here?"

"Not really," Wylder said, "Look for a blue spark. When you get close it will pull you towards it like a magnet."

The three of them looked around and Jessica saw it first. A blue sparkle in the shade where she had been sitting with Wylder. She started walking towards the spark, "Is that the way out?" asked Jessica.

"Hold up," said Wylder, "It's not that simple. I should have thought about it sooner."

"How does it work?" asked Jessica, "Is it a door?"

"Of sorts," replied Wylder, "You have to go through that portal, which we call "the Beyond" from there, you will be faced with the realities you left behind on Earth, something you didn't deal with. Once you come to terms with that, you can go where you want, freely. Until that time you are locked in this quarry like Greg, Jan's husband, is locked in St. David's."

"I have nothing to come to terms with," said Jessica, "I planned this. I have no regrets."

"Well, you have some unfinished business," said Wylder, "or you would have been able to leave the quarry. Jan was the only one who didn't have to deal with anything when she went through the portal, and that was because Jan dealt with all her shit while she was still alive." Wylder looked at Jan, "Sorry Jan, no offense intended."

"None taken," replied Jan with a smile.

"Ok, I'll go through. This should just take a minute," said Jessica.

Jan and Wylder exchanged knowing glances. "We'll wait for you right here," said Wylder.

Jessica clapped her hands together and rubbed them back and forth like she was about to defuse a bomb. She stepped closer to the blue spark and said, "Oh, I feel it. Here we go!"

"It's a little tingly," said Jessica, "like I'm twinkling. Am I twinkling?" she asked with a smile on her face.

And with that, there was a flash, and she was gone.

Wylder sat down and looked at Jan, "You might want to take a seat, we're going to be here a while."

Jan looked up and saw the Swarm, larger

than before, heading back in the direction of St. David's.

UNFINISHED BUSINESS

"Where is she, Wayne? This is not like her. You don't think she ran away, do you?" Jessica's mom paced back and forth while her dad sat on the bed.

"She has done this so many times that I have lost count," said her dad.

"Not like this, Wayne. Never for this long," said her mom.

Jessica stood in the doorway and saw the dark circles under her mom's eyes. She looked out of the window, and the first rays of sun started to peek over the hill.

What day is this? Wondered Jessica. *I don't even remember it.*

Her mom and dad did not sleep that night. They called friends and family, the hospitals, the jail, and the bus station. Around eight in the morning, the doorbell rang. Her mom ran down the stairs to see who it was. When she opened the door, her stomach dropped, and she felt as if she might vomit. The Sheriff stood in his uniform, hat in hand, looking like he had also been up all night.

"Mrs. Kelly?" the Sheriff asked.

"Yes, I am Diana Kelly," said Jessica's mom, holding back tears.

"Mrs. Kelly, we have been looking for Jessica all night. We have an APB out to all the counties nearby. Do you have any idea where she could have gone?"

"No, sir, I don't," She said through tears. "She's ten years old! Where would she go?"

10 years old? Thought Jessica, *I didn't do anything like this when I was 10.*

"Mrs. Kelly, the first 48 hours are the most important when dealing with a missing child," began the Sheriff. "Think, where could she have gone?"

"You think I haven't wracked my brain about where she might be?" Diana started sobbing and her husband came up and put an arm around her. He extended the other to shake the Sheriff's hand.

"Sheriff," said her husband.

"Mr. Kelly," said the Sheriff, as the two men exchanged a firm handshake.

The Sheriff looked at Mr. Kelly, "We have the whole town organizing a walk through the open field near the Williams Farm off 355. We have nearly 100 people from town to walk the 1000 acres, six feet apart. If she's in that field, we'll find her."

"You think she's in the field, Sheriff?" asked Wayne.

"Why would my Jessica be in the field? Do you think she's been taken? Is she dead?" asked Mrs. Kelly, who looked like she might faint.

By now her mom was screaming and crying. Jessica watched the situation in shock and could barely understand the words her mom was saying.

"Mrs. Kelly, we have searched this town high and low, and you have called every place you think she might be. The only place we have not searched is the field. Some kids go exploring in that field and get lost. The corn is taller than they are, and they can't find their way out. All I'm saying, is that if she is there," said the Sheriff, putting his hand on her shoulder, "we will find her."

The Sheriff shook Mr. Kelly's hand and left the house. Jessica looked at her mom, and then her dad.

"I really didn't know it was this bad," she said to them.

The day passed so slowly. Jessica had nothing to do but hear the desperate phone calls of her parents. People stopped by and brought food, offered to clean the house, and keep watch over the phone so they could get some sleep. All offers were appreciated but rejected.

When the afternoon came, her mom and dad got in the car to go and help walk the field. "Diana, why don't you stay here?" said Wayne.

"No," said Diana, "I have to be there when they find her. She'll want her mom."

"I was just thinking," said Wayne, "what if she calls? No one will be here to answer the phone."

Diana looked up, "Yes, you're right," she said, "Of course, someone should be here by the phone."

She got out of the car and walked around to the driver's side. Wayne rolled down the window.

Jessica watched from the porch steps.

"I'll take care of the field, and you stay here in case she comes home, ok?" said Wayne, "We both have an important job to do."

"Yes," said Diana, "I'll stay. I love you. I'll see you both when you get home." Diana began to chew on her fingernails then bent down and kissed him through the open window and watched him until he was down the long driveway and turning onto the road. Diana closed her eyes and took in a deep breath to slow her heart rate. She ran her hands through her unwashed hair, then walked up the steps and went into the house. Jessica followed her.

When Diana got inside, she put on the kettle for some hot tea and brought the phone to the kitchen table. When the teapot started to whistle, she just sat at the table, oblivious to the loud screech that was piercing through Jessica.

Diana ran through all the possibilities in her head, all the places Jessica could have gone, all the terrible things that could have happened to her little girl.

"Mom, get the water!" said Jessica.

As if she had heard Jessica, she stood up and opened the cupboard where the coffee cups were. Jessica stood behind her, seeing all the mismatched cups that had filled that shelf for as long as Jessica could remember. The sobbing sound of her mom broke the trance and Jessica saw her mom slide her back down the wall to the floor. She put her hands over her face and Jessica could feel the sadness and pain in her words.

"Oh Jessica, where are you?" said her mom, "Please be ok."

Jessica started to remember the details of the night.

Something about a dog.

Oh God.

I remember.

****

Wylder and Jan were sitting in the shade when Jessica came back from the Beyond.

"Well, how'd it go?" asked Wylder.

"It didn't," said Jessica, frustrated. "I left. I can't go back. My parents don't know what I did. I didn't know I caused them so much pain. I can't go back."

"You have to go back," said Wylder, "Or you cannot leave the quarry. "You have to face it. Go on! Go back."

"No," said Jessica. "I don't want to be there. I don't want to see them suffer like that."

"Jessica, we don't have time for this!" said Wylder, raising her voice. "Go back. This is bigger than you. We need you. Go," said Wylder, pointing her finger like a mother telling her child to take a shower.

"Ugh," said Jessica. "Fine. I'll apologize and then I'll be back."

"Fine," said Wylder. "Thank you."

"You owe me," said Jessica. "This is going to suck."

"I bet mine sucked worse than yours," said Wylder.

"Fair," said Jessica. "You're probably right."

Before Wylder could respond, Jessica was back in the Beyond.

***

This time she was not at the house with her mom, while the whole community searched for a child that was not missing. This time she was in her dad's old Chevy truck, taking a corner way too fast.

"Hold on," Jessica said to Marleen, who was already holding on.

"Slow down, you psycho!" said Marleen, "Are you TRYING to kill us?"

"Don't be such a wimp, Marleen. Live a little," said Jessica.

"It's dark, Jessica. Please, slow down," said Marleen, with her eyes closed and her hands braced on the dashboard. As they turned the corner, they were coming up on Mr. Turner's Dairy. He was moving the cows to the pasture across the road. "Shit!" yelled Jessica, as she hit the brakes with both feet and the blue Chevy screeched as the brakes tried to slow the speeding vehicle. It was not the brakes that stopped the truck, but the two-thousand-pound dairy cow that was in the middle of the road.

Jessica stood on the road, watching the whole thing transpire. She watched herself open the driver's side door, put her hand to her bleeding head, look at the blood on her hand, and laugh. Still laughing, she returned her hand to her head and walked around the back of the truck to the passenger side, and helped Marleen open the door.

"It's not funny!" Marleen said, as she slipped off the seat and put both hands protectively to her neck. "I think I got whiplash; my neck is throbbing."

"You'll be fine," said Jessica, "but I can't say the same for the cow."

Marleen looked at the dairy cow, and then at the truck. "Or your dad's truck," said Marleen.

"Oh God, he's going to kill me," said Jessica.

Mr. Turner saw the whole thing from down the road and was now within shouting distance, "What in tarnation have you two girls done?" as he started to run to the cow.

"I'm sorry, Mr. Turner," said Marleen, watching Mr. Turner kneel down by the cow, "We were going too fast, and we didn't see her. I am so sorry."

"Well," said Mr. Turner, "You were driving Jessica, what do you have to say for yourself?"

"I'm sorry, but it's just a cow," said Jessica, "You have hundreds of them."

"I'm sure your parents won't have the same response when I send them a bill for $3,000, plus lost revenue for the next six years. Last year I got $1,275 for a side of beef, but retired dairy cows go for less. Let's estimate $500 per side, two sides. $3,000 to buy a new cow to replace the calf she won't have next year, $275 per year in lost revenue times six, plus the lost beef revenue of $1,000 when she retires, is a total of $5,650 that I will bill your father."

Mr. Turner stood from the dead cow to return to the rest of his herd. Marleen looked at Jessica.

"What a jerk!" said Jessica.

"You're kidding, right?" said Marleen.

"Look, Marleen," said Jessica.

"Save it," said Marleen, "I'm going home." She started towards the truck and Jessica went to the driver's side. "I wonder if it will start," she said to Marleen, but Marleen had walked right past the truck and was limping down the road to her house.

Jessica looked at her younger self in the driver's side of the old truck, with steam coming out of the crushed engine.

"I remember this day," she said, walking towards the truck and looking through the broken passenger side window.

Young Jessica was pounding the steering wheel and talking to herself, "This is stupid, it's just a cow!"

"You really don't understand, do you?" Jessica said to her young, irresponsible self. "You took a life, you hurt your friend, you destroyed your father's work vehicle, and you cost Mr. Turner thousands of dollars."

Her younger self got out of the truck, slammed the driver's door shut, and started walking.

Jessica walked next to her younger self. "You caused so many people pain, you hurt so many people. Maybe it was the tumor growing in your head, maybe it was hormones, or depression, or fear of growing up, but you hurt people with your impulsiveness."

The younger Jessica just kept walking towards her house. Jessica looked at her young self and could not find regret or remorse visible on her face. "Your parents will be waiting for you when you get there. Mr. Turner will have called them and explained what happened. Your parents do not have five grand!"

After they walked the long four miles to her parent's property line, they got to the dirt driveway of the house. "Jessica, it takes all your parents' savings to fix this," but the younger Jessica just marched on, as if she had done nothing wrong today. Jessica watched herself go into the house and heard the yelling start.

"I was so horrible to my parents, to Marleen, to Mr. Turner," Jessica said aloud. "If I could go back I would do it so differently. I would apologize for what I had done. I would have worked at the feed store to help pay off the cow, and help my dad fix the truck. I would have apologized to Marleen and told her she was right. Mr. Turner was right. My parents were right."

Jessica watched the scene in the house and thought to herself, *Mom and dad probably don't even know I'm dead yet. I broke my mom's heart the last time I went missing. I was hiding from them for two days because they wouldn't let me get a dog. They had the whole community out looking for me. They thought I was dead, or worse, taken by some crazy person. When my mom found me, hiding in the barn with bags of chips and cases of soda, laughing, she was so angry, so embarrassed. She had to call off the search and tell my father, tell everyone, that she had found me. In the end, she made up some story that I had fallen in the barn and was unconscious.*

I never went to the hospital, so I don't know why everyone believed it. Maybe they couldn't imagine that a 10-year-old would do something so bad as to hide from her parents for days.

All this time I thought I had nothing to face in my life. I believed I left that world with no regrets. Now, I can't even apologize for what I have done. It's too late to fix anything.

Jessica returned her attention to the screaming in the house and walked up the front steps. When she got to the open door, she heard her younger self say, "I wish I was dead!" and slam her bedroom door.

Her mom slumped down on the couch next to where her dad already sat. He put his arm around her, and she put her head on his shoulder. Jessica sat down in the soft chair across from her parents where she used to sit in her dad's lap and watch TV when she was very small.

"Mom, Dad, I don't wish I was dead. I wish more than anything that I was alive, and that I could come back to this moment and apologize for what I did," Jessica said to her parents who were sitting in the silence of the moment, lost in their own thoughts.

"Mom, I am sorry that I worried you when they were looking for me in the field. I was ten. I didn't realize what was happening or that everyone was looking for me. I just thought I would make you worry about me for a few days, and you'd let me have a dog. It was stupid, and mean, and I am sorry."

"Dad," Jessica continued, looking at her father now, "I am so sorry about your truck. I am responsible for the damage and for killing Mr. Turner's cow and for hurting Marleen. I wish I could ask your forgiveness."

There was a knock at the door and her mom looked up, it was Marleen. Her mom wiped her eyes and stood to go to the door.

"Come in Marleen," said her dad.

Marleen stepped through the open door and walked over to Diana and hugged her. Marleen turned to Jessica's dad and stood up straight. Nervous, her hands shook, and she crossed her arms to hide it.

"Mr. Kelly," said Marleen, her voice cracking, "I am so sorry that I had a part in ruining your truck. It was irresponsible of me to go for a ride with Jessica when we did not have your permission. I would like to help pay for the repairs. I have already been to see Mr. Turner and I have worked out a deal with him to help pay for the cow so you should not get billed for my half. It will take me a long time, but I have a job and I could pay you a little each month until my debt is paid."

Jessica looked at her dad and saw his face soften. His big fatherly smile spread across his face. He shook his head, "Marleen," he said, as he stood to look her in the eye, "that must have been very hard. I can be a mean-looking old man, and you came to me like an adult and took responsibility for your actions. I accept your apology, and your offer to help pay for the repairs on the truck. I wish I could say not to worry about it, but I depend on that truck for work, and I will have to get it fixed right away. When I get the bill, I will take half of it, and put a note on the fridge. Whenever you can give me money, I will deduct that from the total. Does that sound fair?"

he asked.

"Yes sir, it does," said Marleen, "and I will pay you interest."

"Now, that I can say you don't have to worry about," said Mr. Kelly, smiling to Marleen.

He extended his hand to her, and she gave it a firm shake like she had just made a business deal.

"Mr. Kelly, Mrs. Kelly, thank you. I'll be leaving now. I appreciate the kindness you have shown me," said Marleen.

"Oh, you are a pleasure Marleen, you know that!" said Mrs. Kelly. "It was very brave of you to come and talk with us, your parents will be proud."

"I was just taking responsibility for my actions," said Marleen, "If only I could ask the cow for forgiveness."

Mrs. Kelly smiled, "Do you want to go see Jessica? She is in her room."

"No ma'am, I just came to see the two of you," said Marleen, and she walked back out the open front door.

When Marleen had gone, Jessica looked at her parents, they had no expression on their faces, no words were spoken, they just looked at each other for a long moment. "Dad," said Jessica, "Marleen did the right thing, the adult thing. That is what I should have done. I am so sorry. I don't even know how you paid for the truck repairs. I remember seeing the tab on the refrigerator and I didn't even ask what that was. I wish you could hear me. I want to apologize. I want to tell you how sorry I am."

"Mom, dad, sometime in the not-too-distant future you will be gone for the weekend. When you get home, I will not be here. I didn't leave a note or say goodbye. I thought that would be easier. Now I realize it would only be easier on me. If it plays out like I planned, you will never know what happened to me. You might think I ran away, but you will never know for sure. I am so sorry for what I have done to you. I hope you can forgive me. I have left you without a child and I caused you so much pain while I was here. Please accept my apology. Even though I know you cannot hear me, I hope you find some closure."

Behind her mom, across the living room, was the sliding glass door to the back wooden patio and steps to the back 40 acres of the property. They left the door open in the late afternoon to cool the house for the night. It was turning to dusk, and the shadows were growing longer. She could see the shadow of the barn, but not the barn itself. In the warm glow of the setting sun, she saw a blue spark like the one at the quarry. Jessica stood and walked outside to the old patio, remembering the birthday parties, the

Easter dinners, and the time when a Christmas scavenger hunt led to a new bicycle hidden out there. This patio had good memories. *I will take these with me*, thought Jessica.

Jessica ran down the steps towards the barn, and when she saw the spark and felt the pull, she let herself go into the portal.

I know what to ask Wylder.

CAN YOU
HEAR ME?

Wylder and Jan laughed as they played Rock, Paper, Scissors to pass the time at the quarry. When a blue flash lit up the dusk sky, they both turned around to see Jessica standing with her eyes closed and an expression of grief that made her look much older, weaker.

"We should add cards to the list of things we miss," laughed Wylder.

"Jessica," asked Wylder softly, "Are you okay?" she approached Jessica and put out her hand. Jessica ignored the hand and embraced Wylder tightly, and Wylder gently put her arms around Jessica.

"Why can't I cry?" asked Jessica, into Wylder's hair.

"I think that's a thing for the living," said Wylder, "I've never seen anyone cry here."

"But I still feel the pain and heartbreak that I caused my parents," said Jessica, releasing Wylder from her tight embrace, "I don't know how to fix it. I can't go back and undo what I have done."

"I wish you could talk to Michael; he could help you. He also had done something while he was living that could not be undone. Ultimately, he forgave himself and found a way to pay it forward with other souls in heaven."

"Who is Michael?" asked Jessica.

"A friend," said Wylder, "I just wish I knew how to reach him."

"What do we do now?" asked Jessica.

"We get back to Greg, and tell him about the Swarm," said Wylder. "It only came for one of you, it's selecting souls somehow."

"But I don't want to leave yet," said Jessica. "I still need to see my parents, make sure they are ok."

"You can see your parents anytime," said Wylder, "now that you…"

Wylder turned to Jan, "Why didn't the portal close after Jessica went through? When you went through Greg said the Earth shook and the portal closed. He had to go through before you because you were the last one with a reserved place in St. David's."

Jan thought for a moment, "Maybe Jessica is not the last one? Her friend died after her, but he's not here anymore. Maybe the portal is waiting for him, maybe he has another chance."

Jessica looked confused, "Where am I?" she asked, "Am I in Heaven, on Earth, or in the Beyond?"

Wylder started pacing and rubbed her face with both hands. "You're not in the Beyond, you just came back from there. That was where you saw your parents, but that was all in your mind. You are definitely on Earth, the question is are you trapped in the quarry like Greg is trapped in St. David's, or are you in Heaven, free to go anywhere."

"Do you hear that?" asked Jan, suddenly looking up.

"What is it?" asked Jessica, "It's getting louder."

It's the Swarm," said Wylder, "but it's not stopping, look," she pointed up, "It's passing over the quarry."

"It's headed in the direction of St. David's," said Jan. "We have to get back to Greg, now."

"We can't all ride on Blaine," said Wylder, "there is not enough room."

"Go!" said Jan to Wylder, "Take Blaine and go help Greg. I know the way; I'll take Jessica and we'll meet you there."

Wylder ran back to Blaine who was following them up the path. When he saw her, he stood ready to be mounted bareback. Wylder waved as she and Blaine headed up the steep path to the road that would lead back to St. David's.

Jan looked at Jessica and said, "I know the way, let's hurry, it's many miles." Jan started walking quickly and Jessica followed.

"You walk fast for an old lady," Jessica said, sarcastically.

Without turning around, Jan said, "I heard that," smiled to herself and kept walking.

"Was it the same Swarm we heard earlier?" asked Jessica, out of breath from the climb.

"We don't know much about it," said Jan, "but it surrounded your friend."

"Oh God," said Jessica, "Jason is with that thing, right?"

Jan stopped walking and turned to Jessica, "Jessica, I am really not sure what happened to Jason. All I know is that when Wylder and I rode up, you were laying on the ground, and Jason was about 15 feet away. The Swarm was all around him, but they didn't come near you. After a few minutes, they disappeared. You showed up but he never did. The part of him that would have ended up here, never came."

Jan saw the uncertainty in Jessica's eyes, "We will figure this out, I promise, but right now we need to get back to St. David's and to Greg, he will know what to do." Jan turned and started walking briskly, up the steep incline to the road, and continued to talk to Jessica who was walking behind her.

"Tell me about Jason," said Jan, "Maybe we can figure some of this out together while we are walking."

Jessica did not answer. Jan stopped walking and turned around. There was Jessica, standing in the middle of the path looking down at the pit they had just walked from.

"You can't leave?" asked Jan.

"No, I can leave," replied Jessica, "I walked right past where we were when I was thrown back into the quarry the last time."

Jan came and stood next to Jessica, and they both looked down into the vast hole, and asked, "Are you looking for Jason?"

"He has to be here, Jan. He has to be," said Jessica. "Where else could he be? This is my fault too. I apologized to my parents, but I need to apologize to him."

"Jessica, what he did was no fault of yours," said Jan, putting her hand on Jessica's shoulder as they both scanned the quarry for any sign of Jason. "I don't know what happened to him, but when we get back to St. David's we will talk with Greg and Wylder, and we will figure all this out."

"There he is!" yelled Jessica, running back down the path.

"Where?" asked Jan, but then her eyes caught hold of the movement on the far side of the quarry.

Jan took a moment to process what she was seeing. After a moment, she grabbed Jessica's hand and started stepping backward, "Jessica," said Jan in a low strong voice, "That is not Jason. Turn around, let's go, now!"

Jessica looked closer at the movement and saw not one, not two, but many people coming towards them and Jan around the circular interior of the crater.

Jessica turned and started back up the steep and rocky path towards Jan. The two navigated the path to the top and out through the gate where Wylder had exited not long ago.

"I really need to talk to Greg," said Jan, "I wish I could ask him what to do." Jan stopped at the top and started pacing, looking back into the quarry with each rotation of her pace.

"What are we waiting for, Jan? I thought you wanted to go."

"I'm waiting to see if those people can get out of the quarry," said Jan, "or if they are trapped like you were."

Jessica turned to watch the crowd walking up the steep path, "There must be 10 of them," said Jessica.

"Look," said Jan, "they are not running anymore."

"The man in front is holding them back like he doesn't want them to scare us."

"They don't look like they have ill intentions," said Jan, "but I'd rather not stay and find out."

"Maybe they are just curious how we got out?" said Jessica.

"They stopped," said Jan, "but, why?"

"I'm going back to help them," said Jessica. "You go to St. David's, I'll find you later, I know the way."

"Why do you want to stay? You know nothing about them," insisted Jan.

"You and Wylder were here to help me, and I have to help them," said Jessica, "Maybe they can find Jason."

"Are you sure you want to stay?" asked Jan, "We can come back for them after we talk to Greg and Wylder."

"I'm sure," said Jessica.

Jan remembered the feeling of being in St. David's and wanting to help everyone cross over before crossing over herself. "Ok," said Jan. "You need to help them go into the Beyond. They have to go through the blue spark, face whatever is in there."

"OK," said Jessica, "I got it, you go. Go help Greg

and Wylder and then come back here. I will wait here for you."

"I'll be back. Don't leave!" said Jan. "You are not bound by the quarry anymore, and if you leave, I won't know how to find you. When I get back, I'll tell you all the rules that we have been able to piece together."

"OK, I won't leave," said Jessica.

Jessica turned around and started walking to the group of curious onlookers down the rocky path.

Jan turned and started to St. David's. *Oh, Greg, how I wish you were here,* thought Jan, desperate.

Jan?

Jan heard Greg's voice and spun around, but he was not there.

"Greg?!" Shouted Jan.

Jan, I'm here. What is it?

Jan looked around again, "Greg, Where are you?" Jan would have cried if she could have. "Greg!"

Jan heard Greg's voice again.

I'm still in St. David's, where are you?

Jan stopped. She was hearing Greg in her head. *Greg,* thought Jan, *can you hear me?*

Jan again heard Greg, clear and loud

Yes, I can hear you. How did you do that?

"I don't know," said Jan, "but I think we just discovered Heaven's communication system."

JASON

"Jessi," said Jason, "Are you sure you want to do this?"

"I'm sure," said Jessica, "I've had a long time to think about it."

"I understand the reasons why, I really do, but you are assuming the worst-case scenario," Jason said, "It's likely not going to be that bad."

"Jason, I know you love me, and this must be hard for you, but I am asking you to do this for me," said Jessica softly, her hand on Jason's face, "I know what I am asking. You don't know how grateful I am that you are saving me from a life confined to a wheelchair. Right now, I am young and strong, and I can feed myself. That is how I want everyone to remember me. I release you from any responsibility for this act."

Jessica looked up and cupped her hands around her mouth, and yelled, "God, if you are out there, I take full responsibility for what is about to happen here. I am the one in control. I am here of my own free will. I release Jason from any and all responsibility today and every day forward, for the rest of his life."

Jessica looked at Jason, and then added, "Amen."

Jessica stepped closer to Jason and hugged him. He sighed and returned the embrace. Jessica put his hand in hers and extended it out, putting her cheek to Jason, they danced cheek-to-cheek like she had seen her parents do.

Jason smiled and spun Jessica, who dramatically rolled from his embrace to the full length of their arms, and then rolled back to him and kissed his cheek.

"I love you, Jay," Jessica said, "Not like puppy dog love, which kids our age normally have. I mean I LOVE you like I have known you for many lifetimes. We found each other in this life, and we will find each other in the next life. I will scope it out and learn all the tricks. When you get there, I'll know everything there is to know and I can show you the ropes."

"Deal," said Jason, "But we better get this over with before I change my mind."

"Ok," said Jessica, "I'm ready." She stepped a few feet from him and asked, "How about here?"

"Jessi, it doesn't matter where you stand," Jason said, slightly irritated.

"I only ask because I want the flood to wash me away," said Jessica, logically.

"It's fine Jessi," said Jason, "Where you are standing is fine. You are my best friend. I have loved you since we were little kids. I will miss you so much, I will…"

"Wait, Jason, we talked about this," said Jessica. "No mushy stuff. This is not goodbye, it's see-you-later, right?"

"Right," said Jason. "OK, on three?"

"On three," confirmed Jessica.

"One," said Jason, pointing his father's pistol at Jessica.

BANG! The gun went off and Jessica fell to the ground, Jason rushed to her side and held her hand.

The blood was pooling beneath her, but she was still conscious.

"I thought you said on three," laughed Jessica.

"I thought it would be easier on you if you didn't expect it," said Jason.

He looked at Jessica, but the life had left her eyes. Jason started to shake. He dropped her hand to the ground and stood up. He backed up a few steps, keeping his eyes on Jessica, then without warning he vomited on the floor of the pit.

"What have I done?" yelled Jason, to the sky.

He ran back to Jessica, but it was clear that she was no longer with him.

"Oh Jessica, I am so sorry, I am so sorry." cried Jason, "I, I should have said 'no'. I should have talked you into the surgery, I, I…"

Jason pointed the old pistol at his heart, and crying, he said, "This is of no use to me anymore," and pulled the trigger.

Jason fell to the ground, his blood pouring out on the ground beneath him. "I'm coming, Jessi, wait for me."

THE ELSEWHERE

You did the right thing

Who's there?

You put her out of her misery

Who is that?

She was a burden
She was dying anyway

Jessica?

She was in pain

Hello, who's there?

You did the right thing
She wanted this
You decided she was ready to die

it was her choice, her wish
but you did kill her
You belong with us

What do you want with me?

Come on Jason, you belong with us

Who are you? Where's Jessica?

She's dead
You killed her
Come on Jason, you belong with us

I don't want to go with you, I want to see Jessica!

You can't see her Jason
You killed her
You belong to us now

No! No, I'm not going with you. No.

This won't hurt a bit Jason
Nothing like what you did to Jessica
You belong to us now

We will explain everything in due time

*But you should find comfort in the
knowledge that you did the right thing*

THE FUNERAL

Greg sat in Old St. David's on the stone benches, thinking of Maddie when the sound of a tractor broke his concentration. Cemetery workers shattered the hard earth as Greg walked over to watch.

"What do we have here?" asked Greg out loud, to the cemetery workers who did not respond. When the hole was dug, and they had completed their task, they left without a single word to each other.

Greg looked at the hole, *I wonder who is arriving,* thought Greg, *this is kind of exciting*.

The approaching Swarm was quiet at first. Greg turned his attention towards the uneasy sound. The Swarm's arrival brought a feeling of grief and anger. The entity hovered over New St. David's, pulsing in and out like a heartbeat over the new gravesite.

Greg focused on the entity sitting in wait above him, *this is not good,* thought Greg.

Cars began to pull up on the new cement drive and they crossed under the archway and proceeded to the Committal Service Shelter set in the back of New St. David's.

The attendees walked the short distance to the open-air pavilion and took a seat. Greg watched from behind the benches as the crowd quieted.

A uniformed Honor Guard stood vigil over the closed casket. A Chaplain, seated in the front row, stood up to start the service, which had now filled the capacity of the shelter with nearly 50 people. Many of the attendees, old and young, men and women, wore military uniforms.

The Chaplain cleared his throat, wiped the perspiration from his forehead, then began to speak in a loud and commanding voice, "Friends, family, military colleagues, we are here today to honor Major Miller, a fallen soldier who was taken too soon."

The Chaplain looked directly at a woman in the front row who could not return his gaze. "Your son is a true hero and a credit to you and the memory of your husband. He made the ultimate sacrifice and brought honor to the uniform he wore. His contribution shall never be forgotten."

The Chaplain cleared his throat again and continued. "We are all in mourning with you. And although our condolences offer little comfort, we are in debt to your son and the sacrifice he made for our freedom."

The Chaplain's eyes shifted to the back of the pavilion where a young woman in an Army Service Uniform and short haircut, quietly took a seat in the back row. A golden retriever followed close behind.

Greg looked over and saw Summer and Daisy.

"Daisy!" said Greg.

Daisy ran to Greg and started barking and wagging her tail.

Greg bent down to greet the dog. "Shhh…" he whispered to Daisy, laughing.

Summer looked over at the dog, with a confused look on her face.

"Ruby, come," said Summer in a strong whisper.

Daisy looked at Summer and then at Greg.

"Go ahead girl, go to Summer," said Greg, "You got a new name! It suits you, Ruby" using her new name, "It's so great to see you."

Ruby went over and lay at Summer's feet. She reached down to pet Ruby, who licked her hand in return.

Now that the short distraction was over, the Chaplain went on with the service.

"The loss of your son was not in vain. He gave his life for the country he loved. He is a hero, and he will always be remembered as a courageous leader.

Greg heard the jet engines in the distance before he saw the F-16s. As they flew over, he saw they were arranged in a traditional Chevron formation. The third plane climbed high in the sky, a salute to the missing man. The Honor Guard marched forward in unison to the edge of the pavilion and took their place on the rectangle cement surface which looked as if it had been designed for this purpose.

"At this time, we will honor Major Miller with a 21-gun salute," said the Chaplain. "The three rounds fired represent duty, honor, and country."

Seven men in crisp uniforms stepped forward, aiming their rifles to the sky above the casket.

"Fire!" the rifles shot in perfect unison.

"Fire!" the rifles shot in perfect unison.

"Fire!" the rifles shot in perfect unison.

As a woman in formal military uniform stepped forward to play Taps, the Honor Guardsmen collected their rifle casings. The flag, which was draped over the casket, was folded in the traditional triangle by the Honor Guard, with the flag edge tucked inside. With both the flag and the casings, the Commanding Officer stepped forward to present them to the mother.

When the Bugle stopped playing, the commanding officer spoke to the mother, "Mrs. Miller, on behalf of the President of the United States, the United States Army, and a grateful nation, please accept this flag as a symbol of our appreciation for your son's honorable and faithful service." The officer handed the folded flag to the mother and saluted.

When the service ended, each person who attended the funeral came to the front to give their condolences. Mrs. Miller solemnly accepted their sympathy. As the friends, family, and fellow military had paid their respects, they quietly left New St. David's until only Summer and Ruby were left.

Summer silently walked to the front and sat next to Mrs. Miller, careful not to disturb her, but Ruby went up and put her chin on Mrs. Miller's knee. Without looking at Ruby, she patted her head gently.

After a few moments, Mrs. Miller looked down at the dog and said, "You can always make me feel better Ruby Tuesday."

"Are you doing ok?" asked Summer.

"I'm hanging in there," Mrs. Miller responded. "This is twice I have been handed a flag. I am not sure there is a more painful gift to receive. Such an honor, and yet, it's like ripping flesh when you receive a flag and become a Gold Star Wife. It sounds very official, but ultimately it means that you lost a spouse in battle. They have a similar term for losing your son while in service, it seems I am also a Gold Star Mother."

"I'm sorry," said Summer, "I can only imagine what you are going through."

"Mason, you know, was only 42. He was in the Army for over 20 years," Mrs. Miller said, as she shook her head, tears in her eyes. "He wanted to join the military and follow in his father's footsteps. I tried to talk him out of it, but on his 18th birthday, he enlisted. He was such a sweet boy. I told him the military was not for him, but he wanted to make his dad proud. There was no changing his mind. If there was one thing that he inherited from his father, it was his stubbornness."

"I remember a story about Major Miller, back when he was enlisted," said Summer. "At one point he was responsible for the personal appearance and cleanliness of the soldiers. That was a thankless job, but he took it very seriously. He said cleanliness was next to Godliness. I heard that if a soldier's hair touched his ears or his collar, he would personally give that soldier a haircut. It was not long before soldiers realized that they did not want a haircut from Miller, and so they kept their hair in regulation." said Summer. "When I was under his command, he was the most badass leader in our battalion. One time when I couldn't hold my own in hand-to-hand combat, Major Miller trained me at night when the other soldiers wouldn't know. When it was my turn to test, they were not going to go easy on me. I relied on his training, and I made it through."

"What did he teach you?" asked Mrs. Miller.

"How to kick their ass," laughed Summer, "I'm going to miss him, I can't believe he's really gone. He was a good man."

"His father was a Lieutenant Colonel when he died," said Mrs. Miller, "I remember, when I opened the door and there stood men in their formal uniform, I knew why they had come and felt the blood drain from my head. I thought I might faint. The officer at the front asked me to confirm my full name. A man I recognized, as Richard's friend and commanding officer, stepped forward and asked my permission to come inside. I opened the door and they walked in, each making eye contact with me, each with a look of sadness I will never forget. We sat on the couch together and the officer said. "The President of the United States has entrusted me to express his deep regret that your husband Lieutenant Colonel Miller, was killed in action in Vietnam yesterday. He was in a military vehicle that was the target of enemy fire. There were no survivors. The president extends his deepest sympathy to you and your family in your loss.'"

"Last week, I opened the door of the same old house and saw the officers in uniform, I just stepped back to let them in," said Mrs. Miller, her voice breaking. "Once they confirmed my full name, they stepped in silently. I knew what was coming, they took a seat on the couch and said that Mason had died in combat. I was in shock. I don't even remember the words they said after that."

Summer listened, and Ruby put her nose under Mrs. Miller's hand asking to be pet and she responded affectionately.

"We can stay as long as you like," said Summer.

"I'm ready," said Mrs. Miller. "I don't want to be here when they lower the casket."

"Ok," said Summer, standing, and helping Mrs. Miller to her feet.

As Summer helped Mrs. Miller out of the pavilion, Ruby walked to where Greg was standing. She wagged her tail and Greg bent down to speak to her.

"Hi Ruby, are you getting lots of peanut butter?" asked Greg.

Ruby barked once.

"I thought so," said Greg. "Well, you look great! I am so glad I got to see you again."

Ruby barked once.

Summer walked with her arm around Mrs. Miller, and called out "Ruby, it's time to go." Ruby turned and followed Summer to the old Honda Civic.

"Good girl, Ruby, let's get Mrs. Miller home,"

said Summer.

After Summer helped Mrs. Miller into the passenger seat, she opened the back door for Ruby. Ruby turned back towards Greg and barked once. Greg waved goodbye as they drove away. The windows were rolled down and Greg could hear Summer say to Ruby, "You got yourself a ghost friend there, Ruby?"

Ruby barked once.

"I thought so," said Summer, smiling.

When Summer and Ruby had left, Greg returned his attention to the growing Swarm over the casket that had yet to be placed in the ground.

The Swarm grew louder, and Greg watched from a distance. When he got too close to the swarm, he felt a pain, an ache in his bones, that he had not felt since before he passed. It was as if he had been carrying a heavy load for miles, and he just wanted to lay it down.

He heard a horse galloping behind him, but he couldn't take his eyes off the Swarm.

Wylder slowed to a trot when she saw Greg staring at the pulsing swarm in the sky. "Greg, everything alright here?" asked Wylder as she dismounted Blaine.

"Do you feel that?" asked Greg, without taking his eyes off the Swarm.

Wylder stood still and focused on how she felt. "I feel tired all of the sudden," she said, "Is that what you mean?"

"It only gets worse, the longer it's here," said Greg, "but, it's dissipating."

Greg and Wylder watched as the Swarm dissolved in front of their eyes, leaving the casket untouched.

"The casket looks the same as it did when it was placed there," said Greg. "Did the Swarm get what they came for or did they give up?"

"I don't know, I couldn't see the person, but if the Swarm is here, you can bet they got what they wanted," said Wylder.

Greg looked away from the now clear sky and walked towards Old St. David's. Wylder followed with Blaine close behind. When they sat at the benches, Wylder said, "aren't you going to ask where Jan is?"

Greg smiled, "I know where she is, she told me about Jessica. She's on her way now but she is walking so she will be a while."

Wylder looked at him with Shock. "What!? How do you know about Jessica?"

"Jan told me," said Greg, with a coy smile on his face. "We figured out Heaven's communication system."

"Oh my God, are you kidding me right now?"

said Wylder, with a big smile, "That is dope! How does it work?"

"You just focus on the person and speak to them in your mind. It's that simple," said Greg.

"Ok, let's try it," said Wylder.

Wylder closed her eyes and thought of Greg. **Hello? Greg?**

Nothing.

"Did you hear that?" Wylder asked Greg, aloud.

"No," replied Greg, "Nothing."

Wylder tried again, **Hello? Greg, are you there?**

"How about that? Did you hear that?" Wylder asked.

"No," replied Greg, "Still nothing."

Wylder focused her mind and tried a third time, **Hello? Greg, can you hear me?**

She opened one eye and could tell that Greg did not hear her.

Testing one, two, three. But you can't hear me. I'm a poet and didn't know it.

Wylder laughed, "Did you hear that?"

"No," replied Greg, laughing "but I am not sure I wanted to."

"I was just being my sarcastic self," smiled Wylder. "Well, at least you and Jan can communicate. When Jessica and Jan get here we need to decide what to do next."

"Jessica's not coming. You have to go back to the quarry and get her," said Greg.

"Oh no, I didn't stay long enough to be sure she could get out," said Wylder.

"She can get out," said Greg. "She doesn't want to leave."

"What is with you two?" said Wylder, irritated.

"We don't have time to be playing these games," said Wylder, standing. "There is clearly something more important going on. Can you please go and deal with your shit so we can focus on the obviously significant Swarm? Fuck!"

Greg looked at Wylder, "I don't expect you to understand why I can't go back to the Beyond, but Jessica can leave, she is just choosing not to."

"What do you mean?" asked Wylder. "What is she waiting for?"

"There are others in the quarry, she wants to help them, like Jan and I helped the people in Old St. David's, to cross over."

"That's just great," said Wylder, with heavy sarcasm, "God knows how long that will take."

"We'll figure this out Wylder," said Greg, calmly. "Jan is on her way here now. We will put our heads together and come up with a plan."

Wylder folded her arms and sat down,

dramatically, "Fine," said Wylder.

"Fine," said Greg, smiling.

THE ELSEWHERE

This is your fault

Who's there?

You put your whole battalion at risk
Yes, this is your fault

Who is speaking? Identify yourself.

You still have bad judgment
They should never have trusted you
with the lives of those soldiers
This is all your fault

Private Johnson, are you hurt?

Oh, yes, he is hurt
He won't be answering

Private Keller, answer me!

He won't be answering either
They trusted you
They followed you
They were so young
They had their whole lives ahead of them
You killed them
You belong with us

Who is speaking?

Come, Mason. You belong with us

How do you know my name? Where are my men?

They're dead
You killed them, just like you killed the man in the forest all those years ago
Come, Mason. You belong with us

I'm not going anywhere without my men

You can't see them Mason
You killed them with your bad judgment, but that is not why you are here

I am Major Mason Miller of the US Army, and I demand that you take me to my soldiers, you PIECE OF SHIT.

> *That is not happening Major Miller*
>
> *Unlike your men, who did nothing wrong, you belong to us now*

Where am I?

> *Not in a good place*
>
> *But you should find comfort in the knowledge that you did not bring your men here with you*
>
> *You belong to us now*

Why am I here?

> *Finally, you are asking the right question*
>
> *Because you killed the man in the forest intentionally, all those years ago*

The asshole? He deserved it

> *Perhaps, but it was not your choice to make*
>
> *Deep down, you knew that*
>
> *You chose to kill him anyway*

Yeah, and I would do it again

Yes, Lieutenant Miller, that is why you are here

RECRUITING

When Jan made it back to the main road that led back to St. David's, she sang to pass the time. The paved road was deteriorating. The fields went on in all directions, as far as the eye could see. The old country roads had the stereotypical tractors driving on the shoulder with the lights flashing. Jan could walk faster than the tractors drove.

Jan sang the lyrics from a John Denver song:

Country road, take me home, to the place I belong. West Virginia, Mountain mama, take me home, country road.

Jan saw a man in a civil war-era uniform, sitting in the shade of a large tree. Legs extended, crossed at the ankles, hands folded in his lap. The man looked at Jan and she looked back at him.

"Ma'am," said the man, standing, "Can you see me?"

"Why, yes, I sure can," said Jan with a smile.

The man stood, removed his hat, and approached Jan, "Ma'am," said the man, "I don't mean any harm. I am Captain Noah Jones of the

United States Army. Who do I have the pleasure of meeting?"

"I am Jan," she replied, smiling. "You look lost. Can I help you?"

"Ma'am," said the Captain, "You'll have to forgive me for staring, I don't mean anything by it. I am genuinely shocked that I am speaking to you right now."

"I understand," said Jan, "I am on my way somewhere. Would you like to join me? I really must be going but I want to help you if I can."

"Yes, Ma'am," said the Captain, "I will join you."

Jan started walking briskly in the direction of St. David's and the Captain kept pace next to her.

"So," said Jan, "how did you get out here on this road."

"It has been a long time, I'm afraid," began the Captain.

"Why don't you start from the beginning, we have a long walk ahead of us," said Jan.

"Yes, ma'am," said the Captain, "But first, do you mind me asking where we are going?"

"We are going to St. David's Cemetery," replied Jan.

"Ma'am," laughed the Captain, "I could be wrong, but aren't we trying to get away from a cemetery?"

"It's a long story," said Jan, "You go first, and

then I will tell you all about St. David's."

"Alright then," began the Captain, "It started about 50 years ago, I'd say. When I died."

"Yep," laughed Jan, "That's how it starts. Funny that when you are living you think that death is the end, but here, we all start our stories with the way we died."

The Captain nodded his head in agreement, chuckled, and continued, "I was a Captain in the US Army, and I died at the old age of 62."

Jan interrupted him, "Sixty-two is not old," said Jan.

"I was being facetious ma'am," the Captain said with a laugh.

"Oh, I see," said Jan, "I apologize, please continue. I shouldn't have interrupted you."

"No need to apologize, ma'am. Please ask anything you wish," said the Captain, "as you say, we have a nice long walk ahead of us."

"Ok," said Jan, "So you were saying that you had a career in the military?"

"Yes," continued the Captain, "when I died, I was given a military funeral at Arlington National Cemetery."

"In Washington DC?" asked Jan.

"In Virginia, ma'am," said the Captain proudly.

"That is such an honor," said Jan, "Thank you for your service. I understand that in-ground burial is reserved for heroes."

"Well, ma'am, I wouldn't say I was a hero, but I was wounded while serving, I received a Purple Heart, presented to me in the name of the President of the United States."

Jan stopped walking and extended her hand to the Captain. He took her hand, and she gave him a firm handshake then placed her other hand on top. She looked the Captain in the eyes and said, "It is an honor to meet you, Captain, I mean that."

"Thank you, ma'am," he said with a genuine smile and bowed his head in thanks.

"What did you do to receive the Purple Heart?" asked Jan.

"I was captured by the enemy when I was on active duty. I suffered broken bones and lost my hearing in one ear. I was placed in a POW camp with other US soldiers. We were given only water and rice. We were kept in large pits that, together, were the size of a football field. Many of the men started to go crazy and I knew we had to escape. We started digging a small tunnel in the back of the pit, taking turns digging or keeping watch. The first three attempts only got us from one hole to another. When I managed to get through a dirt wall to another pit, I met a young soldier, who was maybe 20 years old. He had lost his arm as punishment for trying to escape. He had the heart of a warrior; he was not giving up on escape for himself and all the other soldiers in the camp. He had discovered which wall of the pit led outside the POW camp. The captors were not concerned about the tunnels that connected the pits, so we had a small community of rebels who were committed to the escape plan. The young soldier never told me his name, but I called him Sam, for Uncle Sam, a recruiter for the US Army. Whenever we were at risk of being seen, he would cause a distraction or pick a fight with the enemy on watch. He often took a beating for his actions. It felt like a year before we had the tunnel long enough to get into the brush outside the camp."

The Captain stopped speaking, and Jan stopped walking. She saw the sadness in his eyes, and said, "It sounds like Sam was a good man, brave and courageous."

The two continued walking down the road and the Captain went on, "One night, when it was pouring rain, freezing, and windy, the enemy who stood guard left the soldiers unattended. That was our chance. We went through the tunnel, one by one. Sam and I were the last to go. I told him to go through and I would help him from behind. As we were talking, the enemy had come to check on the POWs and Sam saw that he was going to notice the missing men. He ran straight into the line of sight of the guard on watch, yelling that he was going to kill him. The guard took aim and shot Sam, right in the head. I saw his body fall to the ground, and the blood spilled beneath him. When I knew he was gone, I went through the tunnel. Before the guard realized what had happened, I was out the other side and helping the 30+ men get to safety."

"I am so sorry to hear that Sam didn't make it," said Jan, "I hope you find comfort in the fact that together you saved thirty men."

"That is why the President presented me with the Purple Heart," said the Captain. "I never knew Sam's real name, so the Army could never tell his family that he was the real hero."

"Thank you for sharing your story with me, Captain," said Jan, "I would like to meet Sam one day."

"I would like that too, but I don't see how that could ever happen," said the Captain.

"Maybe you will change your mind once you hear my story," said Jan.

"Then please," said the Captain, smiling widely, "do tell!"

Jan smiled and began, "It all started with my death," she laughed.

Jan told the Captain about St. David's. She started with the way Nala and Wylder met. She explained that they would go through the portal to ride a horse named Cinder. She explained about The Beyond, a place to come to terms with the decisions and choices each person made in life. "Did you ever see a blue spark in Arlington Cemetery?"

"Yes, actually, there was more than one," replied the Captain. "When you got near one it would pull you towards it, so soldiers stayed away. They thought it would take them to Hell since many of them had killed countless men while in the service of the US Army. Those who went through, and there were not many, never returned. This just reinforced the belief that the spark was a place not to be approached. I was curious and bored, so I decided to investigate. I walked towards the spark, and I felt a force pull me. I resisted at first, but when I let it take me, I saw a flash of light, and then I was back in that dark pit with Sam. I thought I had indeed gone to Hell. My mistakes had caught up with me. I saw Sam and myself, I wished I could have saved him. I thought that was my punishment for not saving Sam, reliving the day he died from outside my body. As I watched the scene play out, I realized that Sam knew exactly what he was doing. He was decisive, and strategic in his plan. He led the guard away from the tunnel entrance. He made noise to cover the sounds of the men in the tunnel. I could hear Sam more clearly. He did not say he was going to kill the guard; he was telling me that the guard was going to kill the other men. He was signaling me to save them.

At that moment, I knew I did not leave behind a soldier, but I watched a man become a hero. We all made it out because of Sam."

"Maybe we can find Sam," said Jan, "But first we need to get to Greg."

"Who is Greg?" asked the Captain.

"He is my husband, and the smartest man I have ever known. He will know what to do," said Jan.

"What to do about what?" asked the Captain.

"About what is happening right now. When we were all in St. David's everything was so pleasant. We helped everyone cross over and then we were going to spend our second life together in heaven," said Jan, "But it turned out that we were in a bubble. We were unaware of the real situation."

"What is the 'real situation'?" asked the Captain.

"It seems that there is more to it than just going to face your decisions. Not everyone gets that chance. The Swarm takes some people and not others. We have not figured it out yet," said Jan, "We need to talk to Greg."

"The Swarm?" asked the Captain, "Is that the thing that looks like a colony of bats?"

"Yes, I imagine it is the same thing we call the Swarm," said Jan. "We think it's evil in some way.

When the Swarm comes near, it brings with it a feeling of dread, anger, and hate. It has a target, a soul that it came for. When it finds that soul, the swarm consumes it and then disappears. The terrible feeling goes away once the Swarm is gone."

"I've never gotten that close to it," said the Captain. "Why doesn't it come after you or me?"

"I am only guessing, but it seems that some souls are given a choice," said Jan, "They can stay where they were buried, limited to the boundaries of the cemetery, or they can go to the Beyond, which is not 'real' but a place in the mind where the soul must come to terms with their life on Earth. The place you went when you relived the day of Sam's life, is what we call the Beyond."

"It has a name?" said the Captain.

"We call it the Beyond, but it must have many names. From all the experiences we have heard about, we think a soul can bounce back and forth between the cemetery and the Beyond. Some people choose to stay in the Beyond since they can make it whatever they want. It's not real. The rest, who are willing to see their life from a new perspective, understanding the impact of their choices, can go on to Heaven. A better way to say it is "Heaven on Earth". Heaven, like we are now, is real and on Earth, with real living people. In Heaven, you can choose to stay there, in what I call "the universe" since I don't have a better term for it or visit family and friends back on Earth. You can watch your children and grandchildren grow up. That is what Wylder, and I, chose to do. While the others stayed in the universe of Heaven, we chose to come back to Earth to get Greg."

"Was he taken by the Swarm?" asked the Captain.

"We didn't know what exactly happened," said Jan, still walking with intention ahead of the Captain, "The portal was closing but Greg was still on the other side. He didn't make it through before the portal closed completely. Wylder and I came back to Earth to get Greg," said Jan.

"Where does the Swarm come in?" asked the Captain.

"That is where it all went haywire," said Jan, "As Greg and I were getting ready to cross over, the Swarm came. Greg pushed me through and then the portal closed leaving him in St. David's. Wylder and I were on the other side of the portal, in the Universe. We found a way to leave the Universe and come back to Earth, but he is still trapped in St. David's. The good news is the Swarm left; it did not take him. We really don't understand it. The other development is that they built a new area of St. David's cemetery. When it was expanded, a new portal appeared."

"Why doesn't he go through?" asked the Captain.

"Good question," said Jan. "He did go once, and he came back to St. David's. He saw a part of his life that he believes doesn't deserve forgiveness, and he is prepared to stay in St. David's for eternity."

"What did he do?" asked the Captain, "Please don't answer that. I apologize for asking such a personal question. It was inconsiderate, given that we have just met. Let me ask a different question. I still don't understand the function and purpose of the Swarm," said the Captain, "Can you tell me more about that?"

"Yes," said Jan, "I got a front row seat in the quarry. A girl named Jessica went to the quarry to be killed by her friend Jason."

"What?" said the Captain, who stopped walking to look at Jan.

"Yes," explained Jan, "Jessica asked Jason to help her commit suicide. She had a brain tumor, and she wanted to leave this life with full function of her body."

"What happened?" asked the Captain. "Again, I am sorry for asking such a personal question. I am a curious man; it is my nature."

"Well, he went through with it," said Jan. "Wylder and I rode up right after it happened. We saw the Swarm come to Jason and just consume him. I cannot think of another way to say it. It left Jessica without so much as a notice."

"What do you mean, you 'rode up'?" asked the Captain.

"We were on Wylder's horse, Blaine," explained Jan.

"A ghost horse?" clarified the Captain, an incredulous look on his face.

"Yes, a ghost horse," laughed Jan, "There are animals in Heaven."

"I should have caught on to that when you shared about how Nala and Wylder met. Back to the subject at hand, are you suggesting that the Swarm took Jason to Hell?" asked the Captain.

"That is what I need to talk to Greg about," said Jan, "Wylder and Blaine left the quarry before me, I stayed back with Jessica. They are probably already there. She is going to tell Greg everything and we are going to need a plan, but first, we need to go back and get Jessica."

"Why didn't she come with you?" asked the Captain.

"Jessica stayed because she wants to save Jason, she doesn't want to leave without him," explained Jan.

"How can you save him?" asked the Captain, "You said he was consumed."

"I don't know," said Jan, "But as Jessica tells it,

he was a good person and only doing what she asked him to do. He was never supposed to shoot himself. That was not part of their plan."

"Do you think that he was taken by the Swarm because he committed suicide?" asked the Captain.

"I don't think so," said Jan, picking up the pace, "Michael committed suicide and he got the chance to go to the Beyond. Eventually, he made it to Heaven."

"Who is Michael?" asked the Captain, "It is hard to keep all this straight."

"Michael is Wylder's friend," said Jan. "You can ask her about him yourself, we are almost to St. David's."

"Do you think Sam is here somewhere?" asked the Captain.

"I think it is possible," said Jan, slowing down and looking at the archway that served as the entrance to New St. David's. "We're here. Before we go in, I want to ask you. Do you want to join us? I don't know where this will all lead. It may not end well."

"Ma'am, it would be my great honor to serve alongside you and your friends," said the Captain.

"Alright then," said Jan, "Let me introduce you to my Greg."

The two walked under the arch and down the path to where she and Wylder left Greg. When she saw him and Wylder talking, she ran towards them, and Greg stood to greet her with an embrace and a swing in a circle.

"I missed you," said Greg, noticing Noah. "Who is this? You go on one trip, and you come back with another man?" laughed Greg.

"Let me introduce you," said Jan. "This is Captain Noah Jones from the United States Army."

Greg extended his hand to the Captain. The Captain took Greg's hand and returned a firm handshake. "Please, call me Noah," said the Captain.

"It's nice to meet you, Noah," said Greg.

Jan continued her introductions, "This is our friend Wylder." Wylder stood and shook hands with the Captain.

"Noah, it's nice to meet you. Greg and I were just discussing that we may have a fight on our hands. If you walked here from the quarry with Jan, she probably explained that the Swarm is taking good people and we are trying to figure out how to save them. Are you here to join us? We could use someone with military strategy experience on the team."

"Yes ma'am," said the Captain, "I have made it my life's work to defend and protect those who could not protect themselves. I would like the same mission in death."

"Excellent," replied Wylder, "Consider yourself recruited."

"Thank you, ma'am," said the Captain.

"Not ma'am, just Wylder. You are Noah and I am Wylder, ok?"

"Ok, Wylder it is," replied Noah.

MURDER AT ST. DAVID'S

"Wylder," began Noah, "You said I was recruited. What can I help with?"

"We are all together to make a plan, but first, I'd like to recount the facts since we were not together," said Wylder. "Greg was holding down the fort, here at St. David's. Greg, do you want to go first?"

"It started with a funeral, here in the new part of St. David's," Greg began, "like other funerals I've seen since I passed over, cars drove up and people came together for a service. Now there is the pavilion. About 50 people attended this funeral. His name was Mason Miller, and he was a Major in the Army. He was killed in the line of duty. There was a military flyover, a 21-gun salute, and a bugler played Taps. It was a full hero's funeral. I expected to meet this man, but after the people left the Swarm came, it brought the darkness and the soldier never showed up."

"Darkness?" interrupted Noah.

"Yes," said Greg, "It's a heaviness you feel when you're too close to the Swarm, a physical sensation of pain and fatigue that I have not felt since I was alive. It's also a mental pain, a grief, and sadness that is almost unbearable. I don't think I could manage it for very long. Luckily, the Swarm doesn't stick around once it has what it came for, usually just a few minutes."

"What do you think would happen if you stayed in it?" asked Noah.

"I don't know. The longer you are around it, the more feelings of pain, grief, sadness, all pile onto the foundation of anger."

"Why would the Swarm take a military hero?" asked Wylder, "It doesn't make any sense."

Before anyone could answer they heard glass break over in old St. David's and the sound of a man yelling. Everyone stood and Wylder was the first to walk in that direction. Sitting on the stone benches was a young man. Another was standing and shaking a broken beer bottle at the man seated. The group stopped quickly when the man began to speak again.

"Why did you do it, Jimmy?" yelled a man, slurring his words and unsteady on his feet.

"Put the bottle down," said the man calmly, seated on the stone bench.

"I thought you were a good person, but a good person doesn't sleep with my wife, Jimmy."

"You're my brother Will, and I would never sleep with your wife, anyone's wife," said Jim. "Why did we come here Will? Why are we in a cemetery, in the dark, miles from home?"

"I wanted to talk to you in private, where no one would hear," said Will, stumbling.

"You're drunk Will," said Jim, "Let me drive you home."

"I don't want anything from you, except an explanation and an apology," said Will.

"I have nothing to apologize for Will, I did not sleep with Kate," said Jim.

"You did!" said Will, "You're a liar and a fraud, and after all I have done for you, you're gonna pay for what you have done," said Will lowering his voice.

"That's it," said Jim, standing from the stone bench, "I'm leaving. Your drunk ass can walk home. Maybe it will sober you up."

Will lunged at Jim, plunging the broken beer bottle into his neck.

A look of shock crossed Jim's face and Wylder started walking toward the men. Blood sprayed from the wound and Jim instinctively put his hand to his neck and then looked at the blood on his hand before falling to the ground.

"Jimmy? Oh, Jimmy!" Will reached for his brother and stumbled, his skull cracked loudly when it hit the stone bench. Wylder reached the two men as they lay next to each other on the ground, silent, and bleeding.

Wylder bent down near Jim, "hello?" she called, but neither man responded.

The sound of the Swarm started almost immediately and grew louder as it got closer.

"What is that sound?" asked Noah.

"That," replied Greg, pointing to the cloud that passed in front of the floodlight which lit up old St. David's. "is the Swarm. Everyone, back up."

Wylder walked back to Jan and Greg, but Noah walked forward toward the men on the ground.

"Noah!" yelled Jan, but he continued until the Swarm surrounded him. He stood still in the middle of the chaos while the group watched in stunned silence, Jan with her hand over her mouth and Greg's hand on her shoulder.

When the Swarm dissolved, Noah slumped forward. Jan ran to Noah, but it was Wylder who spoke, "Why the hell did you do that?"

"I was curious. It's what you suspected, it's a collective of vile," said Noah. "I felt something like it before when I was a POW. When we got close to a group of enemies, like those standing guard outside the pit, I would feel the evil intentions, the desire to kill us, we all would. But this time, I heard it too."

"What do you mean?' asked Wylder.

"It was not a sound, it was more like a group of voices speaking over one another," said Noah.

All eyes were on Noah when Greg broke the silence, "What did it say?" he asked.

"It said – you were right to kill him. He deserved to die, he slept with your wife," recited Noah.

"I didn't sleep with his wife," said a voice from behind them.

The small group turned around to see a soul seated on the stone bench. It was Jim, looking down at his own body, lifeless on the cement.

Wylder and Jan looked at each other, "This is just like what happened at the quarry," Wylder said.

"What happened at the quarry?" asked Noah.

Wylder walked over to the man and sat down. "You must be Jim," she said.

"How do you know my name? Are you an angel?" asked Jim.

"No," Wylder laughed, "He called you by name," pointing to Will on the ground.

"Oh," said Jim, "Am I dead?"

"Yes," said Wylder, "I'm sorry."

"Where is Will?" asked Jim, "Is he here?"

"No," said Wylder.

"Is he in Hell?" asked Jim.

"I don't really know," said Wylder, "only you showed up here."

Wylder stood and looked at Jim, who was still staring at the bodies on the ground. "Let me introduce you to my friends, and then we will tell you what we know, which is not much," said Wylder. "This is Greg, his wife Jan, and Captain Noah Jones."

Greg and Jan nodded, Noah stepped forward and extended a hand to Jim, "Just Noah," he said, winking at Wylder.

Returning the firm handshake, Jim said, smiling, "Hi 'Just Noah', I am Just Jim."

"You have a good sense of humor for someone who just died," said Wylder.

"I try to make the best of every situation," said Jim, "There doesn't seem much of a point to do anything else."

"A positive outlook on death," laughed Wylder, "I like it."

"What do we do about that?" asked Jim, pointing to the bodies of him and his brother on the ground, "We can't exactly report it."

"I have an idea," said Greg. "maybe I can reach Ruby."

"Who is Ruby?" asked Jan.

"I met her here in the cemetery before you and

Wylder came back to get me," replied Greg, "Ruby and Summer."

"You failed to mention this when you were telling me about your experience," said Jan, with a laugh. "Two women, huh?"

"Oh," said Greg, "You will like them, especially Ruby."

"Hold up," said Wylder, "How are you going to 'reach' them?"

"Jan and I figured out the communication system, I told you about it," said Greg to Wylder.

"It doesn't work," said Wylder, "We tried it."

"It does," interjected Jan, "I talked to Greg, well, in my head, but he responded."

"Interesting," said Noah, "How did you do it?"

Jim looked up at Jan in surprise, "We have a Death-Comm? Cool!"

Jan started to explain, "you focus on the soul you want to talk to; it helps if you really NEED to talk to them," said Jan.

Wylder looked away shaking her head, "it's not as easy as that, or Greg and I would have been able to talk too."

"I want to try," said Jim.

"Let's give it a go," said Noah.

"Ok, I'll try to say something, tell me if you can hear me," said Jim.

Noah and Jim closed their eyes while Wylder, Greg, and Jan watched.

Can you hear me? Asked Jim, in his head.

Yes! Where are we?

Jim smiled, "It's working!"

Noah kept his eyes closed and pinched his face like he was trying really hard to hear Jim.

This is cool, right? said Jim.

No, Jimmy, this is not fucking cool!

Jim opened his eyes and looked at Noah, who was still contorting his face with effort.

"Why did you say that?" Jim asked Noah, with an expression of disappointment.

"I didn't say anything," replied Noah.

Because I am in the fucking dark and I cracked my head open, you asshole!

Will? asked Jim telepathically, eyes wide, looking at the others.

"What's wrong?" asked Wylder.

Yes, you idiot, who the hell else would it be?

ARLINGTON NATIONAL CEMETERY

Captain Garcia stood at attention over the grave of the Unknown Soldier. This he did, every day at noon.

"It is my great honor to recognize you for your service. You represent the multitude of soldiers who are lost each year without acknowledgment by name, but your spirit lives on."

Behind him in the distance sat two young soldiers, listening to the Captain speak.

"Crazy that after all this time he doesn't know it's you in there," said the soldier seated next to Sam, "someone should tell him."

The man jumped down from the ledge and walked up to the Captain.

"Why do you do this every day?" asked the soldier.

"Someone should do it," said the Captain, "why

not me?"

"Do you think there is someone in that grave?" asked the young man.

"I believe there is," said Captain Garcia, "In fact, I think there are many people represented there."

"I agree," said the young man, "But do you think there are any bodies buried there?"

"I don't know for sure," said the Captain, "I would like to think so."

"Oh, but there is," said the young soldier.

"Me," said the one-armed man who walked up to join the conversation.

"Who are you?" asked the Captain.

"They call me Sam, and my body is buried in that grave."

SAM

"All rise! The Honorable Judge Philips is presiding." said the Bailiff.

The people in the courtroom rose to their feet, and the boy in the orange jumpsuit stood at the front of the courtroom as the judge entered.

"You may be seated," said Judge Philips.

"Andreas Atea, you stand accused of aiding a gang member in the act of armed robbery," said the judge. "How do you plead?"

Before the attorney that was appointed to him by the state could respond, Andreas replied, "Guilty your honor."

"I cannot help you," said his attorney, "if you don't let me!"

Ignoring the attorney, Andreas said, "May I approach the bench, your honor?"

"This is highly unusual," said the judge, "but I'll allow it. Bailiff, accompany the accused to the bench."

The Bailiff walked to the table where the accused stood, and whispered, "You have balls of steel man, respect."

Andreas said nothing and followed the Bailiff to the bench.

"You have my attention, Andreas. What is this all about?" asked the Judge.

"Your Honor," said Andreas, "I am guilty of helping the man who robbed the mini-mart."

"You are not helping your case," said the Judge.

"But I had a good reason," said Andreas.

"As I said," replied the Judge, "you have my full attention. For sixty seconds," added the judge.

"I never met the guy before," began Andreas, "I had just pre-paid for gas. He came up behind me with a gun in his pocket, but anyone could tell it was not really a gun. The kid stepped in front of me and pointed his finger through his sweatshirt pocket at the cashier."

"Andreas, I suggest you go back to the table and explain this to the jury," said the Judge.

"Wait!" said Andreas, "This is important." The Judge rolled his eyes. "Continue," he said, "You better not be wasting my time. You have 48 seconds left."

"No, sir," said Andreas, "OK, from the back of the mini-mart, a young girl with a baby carrier on her chest yelled at the boy, "I have the formula, let's go."

The kid pulled his hand out of his pocket and

ran out the back door with the girl. He didn't have a gun, your honor," said Andreas.

"Where do you come into all this, Andreas?" asked the Judge.

"I heard the sirens and saw the lights. I ran outside and got into my car, hoping that I had enough gas to get away. I pulled up to the back door and honked a loud obnoxious honk to get their attention."

The girl looked first.

"'Get in!' I said and pushed the passenger seat forward. She jumped in, wailing baby on her chest. The boy jumped in after, and we sped away," said Andreas.

As they were driving, the girl leaned forward and said, "'Hi, I am Brandy, and this is our baby, Sophie,'" then she extended her hand to me, like I could shake it while making our get-away... Anyway," Andreas said to the Judge sarcastically. "Nice to meet you, Brandy," I said, as I drove so fast the passenger door closed on its own from the forward momentum of the car. I had a Mustang, so I got us out of there before anyone could follow. When I was clear of the cops, I dropped the little family off and went home. Well, I went to get gas at a different station of course, and then I went home."

"They stole formula, Andreas, and you helped them escape," said the Judge.

"Not true," said Andreas, "They didn't pay for the formula, but I didn't get my gas. My gas was $20. The formula was $8 per can, and they got two cans, which is $16. Even with tax, it is less than $20. In fact, the mini-mart actually MADE money on the situation," Andreas said with a smile.

"Go back to your seat, Mr. Atea," said the Judge.

"Wait, Judge, that is a good reason, right?"

The Judge did not respond, and the Bailiff escorted Andreas back to his seat and the hearing continued.

Andreas recounted all the facts that he had told the Judge. After cross-examination, the state-appointed defense attorney could not prove that the perpetrator did not have a real gun. It did not matter that Andreas had left without his gas, what mattered was that he helped a criminal and his accomplice, AKA girlfriend/young mother/Brandy, to get away with robbery.

Andreas was sentenced to 6 months in jail.

The first month resulted in a trip to the infirmary for refusing to give up his cigarettes. The second month left him with a broken hand for eating before the prison gang leader. The third month resulted in a stab wound for refusing to join one of the gangs that controlled the jail. The last three months were riddled with fights and vendettas despite having a reputation for not standing by and watching things happen to innocent prisoners. When Andreas got out, he joined the US Army. Three months later he was deployed overseas. Three months after that, he was at a POW camp. This is where he met Noah, and this was where he died before his 21st birthday.

He was not known by the name Andreas, or the nickname Andy which his parents and friends called him, he was known only by the name Sam, given to him by Noah Jones. When the United States Army was made aware of how he helped so many men escape, they went back to find his remains. When they exhumed Sam's body, they knew they had the right soldier because he was missing an arm. Since they could not identify this hero by name, they buried him in Arlington National Cemetery as one of the "unknown" soldiers. Selections for those buried in this honored tomb were to represent all unidentified American dead, not just those from one battle. He was repatriated with 12 other unknown soldiers who all made the ultimate sacrifice for their country.

WHO'S THERE?

Jim looked shaken.

"Are you okay?" asked Noah.

Jim stood up and rubbed his hands aggressively over his eyes.

"Please tell me you heard that," said Jim, in a desperate voice,

Noah looked at him, and slowly shook his head, "Heard what?" he asked.

"My brother, Will" said Jim, "and he's pissed."

Wylder went to Jim and put a hand on his shoulder then quickly pulled it away.

Wylder continued, "What did you hear?"

Jim paced back and forth, rubbing his face, and mumbling to himself.

Jan tried next, "Jim, maybe we can help you figure this out. Can you tell us what you heard?"

Greg stepped in, and with a calm voice said, "Let's give him some space. Jim, we don't have to talk about this now. If you need some time, we can revisit this when you have had a little while to process."

"The hell we can," said Wylder, irritated. "Obviously he heard something bad, and I want to know what it was. Jim, please tell me what you heard."

Jim looked at Wylder and shrugged his shoulders. He sat back down on the stone benches and put his face in his hands. Wylder went and sat next to him.

"Jim, we are all in this together. If you don't tell us what you heard, we cannot help."

Jim looked up at Wylder, and then looked at the others who had formed a semi-circle around him. "I'm pretty sure I just heard Will, and I'm also pretty sure he was in Hell."

WILL

Kate looked at Ginger and then at Will, "We have to take her to the vet," she said, "Please."

"She doesn't need to go to the vet Kate, she's a dog. Dogs have been having puppies since the beginning of time," scowled Will.

"She's been in labor for a day now, she has not had a single puppy. She's panting and she won't drink any water. Her water broke hours ago. Will, please, can I take her to the vet?" asked Kate.

"Hell no, Kate," said Will, "You know how much that is going to cost?"

"I don't care how much it costs, she is in distress Will, we have to go," said Kate.

"Are you paying for it? Last time I checked you were not employed. You stay home and take care of the kids, watching TV all day. If you had a real job, you might get a say in some of these decisions, but you don't. That means I make the decisions in this house, and we are not going to the vet."

Kate's phone rang, and she answered it.

"Jim? Can you come help? Ginger is in labor, and she can't get the puppies out. We need to take her to the vet," said Kate, as Will ripped the phone from her hand.

"Jimmy, why the hell are you calling my wife?" asked Will into the phone.

"I do answer my phone Bro, but it's in the other room," said Will.

"No, you don't need to come and take Ginger to the vet, she's a damn dog man," said Will.

"Look, Jimmy, don't get in my business. I don't care that you're my brother, this is between me and my wife, butt out." Will ended the call and looked at Kate.

"Why the hell are you talking to my brother?" asked Will. "Are you two fucking?"

"Don't be ridiculous Will," said Kate. "First of all, I would never cheat on you, and second, I'm not his type, if you know what I mean."

"What type is that?", asked Will

"Male!" yelled Kate, "you're so blind."

"Shut the hell up," said Will.

"I'm taking her to the vet, Will," said Kate, "give me the keys to the car."

"What are you going to do for me?" said Will with his tongue out and his hands on his belt buckle.

"Cook your dinner? Take care of our kids? Clean this house? You name it, I do it around here," said Kate, her face hard.

"Come on babe," said Will, grabbing her by the wrist, "A man has his needs, you know that."

"Don't touch me!" said Kate, pulling away and grabbing for the keys that Will held just out of reach.

There was a knock on the front door. "Come in!" yelled Kate, scared.

The door opened and the cold rain followed Jim into the house. He pressed the door shut against the strong wind.

"Hey Will," said Jim. "I can take Ginger to the vet with Kate."

"What is it with you two?" said Will.

Kate picked up the whimpering pregnant dog and walked past Will, towards the front door.

Jim noticed the bruising on Kate's wrist as she walked by. "The car is running Kate, I'll be right there," said Jim.

"Why are you all up in my business, man?" said Will.

"Will, I can take care of this one for you," said Jim. "Women are crazy for dogs, and they have this mother-thing that connects them to other mothers – even dog mothers."

"Fine," said Will, "but I'm not paying for it."

"No problem, Will," said Jim, "I got this. I wanted a puppy anyway."

"I don't understand you, bro," said Will. "You got a good heart, always saving people."

"It's a character flaw," said Jim with a wink, and walked out the door.

***

Three hours had passed, and Will heard Jim's Subaru pull into the driveway. The front door opened, and Kate walked in, eyes red, face swollen, holding a tiny puppy protectively inside her coat. Jim followed behind her with another tiny puppy against his chest.

"Where's Ginger? She'd better not still be at the vet, that is going to cost me a fortune," Will said, then added, "Actually, It's going to cost Jimmy a fortune, he's paying," he said with a laugh.

Kate kept walking into the kitchen, and Jim sat on the couch next to Will with the puppy. "Ginger didn't make it, Will. Kate is pretty upset. You might want to go check on her."

"Can't you see I'm watching the game, bro?" said Will, "She'll be fine. Women are emotional, she'll get over it. Besides, if she thinks she is keeping that puppy she's got another thing coming."

"What do you mean?" asked Jim, "she needs to keep Ginger's puppy. She's calling around to see if she can find another dog to nurse her. There were seven puppies in the litter but only these two survived. The vet techs did all they could to save Ginger and the rest of the puppies, but it was too late. We waited too long to bring Ginger in."

"You can keep both of them because she's not bringing a puppy into my house. She'll be paying too much attention to it and not get shit done around here. I don't even want the kids to see that puppy, or it will be weeks of crying and hollering and it will end up the same way – no dog."

"Kate," yelled Will, "Come in here."

Kate walked in holding the small puppy wrapped in a dish towel. "What do you want?" said Kate, not taking her eyes off the newborn pup.

"Give the dog to Jimmy," said Will.

"No," said Kate, matter-of-factly, "I'm keeping her."

Jim stood up to go, "Bye Will, I'll call you tomorrow."

Jim walked to Kate and kissed her on the forehead, "I'm sorry about Ginger," he said with a sad voice.

"Me too," said Kate, softly, looking up at Jim, "I owe it to her to take care of her puppy."

"I'll take care of this little guy," said Jim,

looking at the puppy in his hands.

"I know you will," said Kate, smiling.

"Go on, bro," said Will, "Time to get going, Katie has to make dinner."

"Bye Kate," said Jim.

"Bye Jimmy, thank you for everything," said Kate.

"No problem, I am happy to help. Let me know if you need anything," said Jim, as he put the newborn puppy in his jacket and opened the door. He protected the tiny bald puppy as he walked out into the cold wind and rain, then shut the door.

Later that night, when the house was quiet, Will got up and found the puppy sleeping in the box at the foot of the bed, warmed with a heating pad and wrapped in a dish towel.

"Come on little thing," he said, and he gently picked up the pup. He quietly walked out of the bedroom, and into the living room. He opened the front door and felt the cold rain on his face. He set the puppy outside on the porch, closed the door, and went back to bed.

ESCAPE FROM THE QUARRY

"Hell?" asked Wylder, "Explain."

Jim was silent as he looked for the right words. "I was trying to talk to Noah. In my head, I asked if he could hear me. I heard **'Yes! Where are we?'** which should have been the first clue that it was not Noah who was speaking, but I hadn't figured that out."

"Go on," said Wylder.

"I thought it was working but I saw Noah with eyes closed," said Jim, "so I closed my eyes and tried again. In my head, I said, **'This is cool, right?'**"

Jimmy's expression darkened and he said, "I heard, **No, Jimmy, this is not fucking cool!'** and I knew something was wrong. When I opened my eyes and looked at Noah, he was still trying to hear me. I thought it had to be him, so I asked Noah why he said that. He said, 'I didn't say anything,' but the voice in my head responded, **'Because I am in the fucking dark and I cracked** my head open, you asshole!'

Jan began to pace back and forth, Greg and Noah looked at each other and Wylder kept her eyes on Jim.

"What happened next?" asked Wylder.

Jim looked at Wylder and said, "I asked the voice in my head if it was Will and it said, '**Yes, you idiot, who the hell else would it be?**'"

Wylder sat down on the stone benches, put her elbows on her knees, interlaced her fingers, and stared at the ground.

Noah spoke first. "Jim, why do you think he's in Hell?"

"Well," Jimmy said, "first, he's not here with us. Second, he's kind of a jerk. I still cannot believe that he actually killed me."

"Facts," said Wylder. "I started thinking about something when Jan and I came back to get Greg. If there is a heaven, there must be a hell. All this time I thought that everyone went to heaven, once they came to terms with their shit, but maybe not. I don't know what I don't know, anymore."

Greg asked Jan, "What do we know about Jessica and her boyfriend?"

"He's not her boyfriend," interrupted Wylder, "He is her friend, and his name is Jason."

"OK," Greg said, trying again, "What do we

DEBORAH ALBERS

know about Jessica and Jason?"

Wylder stood, "We're not going to get anywhere by guessing. Let's go get Jessica, come back, and figure this out together. I'll go with Blaine and get her. It will be the fastest way."

"I'll go with you," said Noah.

"You can't go," said Wylder, "There is not enough room on my horse for three of us."

"We'll take the portal," said Noah, "We can go from New St. David's to the quarry."

"Noah, how do we know we will come out in the quarry?" asked Wylder.

"That is where you come in," said Noah, "You've been there so you just have to picture it in your head when we go through the portal. We will hold hands and you will bring me there with you."

"It must be the same as the way you and I traveled from the Universe to Earth," said Jan.

"The Universe?" asked Wylder.

"I was having a hard time explaining to Noah that we were in Heaven, but also on Earth, so I started calling the place where you go when you exit the Beyond as "the Universe" and that would separate it from the Heaven we are experiencing on Earth."

"Ok," said Wylder, "I guess I get that."

Jan went on, "it seems to me that the mind is

152

capable of a lot in the afterlife, we just need to be focused."

"It can't be that easy," said Wylder. "If we had total control with our minds, then I would have been able to hear Greg when we tried to communicate, and Noah would have been able to hear Jim."

"But Greg heard *me*," said Jan. "Maybe you can only talk to people you trust deeply."

Wylder looked at Jim, "You said your brother is a bad person, do you trust him in the way Jan is saying?"

"I guess I do. He's my brother, and I would take a bullet for him," said Jim.

Wylder looked at Greg, "I trust you," said Wylder, "and we couldn't communicate."

"If Jan's theory is correct, we have to trust them unconditionally," said Greg. "That limits who we can connect with."

"We are only guessing, I suggest we go get Jessica," said Noah.

"Noah's right," said Wylder, "We need to get to the bottom of this and we all have something to contribute."

Wylder walked up to Blaine and put her hand on his face. "Hey boy, can you stay here with our friends, while I go with Noah to get Jessica?"

Blaine let out a soft neigh and bobbed his head.

"Thanks, Blaine," said Wylder.

As Noah and Wylder walked to the portal, Noah said, "I swear that Blaine just smiled."

Wylder smiled and took his hand, "Ready?" she asked.

"Ready," said Noah.

There was a flash of blue light, both of them flickered and they were gone from St. David's like someone blew out a flame.

***

The bright blue light flashed again, and Wylder stood in the quarry, still holding hands with Noah.

"That was cool," said Wylder. "I think I'm going to like this heavenly travel system. Why didn't you tell Jan about it on the way to St. David's?"

"We didn't get to it," said Noah, "There was a lot to talk about while we were walking. When it was helpful information, I brought it up."

"Fair," said Wylder.

"How do we find Jessica?" asked Noah. "We should make this quick. Will might come looking for Jim."

"God, I didn't think of that," said Wylder, looking around for Jessica.

"Up there," said Wylder, and pointed to the

entrance of the quarry where she and Blaine had exited.

There was a small crowd around Jessica, of various ages, but all men.

"She doesn't seem scared," said Wylder.

"I've learned that if you can see them, they're ok. It's the ones you cannot see that you need to be worried about," said Noah.

Wylder looked at Noah, *Noted*, she thought.

"So, you have some experience with this?" asked Wylder.

"I've been on this side of the portal, what you call Heaven on Earth, for a long time," said Noah. "At first, I didn't realize what was happening, because I could not see the bad souls. I only saw the good ones. I'm starting to see that it's much like war. You don't always see the enemy coming."

"That's just great," said Wylder, sarcastically, "invisible demons."

"Wylder!" said Jessica, jogging down the uneven ground, and wrapping her arms around Wylder.

Wylder unintentionally pulled back a little, Jessica let go and said, "I'm so glad to see you. I want you to meet some of the souls here." Pausing to look at Noah, then back at Wylder, Jessica asked "Who is this?".

"I am Noah Jones, it is a pleasure to meet your acquaintance," he said and extended his hand to her.

"Formal, just like Jan," Jessica said laughing, taking his hand, and giving it a firm shake.

"I am Jessica Elizabeth Jones," said Jessica with a smile, mocking his formality.

"Come again," said Noah, "what is your name?"

"Jessica," she replied.

"I mean your full name, Miss," said Noah.

"Jessica Elizabeth Jones," said Jessica again, with a smirk, "Why?"

"I should have been clearer," said Noah, "I am Captain Noah Jones from the US Army. Are you related to one Elizabeth Jones?"

"My great-grandmother was named Elizabeth," said Jessica.

"Amazing," said Noah, "I have a sister named Elizabeth, You could be my great niece."

"Wouldn't that be a coincidence!" said Jessica.

"We have a lot to talk about," said Noah, "But first I'd like to meet your pals."

Jessica turned around to face the curious onlookers who stopped a bit up the hill.

"First, we have Justin, he is 20 and died here at the quarry in a dirt bike accident," said Jessica.

Justin nodded his head but did not say anything.

"Next, we have Mark, Bill, Gary, and Dean. They were all miners who died here over the years.

The group of men all stepped forward together and smiled, then stepped back.

Finally, we have Phil and Peter, who died in a manner similar to me which I won't go into."

Phil and Peter waived from where they stood.

"It's nice to meet you," said Wylder in a voice loud enough to reach the 20 feet between the two groups.

"Have they all crossed over?" Wylder asked Jessica.

"Yes, they crossed over many years ago, but they chose to stay here. Each felt safe in the quarry for one reason or another," said Jessica, "They think that bad things happen outside, but I told them not to worry, it was all fine."

"I'm not so sure about that anymore," said Wylder.

"What do you mean?" asked Jessica.

Noah interrupted, "Wylder, Jessica, we need to get going. Can we discuss this back at St. David's?"

"Will they come with us?" asked Wylder, motioning with her eyes to the new group of men. "We could use a few more souls to help out."

"No," said Jessica. "I already asked. They want to stay together, and they want to stay here."

"Ok, tell them goodbye, and let's go. We have a lot to tell you," said Wylder.

Jessica turned around and faced the group. "Are you sure you don't want to come with us?" she asked, "We are a small group, but we are all nice people. You wouldn't have to be alone anymore."

The men all looked at each other, one at a time, and no one stepped forward.

"Ok then," said Jessica, "I'm going to go with my friends. It was so nice to meet you."

The group waved to Jessica, and she started to walk in the direction of the exit.

"Wait," said Wylder, "Noah showed me a faster way. We can travel through the portal."

"I was wondering how you got down into the pit. We were all waiting for you at the entrance," said Jessica.

When they got to the bottom, where the blue spark was, Wylder held out one hand to Jessica and one to Noah. Noah took her hand. Jessica just looked at Wylder's open palm but did not take it.

"Are you ready to escape the quarry?" asked Wylder.

"I don't want to leave Jason," said Jessica.

"Jason is gone," said Wylder.

"I think I'll stay," said Jessica. "I have to be here if he comes back."

"He won't come back, Jessica," said Wylder, "and we need you. There is some serious shit going on."

"You don't know he's not coming back, do you?" asked Jessica.

"Not technically," said Wylder.

"Well, I want to be here, if there is even a small chance he could return," said Jessica. "Noah, it was nice to meet you. I hope we can talk more soon. I'd like to know more about my great grandma."

"I would enjoy telling you about her," said Noah.

"Are you sure you won't come?" asked Wylder.

"I'm sure," said Jessica. "Once I find a way to save Jason, I'll come find you."

"I guess we'll have to save Heaven without you," said Wylder with a laugh, "but if we find a way to save Jason, we know where to find you."

Wylder turned to the blue spark but stopped for a second and turned back around to face Jessica, "Why do you think Jason's coming back?" asked Wylder.

"I don't know," said Jessica, "I just feel like he might. I have to be here to help him."

"Don't wait too long. There is more going on than we understand," said Wylder.

"Ok," said Jessica, "I'm just not ready to go yet."

Wylder nodded her head. She looked at Noah, "Ready to go back?"

"Ready," said Noah.

Wylder extended her hand to him.

"I know the way to St. David's. I've been there," said Noah, "You don't have to take my hand this time."

Wylder took her extended hand and waved to Jessica instead. Jessica waved back.

The two walked towards the blue light, letting the pull take them without resisting.

Oh, Jason, I hope you're ok, thought Jessica.

I'm OK but scared as fuck, she heard in her head.

THE HISTORY OF OLD ST. DAVID'S

When Wylder and Noah returned to St. David's it was Jan who noticed Jessica was not with them.

"Where's Jessica?" asked Jan.

"She wanted to stay," said Wylder.

"Why?" asked Greg, walking up behind Jan.

"She's waiting for Jason to come back somehow," said Wylder, "She's got some other people in the quarry with her, so she's not alone."

"So, they were good people?" asked Jan.

"Seems so," replied Wylder.

Greg looked at Noah, "Noah, it seems that you have been here the longest, you knew about how the portal system works, have you figured out anything else?"

"We knew about the portal system too," interrupted Wylder, "at least I should have."

"Why do you say that?" asked Greg.

"When my grandma told me about the portals existing, not only in cemeteries, but in places of beauty," began Wylder, "she said I only had to picture it in my mind, and I would go there. That is how Noah and I got to the quarry, I pictured it in my head and that is where we went. Noah said we could go anywhere together, as long as one of us can picture it in our mind, which is easy if we've been there before."

"I can confirm that I have been able to go two places, both of which I knew," said Noah, "Now I know that we can go with someone else who knows the destination. I went with Wylder to the quarry, and I had never been there before, so I could not picture it in my mind as she could."

"You didn't know it would work?" asked Wylder.

"No," said Noah, "not for sure, but I had a feeling it would. It was an experiment."

"We went through the portal because you said it would work! I trusted you!" yelled Wylder.

"Wylder, it was an educated guess," said Noah, calmly, "I had every reason to believe it would be fine."

"You don't know shit!" yelled Wylder, angry, "And you took a chance without giving me the opportunity to decide for myself."

"I'm sorry, Wylder, I should have asked," said Noah, "I was pretty sure it would be fine."

"Save it," said Wylder, putting up a hand, palm out towards Noah, and walked briskly towards old St. David's.

Jan started to follow but Greg took her hand as she passed, and Jan stopped to look at Greg.

"Give her some time," said Greg, "She'll come around."

Jan nodded her head when she saw Blaine trotting to meet Wylder, at the old stone benches.

"Noah," said Greg, "what else can you share?"

"I was surprised when I met Jan on the road," said Noah, "I have been out of my cemetery for a very long time, and I have not come across many souls. I still see them trapped in cemeteries, but not walking free like Jan, like me. The ones I do come across, say 'hello' and keep moving."

"Wylder and I just came back to find Greg," said Jan, "I don't think we would have left the Universe if Greg had not been trapped here."

"Trapped here?" asked Noah.

"Yes, Greg is stuck in St. David's," said Jan. "Every soul in St. David's got through the portal except Greg. He held back the Swarm while I went through the portal. When it closed behind me, he was trapped here in the cemetery. Some of the St. David's residents were gathered on the other side of the portal, up in the Universe.

I thought we'd all find one another as soon as we crossed, but Wylder told me there were many souls from St. David's who were not there; Jeanette, Patty, Guy, and the family, Elizabeth, Bo, and Nala."

"Who are they?" asked Noah.

Greg spoke next, "They were the people who were buried in St. David's with us. Come on, I'll show you."

"What happened to them?" asked Noah.

"They all went to different places, I guess," said Greg, "I hope I see them again one day."

Greg took Jan's hand and the group followed them through the newly built walkway connecting the two St. David's cemeteries. They stopped at Greg's headstone, "that's me," said Greg, pointing to his gravesite, "And that is Jan, right next to me."

They walked a little further, out of the stone walls that separated the Jewish section of Old St. David's, and stopped at the bench that was at the foot of Wylder's grave. "Her dad made that for her mom when she comes to visit," said Jan.

As they reached the back of the cemetery, they saw the historical marker than stood at the entrance to the Slave Cemetery. "This is where Nala and Mama were buried," said Greg.

"Nala and Mama?" asked Noah.

"Mama's name was actually Elizabeth, but we first knew her as 'Mama" because that is what Nala called her," said Greg. "Elizabeth was Nala's mother, and she had been in St. David's for about 200 years. She was very protective of her young daughter. They had both been killed by slave owners. Elizabeth couldn't forgive herself for being unable to protect Nala, of course, there was nothing she could have done. Nala was the one who showed Wylder there was a way out of St. David's."

"You mean Elizabeth?" asked Noah.

"No, young Nala," replied Greg. "She used to go out and ride a horse named Cinder. Despite the interference of Elizabeth, the two girls became friends. For years they snuck out and rode Cinder together until Mama found out and put a stop to it. When Wylder tried to go through the portal to see Cinder alone, she was thrown back to the car accident that took her life. That was how we found out the truth about the portal to the Beyond."

"Fascinating," said Noah, "When I went through the portal, I was also thrown back to the day I died. I suppose I had not fully come to terms with what happened."

"Elizabeth did not trust Wylder," said Jan, continuing with the story, "She tried to trap her in the Beyond. Elizabeth thought The Beyond was where the Devil showed you your deepest desire and was able to persuade weak souls to leave the cemetery. When it came time for the good Lord to take the souls to Heaven, she believed anyone in The Beyond would be left behind. In her attempt to trap Wylder, she accidentally trapped Nala instead. It was Wylder who saved Nala, getting stranded somewhere inside the gateway itself."

"How did Wylder get out?" asked Noah.

"It was Elizabeth," said Greg, "She recognized the sacrifice that Wylder had made for Nala, so she let go of the anger. Elizabeth managed to reopen the portal with an act of love, and in doing so, rescued Wylder. Later, when Jan finally went through, the portal to the Beyond closed for good. She was the last one buried in St. David's; the cemetery was full. When she went through, the ground shook and the portal collapsed until they built New St. David's which created another portal, or so it seems."

"Because Jan was the last person buried in St. David's when she crossed over, the portal closed?" asked Noah.

"That was the rumor among the residents," said Greg, "But we don't know where it originated."

"Seems it was true," said Noah. He walked towards the center of the circular drive that served as the entrance and exit of Old St. David's. "This is a beautiful tree," said Noah, pointing to the Yew tree, "It must be hundreds of years old."

"That is where Patty and Guy would sit," said Greg. "Guy was a detective and Patty was his wife. It was Guy's detective work that figured out the puzzle that the Beyond was a good thing, a way for souls to move on to a better place. Patty was his biggest fan. She organized all of us at St. David's and held meetings until we had a plan to get all souls to heaven."

"The residents were not waiting on the other side for you?" asked Noah.

Greg looked at Jan and asked, "Who did you see on the other side?"

"It was only Wylder, Michael, and three kids," said Jan, "and of course, Blaine."

"Three kids?" asked Greg.

"Yes there were three," said Jan.

"Wylder only left with one," said Greg, "Who were the other two?"

"I don't know," said Jan, "We were only there a few minutes before we came to find you."

"Wylder came with a child?" asked Noah.

"Come with me," said Greg, and he led the group to the reflection area in the corner of the cemetery, to the tiny gravesite under a beautiful tree.

"This is where Wade was buried," said Greg, "He looked to be about three years old. He showed up right as we were leaving. He took to Wylder right away and she took him through the portal."

"She took him to the Beyond?" asked Noah, "At least he didn't have to go alone."

"It seems that children do not have to go to the Beyond, they can go straight to Heaven," Greg said. "When Wylder and Wade left, it was only Jan and I left from our small group in the main part of St. David's. We stayed behind to help the people from the Dark Side of St. David's cross over."

"The dark side?" asked Noah.

"It was the part of St. David's where the slaves were buried, like Elizabeth and Nala," said Greg, motioning for the group to follow, "because it was hidden by the trees and the residents kept to themselves. They had all been buried there when it was a slave cemetery."

Greg led them to the small space in the back of St. David's and Noah read the historical marker aloud.

This one half acre site of old St. David's cemetery was reserved for slave burials. Marked by oak posts and hand barbed wire, graves are marked head and foot with bricks made by hand of mud and rock. Some bricks are marked with names and dates, although most of them are no longer legible. The oldest legible stone marked the grave site of a 12 year old girl named Nala Jones whose cause of death is not recorded. Although the main cemetery is still in use, no former slaves were buried here after 1900.

"Nala and her family were buried here?" asked Noah.

"Yes, along with others. Jan and I stayed for a long time to help them all get through the portal to their heaven," said Greg.

"*Their* heaven?" asked Noah.

"What we learned was that the Beyond can be anything you want it to be, because it's all in your mind, it's not real. You can be there with your loved ones, even if they are alive and well on Earth," said Greg.

"Why would you leave?" asked Noah, "If you could have anything you want, wealth, good looks, love? All the things you couldn't have on Earth?"

"Because there is more to the afterlife than just hot guys and Cosmos," said a voice from behind them.

"Steve? Brian?" said Greg with a smile, "How are you guys?" Greg said, extending a hand to

Steve, and then Brian, giving both men a firm handshake. "Where did you come from?"

"Who do we have here?" asked Brian, motioning to Noah, "I love a man in uniform."

Noah stepped forward and extended a hand to Brian, "Captain Noah Jones of the United States Army, at your service."

Next Steve shook Noah's hand slowly and smiled, "Great skin," he said.

Jim stepped forward, "I'm Jim," he said, "Nice to meet you."

"Nice to meet you as well," said Steve, "So many new faces. Where is Wylder?"

"She is at the stone benches," said Jan, "cooling off."

"Oh," said Steve, "Did we have a little afterlife drama?"

"I'm afraid it was my thoughtlessness that has her upset," said Noah.

"You're a little old for her, aren't you?" asked Steve with one eyebrow raised.

Noah looked horrified, "No, it was not like that. I took her through the portal, and I was not 100% sure where we would end up."

"I see," said Steve, "So you isolated a young woman from the only people she knows and took her through a doorway that could have gone anywhere, and you didn't know if you could get back?"

"When you put it that way, it sounds pretty bad," said Noah.

"That's because it was bad, Captain," said Steve, in a protective tone.

"Please call me Noah," said Noah, "I'll go talk to Wylder."

Noah walked away and Steve whispered to Greg, "I see we have some juicy drama to catch up on. Anything else happen while we were away?"

"Well, we may have stumbled onto Hell," said Greg, watching Noah sit next to Wylder on the stone benches.

"Do tell," said Steve, who turned to Brian and whispered, "I told you we should come back and find our friends."

I DON'T BELONG HERE

"Jason?" cried Jessica, "Oh my God, Jason!"

Jessica, I'm so sorry, I shouldn't have done it

Dude, I am so glad to hear your voice, even if it's in my head

Jessica, listen to me

Wait, Jason, I never should have asked such a thing of you

Jessica, I am scared

Where are you?

I don't know, but it's dark and hot

Look for a blue spark, do you see one?

No, Jessica, I can't see anything, it's like it's just my mind and not my body. Jessica, I don't belong here, I can feel the hate and anger

I'm going to get you out of there, Jason, this is all my fault

Jessica, there are other things in here

What things, Jason?

I don't know, Jessica, they talk to me, they say I belong to them now

You do not belong to them, Jason, I'm going to find a way to get you back.

Hurry Jessica, they are getting louder, and I feel myself being pulled.

Hang on Jason, I'm coming

Jessica sprinted towards the entrance of the quarry. Without the fatigue of a physical body, she was at the top in a short time. She got to the main road and kept up her pace, heading for St. David's Cemetery.

THE PRICE YOU PAY IN HELL

In between lives, Dave could see so clearly, he was aware of what was coming. The same yet different pain, the fear, the rape, and finally the death.

When he was alive, he was the aggressor. In death, he was cursed to relive the pain he had caused his victims the night he killed them – but through their eyes, and their skin, unaware of what was to come...

When one death was done, the next was waiting. It never ended. Aside from the brief clarity that he was moving from being one of his victims to the next, there was no time to recover.

The bruises and scars, the feeling of broken bones, they didn't heal before he jumped to the next life, the next death.

At least for his victims, when they died the pain stopped. Not for Dave, the pain accumulated in his soul as he jumped from victim to victim. This time, Dave knew, he was going to be Sylvia when the awareness faded, and a beautiful sunset appeared directly on the trail in front of him. Breathtaking.

***

Sylvia was jogging on the trail, and it was getting dark, *I better turn back.* She stopped and put her hands on her knees taking deep gulps of air to slow her heart rate from the run up the steep mountain trail. She stood at the top of the mountain, watching the colors in the sky turn from blue to yellow, to orange, and finally red. When the darkness set in, she pulled the small flashlight from her pocket and turned it on. She would walk the 5 miles back to the car, careful not to fall.

The walk was slow, and the sounds of the night began to surround her. These sounds reminded Sylvia of growing up in the country. They were comforting. She turned off her music and let the crickets and cicadas be her playlist. Careful to plant her feet firmly on the path and not twist an ankle, she took her time but did not stop to rest. As she came to the low water crossing, she tried to avoid the slick moss that was under the inch of water that had been the reason for her wet socks and shorts. On her tippy toes, she slowly crossed, and the water flowed over her new running shoes. Despite her caution, the moss again caused her to slip, and she splashed down into the water, soaking her backside and hair.

"Need a hand?" asked a man on the other side of the crossing.

Startled, Sylvia looked up and saw a man, clearly a runner, and a handsome one. Sylvia felt her cheeks turn red, even more than the blush from running.

"I got it, thank you," said Sylvia, embarrassed.

When she started to slip again, the runner jumped in and steadied her.

"It's those shoes, you know," he said. "They are not trail shoes so they will slip in water like this."

"So, I am learning," said Sylvia.

"What are you doing all the way out here after dark?" asked the man.

"I lost track of time," she said, "The run was going so well, I didn't want to turn back."

"The sunsets are beautiful out here," he said, "I like to watch them before I go home."

"I can see why," said Sylvia, walking gingerly to the other side of the crossing.

"You're limping," said the man, "Did you hurt yourself?"

"No, it's just a twisted ankle. I'll walk it off in no time," she said.

"How far is your car?" he asked.

"It's still a few miles up, but I'll be fine," she

said.

"Don't be silly," said the man. "My house is half a mile away. I'll help you get there and then I will drive you to your car."

"Really, I am OK. I appreciate your offering," she said and turned to go.

"Alright, I hope you feel better soon. Have a good night,' said the man.

"You too," said Sylvia.

"I'm Dave, by the way," he said.

"I'm Sylvia," she said, "Nice to meet you."

"Likewise," said Dave.

Sylvia stood there while he walked away. He looked back, but then kept walking through the trees.

Sylvia picked up her flashlight that had dropped on the ground and started slowly towards the car. Her ankle swelled with each step and the pain got worse as the minutes went by.

She sat to rest on a large rock that blocked part of the trail. She heard Coyotes in the distance, *that's just great*, she thought.

After a few minutes of elevating her foot, she stood to continue her long trek back to the car when she heard a branch break nearby. "Hello?" she said to the night.

After not hearing movement from the small animal or whatever had made the sound, she continued to limp down the trail, one small hop at a time.

Crack

Sylvia stopped again to listen, "Hello, anyone there?" she asked.

When there was no response, she picked up the pace, despite the pain. For the third time, she heard movement in the brush and stopped. "Dave?" Dave stepped out from the brush, "What are you doing?" asked Sylvia.

"I didn't want to be creepy, but I wanted to be sure you made it back to your car ok," said Dave.

The light of the moon lit up his face, *you are really handsome,* she thought.

"Thank you," she said, "This is taking longer than I expected."

"Can I help you?" he asked.

"Sure," said Sylvia, and he put his left arm around her waist, and she put her right arm around his neck, lifting her swollen ankle between them and leaning on him for support.

In what seemed like one second, he covered her mouth with a cloth, and the little bit of light there was closed in around her and everything went black.

When she woke up, she was sitting with her wrists tied behind her and each ankle secured to the front leg of the chair. She felt her ankle throb and her heart pound. She could smell bacon cooking and heard classical music playing in the other room.

Dave walked in with a plate and sat on the bed next to the chair. "Are you hungry?" he asked her.

"Untie me right now," said Sylvia.

"We'll get to that in a little bit, but I made you some food. You must be starving. I did the math; you ran from your car on Wilson Road uphill to the top of the mountain. That's over five miles. You'll need some protein to help your muscles recover. I made you some bacon."

He held out a piece of bacon close enough that she could take a bite, but she turned her head. "Untie me," she said again, "Now, Dave."

"Sylvia, I went out of my way to cook for you. Damn, you are just like all women: stubborn, bossy, and ungrateful."

Dave stood up and walked in front of the chair to look Sylvia in the eyes and took off his shirt exposing his fit body.

Sylvia began to sweat, and her heart was pounding, her mouth was like cotton, "Get away from me!" she managed to say before he tried to shove a rag in her mouth. As he tried to silence her with the rag, she managed to bite the side of his hand, hard, and the taste of blood was satisfying knowing it would mark him, leaving a deep scar as a warning to other women. He yelled out in pain and hit her in the head with the pan that held the bacon. Sylvia fell backward and felt her wrist break under the pressure of her weight on the chair. She tried to scream, but the pain choked her. He took her shoes off, then her socks, exposing her feet and one black and blue ankle. "Let's get to it, shall we?" he said, and she began to cry, then spit in his face.

The spit brought an awareness to Dave that he was seeing himself through Sylvia's eyes, feeling the sharp pain of her broken wrist and the helplessness to stop what was to come.

If there is a God, please make it stop, *he heard Sylvia thinking,* but Dave knew it was just the beginning.

When the darkness had closed in on Sylvia, and her pain had registered in his soul, it began again. *This time I will be Cynthia.*

Cynthia laced her shoes and stretched her arms over her head. This was going to be an epic run.

She took three deep breaths and hit the trail. Dave followed in the shadows.

CONNECTING TO THE ELSEWHERE

Wylder and Blaine were at the stone benches when Noah walked up.

"Wylder," began Noah, "I owe you an apology. I should not have told you to take me through the portal when I was not sure that we would come out where I expected. I am sorry. Steve gave me a new perspective on the situation from your eyes. I had not thought about it like that."

Wylder looked up, "Steve?" said Wylder, with a smile.

"Yes," said Noah, "Two men came through the portal while you were here in Old St. David's, Steve and Bill."

"Brian," corrected Wylder, "Steve and Brian. They're here? We didn't know what happened to them."

"They are in New St. David's; do you want to go talk to them?" asked Noah.

"Yes!" said Wylder, standing, "And we are

good. Thanks for the apology."

"Thank you, Wylder. I really am sorry," said Noah, "It is my nature to take risks."

"Me too," Wylder said, "If you had told me ahead of time, I still would have gone with you. Next time, include me so I can decide for myself."

"I will," said Noah.

As they started walking back to New St. David's, Wylder saw Jessica running up to the front gate and ran to meet her. "What's wrong?" asked Wylder.

"I found Jason," said Jessica, "and we have to save him."

***

Wylder and the group surrounded Jessica to hear the story of how she found Jason. When she was done explaining how she heard him speaking in her head, and that they had a full conversation, she looked around at the shocked faces and asked, "Will you help me save him?"

"Jessica," asked Wylder, "how do we do that. We don't know where he is."

"Well," Greg said, "we do have some experience in opening portals."

"To the Beyond," said Wylder, with a hint of sarcasm, "This is somewhere else entirely."

"You were trapped in a portal, Wylder, and you were rescued by those who were still in St.

David's," said Greg, "There is no harm in trying,"

"You were trapped?" Jessica asked Wylder, "How did you get out?"

"I went in to save Nala and I got trapped between St. David's and the Beyond," said Wylder, "Elizabeth pulled me out."

"What we believe to be true is that a group of people, with a common goal and motivated by love, can open a door for the person who is trapped," added Greg.

"Please," said Jessica, "I have to save him. It's my fault he is there."

"Is where, Jessica?" asked Wylder.

"Well, he's not here," said Jessica, "It's like you said, Wylder, he's... somewhere else but I can still hear him. We need to go there and get him."

"Elsewhere?" asked Noah.

"Yes," said Jessica, "Good description, elsewhere."

"Jan," began Greg, "sing a song."

"Why?" asked Jan, laughing.

"Because when Elizabeth was singing," said Greg, "it was then that the spark appeared, and it led to rescuing Wylder."

"OK, what should I sing?" asked Jan.

"Something we all know," said Greg.

Jan began to sing:

Country road, take me home, to the place I belong. West Virginia, Mountain mama, take me home, country road.

"Join in anytime," said Jan, sarcastically, "I don't want to sing alone."

"I don't know that one," said Wylder, "How about this one?"

Wylder cleared her throat, and began to sing:

"Amazing Grace, how sweet the sound," sang Wylder.

"That saved a wretch like me," added Noah.

"I once was lost, but now I'm found, was blind, but now I see," added Jim, in a deep baritone voice.

Jessica looked at the group of strangers and smiled a grateful smile. "So, you'll do it?" asked Jessica, "You'll help me?"

"We'll try," said Wylder, "Let's try to recreate the situation that saved me."

"Ok," said Jessica, "Anything. What's the plan?"

Wylder looked at Greg and said, "I was trapped, but you saw what happened. Where should we start?"

Greg thought for a minute and then said, "It was all connected. Elizabeth was singing Amazing Grace. The whole group joined in. We saw a blue spark, fade in and out. Everyone sang with conviction, with hope, with love for Nala. The spark grew and Elizabeth was able to make the portal grow enough for Wylder to reach in and get Nala. In the process of saving Nala, Wylder was pulled in, and was trapped somewhere between St. David's and the Beyond."

"Do we need to go back to the quarry?" asked Jan, "That is where his portal is."

"I don't think so," replied Greg. "Jason was not taken through a portal. Jessica, can you hear him now, while you are here in St. David's?"

"No," replied Jessica, "I don't hear him."

"Can you try to reach him?" asked Jan, "When I was able to hear Greg, it was because I was intentionally focusing on him."

"When I heard him last time, I was desperate to talk to him," said Jessica, "I'll try."

Jessica closed her eyes, "Jason?" she said, aloud, "Can you hear me?"

Jessica? Is that you? Where did you go? I'm scared. This place is bad, Jessica, I don't want to be here.

"Jason!" said Jessica, opening her eyes and looking around. "Did anyone else hear that?"

The group all looked at one another, and then back at Jessica, shaking their heads.

Jessica closed her eyes again and spoke, "Jason, keep talking. I don't want to lose you. Tell me where you are. What does it look like? Is anyone else there?"

It's dark. It's hot. I cannot see anyone, but I can hear voices. I feel a presence or a collection of spirits. I feel their anger, their hate. Jessica, I don't belong here. How do I get out?

Jessica opened her eyes and looked at Wylder, "He doesn't know where he is. He said it's dark and hot and he can hear and feel others, but he cannot see anyone. How can we go get him?"

"If he can hear you, he's not totally lost," said Wylder, "Right?" she added, looking at everyone. "Ask him if he can hear any of us." She looked around at the group, "Try to talk to him, let's see if he can hear us."

"Jason, I am here with a bunch of people who will try to talk to you, let me know if you can hear them," said Jessica.

Quietly, each person closed their eyes and thought of Jason.

"Jason, anything?" Asked Jessica.

No, Jessica, I only hear you. Thank God, I can hear you. Don't leave me here Jessica, please!

"Maybe we can't focus on someone we have never met," said Wylder, "But I have an idea." She closed her eyes and began to sing.

"Amazing Grace, how sweet the sound," sang Wylder.

"That saved a wretch like me," added Noah.

All the others joined in, "I once was lost, but now I'm found, was blind, but now I see,"

"Jason, did you see anything? Hear anything?" asked Jessica.

No, Jason said, **Nothing. Jessica, I think I am in Hell. I don't think I can get out**.

"It's not working!" said Jessica, to Wylder, "He can't see a way out."

"If he cannot get out, maybe we can get in," said Wylder.

"Now you're speaking my language," said Noah, "A good old-fashioned rescue mission."

THE PLAN

"Tell Jason to hold on," said Wylder to Jessica, "We need a plan."

Noah stepped forward, "Rescue missions were my specialty; I'd like to assist," he said to Wylder.

Wylder nodded, "Go for it."

Noah looked at the group and started to list the facts on his fingers.

"We know that communication with someone in Hell must be initiated by someone here in Heaven," said Noah.

"Please don't call it Hell," said Jessica.

"Ok," said Noah, with compassion, "Pick another name."

"Call it 'the Elsewhere'," said Jessica.

Noah started over, "We know that communication with someone in the Elsewhere, must be initiated by someone here in Heaven."

"I don't think that is accurate; I spoke with Jan," reminded Greg.

"I initiated the conversation, remember, called out to you," said Jan, her face heavy with the weight of Greg's actual meaning.

"Let's test this," said Noah. "Greg, try to reach Jan telepathically."

Greg closed his eyes, and Jan waited to hear him.

"Anything?" Noah asked Jan.

"No," said Jan, sadly.

Greg opened his eyes, with an unsettled look on his face.

"Jan, try to reach Greg," said Noah.

Jan closed her eyes and smiled.

Greg replied aloud, "I love you too, honey," with the same unsettled look on his face. "This is the first time I felt like I was not with the rest of you." He looked at Jan, "I have not gone through the portal, so I am not in Heaven. I can't leave St. David's, so I cannot help to rescue Jason."

"I can't either," said Jim, "I only just arrived. For us to be of any value, Greg, it sounds like we need to go through the portal and be released from our sins. Then, we can help the cause. I, for one, do not want to be trapped here in St. David's while there is work to be done."

Jessica jumped in, "It's hard to face your demons, but it's also freeing. When we have all done this, we can get to the work of freeing Jason from the Elsewhere."

"If we can free Jason," said Jim, "maybe we can

free Will too."

"Jim," said Greg, "Will killed you. Are you sure you want to rescue him?"

"He accidentally killed me," said Jim.

"No," corrected Steve, "He killed you on purpose; he accidentally killed himself. There is a difference."

Noah interjected, "Let's continue to gather the facts."

"You remind me a little of Guy," said Wylder, "He was always collecting the facts and testing them."

"Greg mentioned Guy also. Who is he?" asked Noah.

"He is a friend that was in St. David's," said Wylder, "He helped sort out all the details about the Beyond. Like you, he was a problem solver. He was curious and thoughtful about his actions, but a total risk-taker."

"It's a strategy that has served me well," said Noah, then he continued, "It seems that if you murder someone, you are taken by the Swarm, and not held in the cemetery where you are buried."

Jessica spoke up, "We were not buried in the quarry, and neither were any of the others I met there."

"True. Still," said Noah, thinking of another

connection, "it was the place where you both died. You were given the chance to go to the Beyond, and Jason was not. Can you think of another reason why he would have been taken to the Elsewhere? He killed you, didn't he?"

"Technically," said Jessica, "but I was already dying. I guess, he killed me because I asked him to do it. That's not fair!"

"Let's figure out how this all works, then maybe we can save Jason," Noah said to Jessica. "Let's keep going, ok?"

Jessica nodded her head.

"Each person in the Elsewhere can only hear one person," added Noah.

"We don't know that for sure," added Wylder. "It is more accurate to say that the person on this side of the Elsewhere can connect to someone on the other side if they are trusted by the trapped person. Since we don't know each other well enough to build significant trust, we are just assuming that only one person can speak to someone trapped in the Elsewhere. We can't really test that theory."

"What if the Elsewhere is the opposite of the Beyond?" added Steve.

"What do you mean?" asked Noah.

"Brian and I were in the Beyond for a long time, intentionally," said Steve. "We built this great place with hot sun, and cool water, chiseled pool boys delivering chilled Cosmopolitans. It was all in our imagination. What if the Elsewhere is also in the imagination, but the bad part?"

"Didn't you have to go *through* the Beyond?" asked Jessica, "And deal with the choices you made on Earth?" she added.

"I knew I was dying," said Steve, "I took what little time I had and made amends, apologized, and forgave people I needed to forgive."

"When Steve passed, I took the opportunity to do the same," said Brian, "It did so much good for Steve, I wanted that freedom too."

Jan stepped in and added, "So another fact we know is that if you cross over having come to terms with your life, you don't have to go through the Beyond. Steve, Brian, and I are proof of that. When you die suddenly, or if you never came to terms with your life while you were living it, you have the chance to do so after death."

"That would make the Elsewhere a place where you are forced to come to terms with the pain you caused others, no option given," said Noah.

"But what about the soldier that was taken," added Greg. "I saw the funeral and I saw the Swarm take him. He was a good soldier. Do all military people have to go to the Elsewhere if they took a life in the process of doing their job, protecting their country?"

"I did not go to the Elsewhere," said Noah, "and I am a soldier. What else do they have in common: Will, Jason, and the soldier?"

"They are all men, they are all young, and they all killed someone," said Wylder.

"None of those things, on their own, are unique to them. Many of us are men, some are young, we did not go to the Elsewhere," said Noah. "I have killed people in battle, and I am here. Has anyone else killed someone?"

Wylder said, "Not me."

"No," said Brian.

"Me either," said Steve.

"Not me," said Jim.

"Nor I," said Jan.

The focus of the group moved to Greg, whose eyes were looking down at the dirt.

"I have killed someone," said Greg, "A child. If anyone deserves to be in the Elsewhere, it's me."

"Wait," said Jan, "What are you talking about?"

"I started to tell you when you arrived with Wylder," said Greg, still looking at the ground. "When I went into the Beyond, I was back at home with my parents. I was seventeen and my little sister was twelve. I took my dad's new car for a drive without asking. My little sister, Madeline, tried to stop me but I talked her into going too."

"She was twelve," said Wylder," I am sure she wanted to go with you. There was probably no persuasion needed."

"She had Down Syndrome, Wylder," said Greg, "She didn't know clearly what the risks were. I was the one responsible. We wouldn't have been on that street when the driver ran the light if I had not taken the car without permission."

"Greg, I am sorry to hear about your sister. It must feel devastating to realize you had a part in her death," said Noah, "But that is not like Jason or Will; you did not intentionally kill someone."

"The end result is the same," said Greg. "A person died because of my action. It was my fault and I accept full responsibility. I do not belong in Heaven with the rest of you."

"Greg," said Noah, "We have just met, and I am only stating what we believe to be true, but you are here in St. David's and the others are in the Elsewhere. God, or whoever sorts souls into their rightful place after death, has chosen to give you the chance to go through the Beyond. You have been forgiven. Now you need to forgive yourself. If you want to help us rescue Jason, you have to go back to the Beyond and face your sister's death."

"What about me?" said Jim, "I want to help."

"Well, can you hurry up and go then?" said Jessica, "Jason needs us."

"Sounds like we have work to do," said Noah, "I'll come up with a plan. I love…"

"We know," interrupted Jessica with a laugh, "You love a good rescue mission."

Greg looked at Jim, and then at Jan, "Jan, I want to tell you about everything before I go. I am sorry I did not tell you sooner."

Jan took Greg's hands and stood in front of him looking up into his eyes. "Greg, in life I knew your heart, in death I know your soul, you are a good man."

Greg took Jan in his arms, and rested his chin on her head, "I don't deserve you," he said and held her close. Jan returned his embrace. "I'm ready," he said to Jessica.

"I'm ready too," said Jim, "What do I do?"

"Jim, you go first," said Wylder, "then you go, Greg, OK?"

Jim nodded.

"Walk towards the portal," said Wylder, "You will see a blue spark and it will pull you towards it. When you get there, reach for the spark like the handle to a door; you will go into the Beyond. If you are not ready to face it, you can come back anytime just by wanting to be back here in St.

David's."

"I understand," said Jim, as he walked towards the portal, "Wish me luck."

As Jim walked closer, he said, "I feel it." In a few seconds, there was a flash of light, and he was gone.

JIM

"How many times do I have to tell you not to let the dog out?" said his father, taking off his belt.

"I'm sorry dad, I didn't mean to, he ran right past me when he saw a cat. I'll be more careful next time," said Jimmy.

"There won't be a next time, right James?" said his father.

"Right, dad," said Jimmy, "There won't be a next time."

"Let's get this over with," said his father, looping the belt around his hand.

"Dad, I won't let the dog out again, I swear," said Jimmy, with tears in his eyes.

"I bet you won't," said his father.

Jimmy could see Will through the open door of the bedroom behind his father, sitting on the bed looking at the floor.

"Bend over," said his father.

"Dad, I promise," cried Jimmy, "I will never do it again."

"That is what you said last time, Jimmy, you lied," said his father. "You get one for letting the dog out and one for lying. I am adding one more since you are being disobedient. Now come over here and bend over."

Jimmy looked at Will through the open door, helpless. Jimmy walked over to his father and laid down across his lap.

Jimmy cried out in pain when the belt hit his lower back and not his backside. He moved his hand instinctively to cover the pain.

"Move your hand, Jimmy, or we will start over," said his father.

Jimmy moved his hand, and the belt came down again with a loud snap and the yell that followed was not from Jimmy, but from his father.

Will had taken a pan from the kitchen and hit his father over the head with a sound that reminded Jimmy of a bell.

"Run!" said Will, as he took another swing of the pan.

Jimmy ran outside and down the street. He kept running until he could not run anymore. His heart was beating so hard he could not stand. He collapsed on the grass of a neighbor's lawn.

"Are you okay, son?" asked a man, who stopped mowing the lawn and bent down to check on

Jimmy.

"What happened to your back?" asked the man.

Breathing heavy, with tears in his eyes, Jimmy said, "I let the dog get out."

"Stay here," said the man.

Jimmy could hear the man inside his house on the phone with the police. After a few minutes, the nice man walked back outside and sat down on the grass next to Jimmy. It was only a few minutes before they could hear the sirens. A police car arrived with two officers, a man, and a woman. The neighbor stood to meet the officers.

"Hi, I'm officer Luca," said the officer. "What is your name?"

"I'm Jimmy," replied the boy.

"Where do you live?" asked the officer.

Jimmy pointed down the street.

"What happened to your back, Jimmy?" the officer asked.

"I got a spanking for letting the dog out," replied Jimmy, taking short quick breaths to stop the crying.

"That looks like more than a spanking," said the officer, "Do you mind if I take a look?"

Jimmy lifted up his shirt to show the raw red band of skin that went from side to side like someone had painted a stripe across his back.

"Who did that?" asked the officer.

"My father," said Jimmy.

"Where is your father now?" asked the officer.

"At my house," said Jimmy, wiping the tears with his dirty hand.

"Is anyone else at the house with your father?" asked the officer.

"My brother, Will," said Jimmy.

"How old is your brother?" asked the officer.

"Eleven," said Jimmy.

"How old are you?" asked the officer.

"Eight," replied Jimmy.

"Is your brother ok?" the officer asked.

"He hit my dad in the head with a pan to get him to stop hitting me," said Jimmy, "He told me to run so I did."

"Let's go check on your brother," said the officer who had just walked up. "Can you show us where you live?"

"Yes," said Jimmy.

"Have you ever ridden in a police car?" asked the officer.

"No, sir," said Jimmy.

"Well, you are in for a treat. Jump in," he said.

Jimmy got into the police car and buckled the seatbelt. In about a minute, they arrived at the house. The officer said, "Wait here, ok Jimmy?"

Jim watched the officers walk to the front door. He heard them knock loudly and say, "Travis County Police, open up."

When there was no answer, they spoke again. This time they were almost yelling, and they drew their guns. "Travis County Police, we have reason to believe there is a child in danger. Open the door or we will enter by force."

When there was no answer, the front officer kicked at the door. After four attempts, the door gave way and opened, slamming against the wall. The police entered the front door and Jimmy watched from the patrol car.

A few minutes later, one officer helped Will limp out. He was bleeding from the head, his jaw was bruised, and one eye was swollen shut.

Jimmy unbuckled the seatbelt and tried to open the door, but it was a police car. Even though he knew police cars did not allow prisoners to open the door from the inside. Jimmy violently pulled at the door handle without success. By this time the police officer had arrived at the car with Will and opened the car door. Jimmy jumped out and wrapped his arms around Will's stomach. Will grimaced in pain but returned the hug.

"I'm so sorry Will," said Jimmy, "I shouldn't have run."

"No way, little bro," said Will, "I'm glad you got out. Dad was going crazy on you."

"But he hurt you," said Jimmy, starting to cry again.

"I'll always protect you, Jimmy, you're my brother," said Will.

Jim watched the situation unfold from the front lawn. He walked up to his younger self, and his older brother. "You were my hero," he said to the young Will, "You took a beating for me, time and time again."

"Let's get you to the station," said the officer.

"Where is our dad?" asked Will.

"I'm not sure," said the officer, "but he is not in the house."

Will and Jimmy got in the backseat of the patrol car and Jim walked to the street and looked through the window at Will. *When dad came after me, you would instigate a fight to distract him and direct his anger on you instead. I probably owe you my life*, thought Jim.

Inside the car, Will scooted to the middle seat and buckled his seatbelt. Jimmy turned to pull the seatbelt around him and winced. "Jimmy are you okay?" asked Will.

Jimmy pulled up the back of his shirt to expose the black and blue stripe across his back.

"That bastard," said Will.

"It's ok," said Jimmy, buckling his seatbelt.

"It's not ok," said Will roughly, putting his hand on his broken jaw.

Jim put two hands on the roof of the patrol car, "I never thanked you," he said to Will through the closed window. "Thank you for protecting me, Will."

The Police car engine roared to life, and Jim stepped back. As the police car drove away Jim said, "I love you, Will. You were a good brother."

Standing in the road, watching the car reach the corner, Jim saw the spark. When the police car was out of sight, Jim reached for the light and found himself back in the cemetery with a newfound gratitude for his brother.

***

Back at St. David's, Jim walked from the portal to where the group had been, but St. David's was empty.

"Wylder?" called Jim, "Noah?"

Where did everybody go?

NOT YOUR TIME

"Are you ready, Mrs. Miller?" asked Summer.

"Yes, dear," Mrs. Miller said.

"Are you ready, Ruby?" Summer asked her dog.

Ruby barked once.

The three of them headed to Summer's little Honda Civic, parked on the street. Summer opened the back door and the dog jumped in. She opened the passenger door and helped Mrs. Miller into the seat before closing the door and walking to the driver's side.

When she started the car and buckled her seatbelt, she looked at Mrs. Miller.

"Mrs. Miller, are you sure you want to go to St. David's?" Summer asked, "After what happened there? You know there was a murder only a few weeks ago."

"I want to visit Mason," said Mrs. Miller, "Besides, I am with you, and you are a..." Mrs. Miller cleared her throat and said in a whisper, "bad bitch."

Summer let out a loud laugh and shook her

head, "Mrs. Miller, you are one awesome lady. I am a bad bitch, and I will take you to St. David's, killers be damned."

"Thank you, dear," said Mrs. Miller, and looked forward again, out the windshield.

They went through the sleepy town, and out into the countryside. When they had pulled onto the road which led to the cemetery, Mrs. Miller said, "Well look there, dear. You don't see that every day."

Just outside of the cemetery entrance was a car, upside down, with smoke coming out of the engine. Summer quickly pulled over the car and jammed it into Park, turned off the engine, hit the emergency flashers on the dash, opened the door, and ran towards the overturned vehicle. Ruby jumped into the front seat and out the door, following Summer.

As she approached the scene, Summer looked around. There was no sign of what had caused the accident. There was no other vehicle, no people, no wires down, nothing in the road; there was only a large boulder sunk deep in the grass on the outside of the cemetery.

Summer lay on the ground and looked into the broken windshield. "Ma'am!" yelled Summer. There was no response. Summer tried again, "Ma'am, can you hear me?"

"Yes," said the woman in a weak voice, "I can't

feel my legs."

"You're going to be ok," said Summer, "I have to get you out; I smell gas."

The woman groaned in pain.

"I'm Summer and this is my dog Ruby," Summer said, pulling down the sleeves of her sweatshirt to her wrist before she crawled on her elbows under the car and through the broken glass of the driver's side window.

"I'm Stephanie," the woman said, coughing.

Blood was dripping from above Summer and pooling on the ground. "Turn off the engine, ok Stephanie? I'm going to release your seatbelt, and you are going to fall."

"OK," said Stephanie, wincing.

Summer worked quickly, positioning herself under the woman. "I got a hold of you the best I can. I am going to release your seatbelt. Are you ready?" Summer asked.

"Yes," said Stephanie.

"OK, here we go," Summer said, and she pressed the release for the seatbelt. Nothing. Summer pressed the seatbelt button franticly, but it did not release the belt.

"Stephanie," said Summer, "It's jammed. I have to go get a tool from my car. I'll be right back."

Summer scooted back out of the crushed vehicle and looked at Ruby and said, "You stay with Stephanie, alright girl?"

Ruby barked once.

Summer ran for the car yelling for Mrs. Miller to call 911.

Ruby laid down on her belly, looking up at the woman, trapped in the driver's side seat, suspended.

"Hi Ruby," said Stephanie, breathless, face red, then her eyes rolled back in her head.

Ruby barked once, then twice, then repeatedly.

Summer was rummaging through a bag in the trunk of the old car when she looked at Ruby.

"I've never heard her bark like that before, dear," Mrs. Miller said to Summer.

"Yeah, me either," Summer grabbed the Swiss Army Knife and ran back to the smoking car.

Scooting on her back until she could reach the seatbelt, Summer said, "Hi Stephanie, I'm back. I'm going to cut your seatbelt and get you down."

Ruby backed out from underneath the car but kept barking. Summer repositioned herself inside the smoking vehicle, sitting on the roof, holding the woman's shoulders.

"Are you ready?" asked Summer, but there was no response. "Stephanie? Shit. Stay with me."

Summer reached up and used the knife to start cutting through the seatbelt. Ruby kept barking continuously, "I know, Ruby, I smell it too." Summer kept at the seatbelt, making slow progress.

Ruby's bark got more urgent, "Ruby, you are not helping," said Summer, sounding irritated as she worked on the seatbelt over her head, with blood continuing to drip from Stephanie.

Wylder ran across the street and stood by the wreck.

Even though Summer could not hear her, Wylder shouted, "Hurry up! Get her out of there!"

Ruby's bark quieted, "Thank you, Ruby," said Summer.

Ruby came up and smelled the ground at Wylder's feet, then looked up at her.

"Can you see me?" Wylder asked.

Ruby barked once.

Steve and Brian ran up behind Wylder, "Oh my God," said Steve, "What's happening here?"

"This woman is trying to save the driver of the car," said Wylder, "and this dog can see us," she added casually. Wylder turned her attention back to the car.

Steve looked at the dog, and asked, "Can you see me?"

Ruby barked once.

"Jan," said Steve, "Check this out." Steve looked behind him for Jan, but she was not there.

Steve looked at Brian, "Where is everyone?" he asked.

Brian looked at Steve and said, "Greg cannot leave the cemetery. Jan is trying to talk him into going into the Beyond, but he doesn't want to go."

"I'll go talk to him," said Steve, and he turned to head back to St. David's, with Ruby right behind him.

Noah and Jessica were crossing the dirt road towards Steve. Jessica smiled, "That dog seems to be following you," she said to Steve.

Summer looked through the broken windshield at Ruby who was now at the edge of the dirt road, facing New St. David's, wagging her tail.

"I think she can see us," Steve said, smiling. "I'm going to talk to Greg. Wylder and Brian are watching the rescue mission over there."

"I love a good rescue mission," said Noah, "I'll go see if I can help."

"Me too," said Jessica, and they picked up the pace to the other side of the road.

Steve saw Jan and Greg at the edge of New St. David's. Ruby ran to Greg and barked.

"Hey girl," Greg said, "What are you doing here?"

Ruby wagged her tail.

"Is Summer here?" Greg asked.

Ruby barked once.

"Is she hurt?" Greg asked.

Ruby barked once.

Summer finally cut through the thick belt and the woman dropped into her arms, knocking the knife out of Summer's hands and onto the ground. Summer put her arms under the unconscious woman and pulled, but Stephanie's feet were still trapped in the crushed dash above.

"Ruby!" yelled Summer, and Ruby left Greg and came running to Summer, "Get the knife, girl, bring it to me, hurry!"

Ruby picked up the knife in her teeth and brought it to Summer. "Thanks, Ruby," said Summer as she grabbed the Swiss Army Knife, reached up as high as she could, and started to cut through the fabric that held the woman's legs in place. When the denim finally tore, Summer found the source of the bleeding. It was not Stephanie's pants, but her leg that was hooked on the jagged piece of metal that was now exposed.

"I'm sorry," Summer said to the unconscious woman, "but this is going to hurt." Summer leaned back and pulled, hearing the woman scream. "You're going to be ok," Summer said to the crying woman, "It's just a flesh wound. I smell gas and we need to get out of here, right now." Stephanie didn't respond, but Summer's military training kept her talking.

"Why were you out here anyway?" asked Summer.

"Were you going to St. David's to visit someone?" asked Summer as she struggled to get them both free of the wreck. There was no verbal response from the woman, but she was rolling her head from side to side, with a weak groan.

"Stay with me," Summer said, pulling the woman free of the car.

Ruby ran back across the dirt road, to Greg, and began barking.

Greg looked at her with a miserable expression and said, "Ruby, I cannot leave her, do you understand?"

Ruby barked twice at Greg, then looked back at where Summer was lying on the ground.

"I have to stay," said Greg, "I cannot get out, even if I wanted to."

Summer, laying on her back, tried to shimmy out from under the vehicle pulling Stephanie, who was unconscious, on her chest. Using her heels to push the weight of two people, she felt rocks cutting through her shirt, blood pooling beneath her. "I'm not sure if that's your blood or mine," said Summer grimacing as she cleared the car, "but we're almost out, Stephanie," Summer said.

As she rolled on her side to get a better hold of the unconscious woman, the heat intensified, and Summer felt the inside of her nose burning, and her hands began to blister. The car let out a loud screech of metal against metal before she heard the deafening blow of the car exploding. Pieces of debris went flying, and broken glass fell down like rain, sparkling in the sun before it hit the women and the ground around them. Summer heard herself scream as the weight of the car pinned her between Stephanie and the ground. Ruby barked loudly pawing at the ground near Summer's head and the sound of distant sirens grew louder, then it all went black.

As metal and glass showered down, Jan left Greg and went running towards the explosion. She passed Steve and yelled, "Talk some sense into him!"

***

An ambulance pulled up, and a fire truck followed behind, partially blocking Greg's view of the scene. As six firefighters jumped from the doors of the huge red truck, Ruby ran back across the road to find Summer.

Greg looked across the road and struggled to see what was happening. Firefighters were working to put out the car fire, emergency personnel were performing CPR on the driver of the car, while other emergency personnel were helping Summer into the Ambulance.

Steve reached Greg and said "Are you just going to stand by and do nothing? That's pretty selfish, Greg. I remember you being the voice of reason, resolving conflict, and facing the hard stuff. What happened to you?"

Greg looked at Steve, who would not break eye contact. After a few long minutes, Greg said, "I'm coming, Ruby," but Ruby was already out of earshot.

Greg looked back at Steve, then turned and walked to the blue spark, letting the force pull him into the Beyond.

FINDING FORGIVENESS

Greg was in the back room of his synagogue, seeing his younger self sitting on a folding chair facing the plain wooden casket. The room was empty, but he could hear the low hum of the Comforters in the main room.

His father knocked on the old wooden door and it made a loud screeching sound as it was opened.

"It's time," said his father, and shut the door, making the same painful noise before latching closed.

Greg sat in the second row, behind his younger self, knowing that he was going to be sitting there for a while, despite his father's announcement.

Greg had no words of comfort to give his younger self. As in the Old Testament, the book of Job, he sat in the presence of the one mourning and in pain, offering only his presence as comfort.

Greg remembered that he had not participated in 'sitting shiva' with his family. The young Greg did not want to be comforted, he did not want to accept Maddie's death, and he did not want forgiveness.

Greg reminded himself why he was here. *This is not for me. My time on Earth has passed. Forgiving myself is the only way to allow me to help those I love in the afterlife.*

As a Jewish man, he knew the traditions that helped the mourning family through the grieving process. He saw the black ribbon, and a pin, sitting on the folding chair next to his young self, untouched.

If this was the Beyond, as he knew it was, he should have full control of the situation. Greg stood and walked in front of his younger self and looked into the tear-filled eyes of the young boy.

You are so young, Greg thought.

Greg picked up the ribbon and began to speak.

"Hi Greg," he said, looking at the child he once was, carrying the heavy burden of his sister's death.

The younger Greg looked up, "I didn't hear you come in," he said.

"It's time," said Greg.

"Oh, I thought that was my father," said the boy, standing.

"May I pin this on you?" asked Greg.

"I do not deserve to wear that," said the young Greg.

"You are Madeline's brother, are you not?" asked Greg.

"Yes, I was," said the boy.

"This is not for you, this is for her," said Greg, "This is to honor her and recognize the loss this world will face without her. Wear it for her."

The boy stepped forward and allowed Greg to pin the black ribbon on his shirt.

"Baruch atah Adonai, Dayan Ha-Emet," said Greg *Blessed are You, Adonai, Truthful Judge*

The young boy recited a passage from the book of Job:

"Adonai natan, Adonai lakach, yehi shem Adonai m'vorach," *God has given, God has taken away, blessed be the name of God.*

Greg put his hand on the boy's shoulder. "Are you ready?"

"Not really," replied the boy, "I cannot sit shiva."

"You can. You must," said Greg, "It is the custom for our people. It is how we honor the dead, and comfort those still living."

The boy walked towards the door and Greg

followed. After the eulogy and concluding prayers, Greg listened to the El Malei Rachamim being recited. Then Greg, along with his younger self and his parents, returned to another private room to await the procession to the cemetery.

Greg knew from experience that the pallbearers would help to move the casket from the chapel to the hearse. He sat in the backseat of the vehicle, next to his younger self, as they drove to the gravesite.

They moved from the car to the folding chairs set up near the gravesite. They stood as the pallbearers made their way from the hearse to the grave, pausing seven times, as is tradition. As the casket was lowered, the rabbi said a prayer and recited a Psalm.

His mother stepped forward and put the first shovel of dirt on the casket. After his father had placed earth on top of the casket he handed the shovel to his son, not letting go until the young Greg looked in his eyes. They were filled with compassion and love. His father let go of the shovel and young Greg painfully took the responsibility of burying his young sister.

Greg felt a slight healing come over him. The pain was somehow diluted in the presence of those around him, those who loved Maddie too. The pain did not go away, but the sharp sting was replaced by a deep grief that took the place in his heart that his sister had occupied.

For the next seven days, both Greg and his younger self sat shiva with his family. In silence, and in the presence of his loved ones, he took part in all the rituals he had refused to participate in on Earth.

Once the week was over, he looked at his younger self from across the room. *I must forgive you; I must forgive myself. I will carry with me the weight of what I have done, but I will accept the forgiveness offered by God and my family.*

A blue spark appeared. Greg looked around at his family. *It would be so easy to stay,* he thought, *here, I could create a place where Maddie could be back.* With that, a realization hit him like a brick. Greg headed towards the blue spark, with a smile on his face and a spring in his step.

I'm going to find Maddie.

THE SEARCH FOR SUMMER

Greg entered New St. David's and walked against the current of the Portal. Each step got easier as he put space between him and the gateway to the Beyond. When he got to the edge of the cemetery, he expected to be thrown back inside as had happened the last time he got too close to the boundary.

This time, he passed right through the gateway and joined Jan and the others in the street, watching an ambulance drive away.

"Greg!" yelled Jan, and she threw her arms around her husband, and he returned the hug. She looked up at him, "I am so proud of you," she said, "I cannot imagine how hard that was."

"I didn't know if you would still be here," said Greg, "I sat shiva with my family for a week. I guess time passes quicker in the Beyond than here on Earth. How long has it been?" asked Greg.

"About an hour, I'd guess," said Noah, walking up behind Jan.

"The first ambulance took the driver of the car, the second ambulance took Summer, and the fire truck took Mrs. Miller home," said Wylder, "Should we go to the hospital?"

"Yes," said Jessica, "let's go."

"I'll go get Blaine," said Wylder.

"We'll meet you two there," said Jan, "I want to hear all about Greg's experience in the Beyond."

"Jessica," said Noah, "Would you like to talk about how to rescue Jason?"

"Absolutely!" said Jessica.

"Can I help?" asked Jim.

"Us too," said Steve and Brian.

"I'll go to the hospital with Blaine and meet you all there," Wylder said. She left the others and started the walk back to Old St. David's. When she arrived, she went to the stone benches where she had left Blaine, but he was not there.

That's just great

"Blaine?" asked Wylder aloud, "Where are you boy?"

She looked around the stone benches, by the Yew tree in the center of the drive, and on the dark side of Old St. David's.

"Blaine, this is no time for hide and seek, we have to go to the hospital," said Wylder, with an edge to her voice.

After a few more moments of looking around, unsuccessfully, Wylder called out again, "Blaine? Are you okay? This is not funny. Where are you?"

I'm here, Wylder, said Blaine.

Wylder spun and looked around, but there was no one there.

"Who said that?" asked Wylder.

I did, of course. Ha! Of course, of course, said the horse. This is rather fun.

"Blaine? Where are you? And how are you speaking to me?" Wylder asked, spinning in circles looking for Blaine.

I have something I must do, said Blaine.

"Why? Ugh! Blaine, we have a lot to talk about," Wylder said, standing still. "How are you speaking to me right now?"

I heard Greg and Jan surmise that you had to trust someone to speak telepathically, someone you'd trust with your life. Well, I trust you, and you trust me, so I thought I would try to speak to you. Look at that, apparently, it works. Brilliant!

"Apparently so," said Wylder, sarcastically, "Everyone is going to think I am nuts If I say I can talk to a horse."

I beg your pardon, said Blaine, **I am not just a horse.**

"You're right, Blaine. Of course, you are more

than a horse. You are my friend," said Wylder.

That's better, said Blaine, **Besides, no one will know you are talking to me unless you want them to – it's telepathic.**

"Right," said Wylder, "I'm going to the hospital to meet everyone and check on Summer. I'll contact you again in a little while."

Very well, said Blaine.

Wylder laughed and started jogging to the hospital with a smile on her face.

So, I CAN use the heavenly communication system, after all, thought Wylder, *I was beginning to think there was something wrong with me.*

There is nothing wrong with you my friend, except that you have trust issues.

"Are you still there?" laughed Wylder, "How do I hang up the phone?"

I am as new to this as you are, said Blaine, **I'm afraid I don't know how to disconnect either.**

"Well then, just don't comment on my thoughts, OK?" said Wylder, still jogging.

Are you running? asked Blaine.

"Yes, why?" asked Wylder.

Because you can barely run a bath, said Blaine.

I think I liked him better when I couldn't hear him, thought Wylder.

I can still hear you, said Blaine, in a sing-song voice.

"Shh," said Wylder.

*****

Wylder kept running until she reached St. David's hospital.

Ironic, thought Wylder, *St. David's is a hospital and a cemetery*.

Without fatigue or burning lungs, and with the surprising conversation with Blaine, the time passed quickly.

One of the ambulances was still in the Emergency bay. The driver was closing the doors to the back of the vehicle and the other EMS personnel were climbing into the cab on the passenger side.

Wylder walked up to the Ambulance.

"What a shame," said the driver to his partner, "She was so young."

Wylder did not stay to hear the rest of the conversation; she ran through the open doors into the bright white light of St. David's hospital.

Wylder looked around for the nurse's station. When she found the circular desk with nurses and doctors on the phone or computer, she saw the patient board in the back, but the names had been coded for the privacy of the patient.

A man rushed to the nurse's station, "Where

is the car accident victim?" he asked, dressed in scrubs with his full tattoo sleeve showing.

"Room 7B," replied another nurse, "She's not awake Dane. She is in rough condition, but she is stable."

"Thanks, Lilly," he said, breathless, and he rushed down the hall.

7B, thought Wylder, *thank you,* and she followed the nurse to the room.

When she arrived in the room, Summer was surrounded by the souls from St. David's cemetery.

Dane stepped right through Greg and checked Summer's I.V. An elderly nurse walked in and said, in a familiar voice, "Her MRI shows no swelling of the brain, and her heartbeat is strong. Honestly, I think she should be alert anytime now."

Wylder stared at the nurse in front of her, as she reached to check Summer's pulse. *Mom?*

"Thank you, I am glad you were here when she came in," said Dane.

"She was trying to save the driver of the car, you know?" said Sage, "She is one brave woman."

"Yeah, she would say she was not so much brave, as reckless," laughed Dane.

"My Wylder would say that too," said Sage.

Holy Shit, Mom!

Wylder stepped closer to the nurse, staring at her with soft eyes and a childlike smile.

"It was brave, don't let anyone tell you differently," said Sage, and she walked out of the room.

Seeing the look on Wylder's face, Jan walked up and said, "Is that your mom?"

"Yeah," said Wylder, "that's her."

"I recognize her voice," said Jan, "She was so kind to me when I was in this hospital," Jan paused, "when I was dying."

"It's been a minute," said Wylder, still looking at the open door where Sage had left the room.

"Is she okay?" asked Greg, as the whole group got closer to the small hospital bed where Summer lay motionless, tubes and machines connected to her.

Wylder did not respond.

"Wylder," said Greg, "Are you okay?"

Jan turned to Greg and said, "The nurse that just left, is Wylder's mom."

The group left Summer's side and surrounded Wylder.

"That's so cool," said Jessica, "You get to see your mom!"

"Yeah," said Wylder, "I just was not ready for it. It took me by surprise."

Dane was sitting in the only chair in the room, holding Summer's bandaged hand. When he spoke, the whole room of souls turned towards him.

"Summer, baby, come back to me," he said softly and gently kissed her exposed fingertips with the chipped black nail polish. "Do you remember when we got these tattoos?" With his free hand, he gently touched her forearm and smiled as he traced the shapes with his finger. "We were just out of the military. We wanted to commemorate the day. We were barely friends then. Now, you are so much more to me. I never told you. Summer, please come back, I want to tell you."

Just then, the long unbroken beep of the heart rate monitor made him jump. He was halfway through the door when Sage ran into him in the doorway. Sage called into the headset that was in her ear and two other nurses filed into the room, knowing exactly what to do.

"Dane," said Sage, "We got this. You're not helping so step back and think good thoughts."

Dane did as he was told and leaned against the wall of the hospital room, staring in Summer's direction, his view blocked by nurses tending to Summer.

"Stupid guy," said Summer from behind Wylder, "I know how he feels about me."

Wylder looked to her left and saw Summer standing there looking at Dane.

"Hi," said Wylder, "You must be Summer?"

Greg turned to see Summer and Wylder talking, "Summer?" said Greg, smiling.

Summer looked at Greg, "Hi," he said, "I am Ruby's friend at St. David's cemetery. It's nice to meet you."

Jan cleared her throat, and said to Greg "No, Greg, we could have waited much longer to meet her."

"Of course," said Greg, "I only meant to say that I am so glad you took Ruby home. The cemetery is no place for a dog to live."

"You are Ruby's ghost friend?" asked Summer.

"I am," said Greg, "I called her Daisy, but yes, I am her ghost friend."

Summer was fading in and out, "Summer?" asked Jan.

Summer looked at her hands, first at the palms, and then at the backs. She looked past Greg to see herself lying on the bed surrounded by nurses, receiving CPR. "Clear," shouted the doctor.

The paddles charged and the nurses stepped back. The doctor pressed the button and Summer's body lurched. Her ghost vanished.

****

Sage stood over Summer with her fingers on Summer's wrist as she felt for a pulse. The steady rhythm of a heartbeat returned to the monitor and relief could be seen on the faces of everyone in the room, both the living and those from St. David's Cemetery.

"That must have felt like a close one, missy," said Sage to Summer, "but, it's not your time yet."

"Dane, you can breathe now," laughed Sage, "She's still here. You're such a tough guy, but when something happens to your girl, you're a bag of mush."

"Very funny, Sage," laughed Dane, "I'm just glad she's ok."

"Yeah, yeah, that's what they all say," joked Sage.

"What happened to the driver of the car?" asked Dane.

"She didn't make it," said Sage, "We don't know who she is so we cannot notify her family. I'm hoping when Summer wakes up she can tell us something."

"I'll ask her," said Dane, "I work tonight, so I'll check in on her as often as I can."

"I know you will," said Sage, "and she is in good hands with any nurse here."

"Thanks, Sage," said Dane, "You saved her."

"It was nothin'." said Sage, "Just doin' my job."

"Well, thanks anyway," said Dane.

"Sure thing, kid," said Sage, "Better get to work."

"Yes ma'am," said Dane.

"Not you, me!" said Sage, "There is a gunshot victim that is just getting out of emergency surgery," and she rushed out of the room to the next patient.

"She's quite a human," Dane said to Summer, but Summer was fast asleep.

Jan stepped closer to Summer, "I'm glad I didn't get to meet you yet," she said, smiling.

Greg took Jan's hand, "I know you will like her," he said.

From the doorway, a voice said, "I'd like to meet her too,"

"Who are you?" asked Wylder.

The driver of the car looked at Wylder and said, "I'm the one she almost saved. I'm Stephanie, the driver of the car. I came to thank her."

"Woah," said Jessica, "Plot twist."

THE ENTRANCE
TO ST. DAVID'S

"This little room is getting quite full of dead people," said Wylder, "Let's let her talk to Summer in private."

Greg and Jan started to wrangle the group to the lobby of St. David's hospital near the sliding glass doors.

"This is when we need Patty," said Wylder when they arrived.

"Agreed," said Greg with a laugh, "This was her strong suit."

"Who is Patty?" asked Jessica.

"She was a resident of St. David's, and she was in charge," Steve said with a smile, "always keeping us in line with group meetings by the stone benches."

Noah walked up and heard Steve explain how Patty would organize the conversations, allowing each person to express an opinion or ask a question.

"Since Patty is not here to herd the cats, I volunteer," said Noah.

Not waiting for permission, he stepped away from Greg and Wylder and tried to whistle as he did to his men in the Army when he needed their attention. Instead of a whistle, a vibration shook the room and the sliding doors opened and closed, opened and closed.

All eyes turned to Noah, even those who were still with the living, "Woah, I was not expecting that," said Noah, "Can all of them hear me?"

"I don't think so," said Greg, "They were looking at the doors opening and closing. Can you do that again? That is the first time I have seen an action in the afterlife affect the real world."

Noah put two fingers in his mouth and tried again to whistle, and for the second time the room vibrated, the doors opened and closed, and the souls looked at one another in surprise.

"It was most certainly you," chuckled Greg as he heard the receptionist call for maintenance to look at the malfunctioning sliding doors.

Everyone gathered around Noah, "Now that I have your attention," he laughed and gestured for Greg to take the lead.

Greg stepped forward, "I'm a little out of practice," he said, and stood with Noah facing the crowd.

Jan stepped up and stood next to Greg on one side, and Wylder stepped forward and stood on the other. Steve and Brian moved next to Wylder and motioned for Jim to join them. When Jim joined the growing line of souls, Jessica stood next to Noah, completing the connection.

All eyes were on Greg when the doors opened, closed, and opened again.

"It wasn't me," said Noah, putting his hands in the air.

Wylder looked at Greg, with eyes wide. Just then, a feeling of dread was obvious on the faces of the living. A baby in the arms of its mother began to wail. A security guard who was looking at the misbehaving door began to curse, the Police dog standing at attention with the officer at the desk lunged forward and barked loudly at the opening and closing doors. It was then that the Swarm came in, much larger than when it appeared in the quarry. It divided into four masses, each going down a hallway of the hospital, lights flickering in their wake.

STEPHANIE

"Was that death?" asked Jessica, her eyes looking in the direction the Swarm had gone, "Did you feel it?"

"Greg, explain," said Steve, matter-of-factly, "What the hell was that?"

Wylder looked at Greg, and said, "You may not be Patty, but you have their undivided attention now."

Greg spoke up, "That was the Swarm."

"Is it taking souls to hell?" asked a voice in the back.

All eyes turned around at the sound of an unfamiliar voice. Stephanie, the driver of the car, stepped forward.

"I saw you all in the hospital room. I'm dead right? I must be, how else could you see me?" she asked, with a skeptical look on her face, "Are you dead too?"

"You're the one Summer was trying to save," said Noah.

"Yes, almost saved," Stephanie said, pushing

her hair behind one ear. "I would have been angry if I had gone through all that, to be denied Heaven."

"You're not in Heaven," said Wylder, "You're in St. David's Hospital."

"Yes, well, at least I'm not in Hell," said Stephanie.

"Did you all die here?" Stephanie asked the group, "in the hospital?".

"I hate to break up this party, but we need to talk about the Swarm," said Wylder.

"Does that," Stephanie looked for the right word, "thing, take your soul if you've done bad things?"

"We've all done 'bad things'," said Jessica, sarcastically, adding air quotes to emphasize her dissatisfaction.

"Yes," replied Wylder, "but it seems a person has to have taken a life, intentionally killed someone, to be taken by the Swarm."

Greg continued, making room for Stephanie to join in the circle and the conversation, "Jason, Jessica's boyfriend,"

Jessica interrupted, "He's not my boyfriend."

Noah continued, "Will, Jim's brother, and Mason Miller, the soldier buried in New St. David's were all taken by the Swarm. That is three that we know of for sure."

"Stephanie," said Greg, "We are trying to understand what to do about the Swarm. It has grown since we saw it last."

"And the dark feeling it brings is growing stronger," added Jan.

"Why is it here?" asked Jessica, "At a hospital?"

"It's recruiting," said Noah, "Where better to get souls right after death than those in a hospital?"

"Why did the Swarm come to the cemetery if it could have just loitered around a hospital waiting for people to die?" asked Brian.

"Maybe it takes souls from here, when it can, and when there is no one here to take it goes out to the other places where people died, like the quarry," said Noah, "but we still have a lot to learn."

"Like what we can do with that whistle," added Wylder.

"Yes, and any other way we can influence the real world," added Steve, "Did you see that the Swarm affected the lights? Maybe we can too."

"I think we need to do some recruiting of our own," said Wylder, "beginning with you, Stephanie."

"No," said Stephanie, "I just want to find my son. I can't stay."

"It's not as easy as that," said Wylder, "You

have not made it to Heaven."

"Can you show me?" asked Stephanie, "What do I have to do?"

"We can give you the Cliffs Notes on how to get to Heaven," said Greg.

"Cliffs Notes?" asked Stephanie.

Jan laughed and looked at Greg, "You're showing your age," Jan looked at Stephanie and said, "The fast version."

"Ahh," said Stephanie, "Yes, I prefer the fast version."

Greg pointed to the sliding glass doors of St. David's Hospital, "Just walk towards those doors. In the bright light of the hospital, you can barely see it, but there is a blue spark that fades in and out. When you feel the pull, like the current in a river, let it take you into the light. You will have to face the biggest mistake of your life on Earth. Once you do that, you can pass through to Heaven."

"That sounds quite nice, but how long will that take? I just want to see my baby. I just want to see Wade. I cannot wait any longer," said Stephanie.

Wylder's head popped up at the sound of the name Wade. "Stephanie, your son is named Wade?"

"Yes, and I need to see him. He was just three

years old when he died. I cannot bear the thought of him lost, and alone, I have to find him," said Stephanie.

"Was he buried at St. David's cemetery?" asked Wylder.

"Yes," said Stephanie, "Thank God. There was no more room in St. David's. All the spots had been reserved but there was no other cemetery in the town, and I was not going to have my boy 40 miles away at the next closest cemetery. I went to see the Mayor. My husband and I offered to start a beautification project for the town, fixing the parks, building modern playgrounds for the children, and improving the school grounds. We only asked one thing in return, that they allow our Wade to be buried in the local cemetery. The Mayor, Rob, pulled a few strings and made all the arrangements for Wade to be buried in the most beautiful spot in St. David's, under a large tree. It wasn't even designed for a gravesite, but Rob made sure it was perfect, with a bench and a view. I planned to go there. I was going to sit with Wade and tell him stories or read him books, but I couldn't face the cemetery. The anniversary of his death came, and the pain was still too much to bear. Jack, my husband, decided to go to counseling but I refused. I was going to handle this on my own. Year after year the thoughts got worse, and I never went to see him. When I finally got the nerve to drive to St.

David's to see him, I had the accident. My tire blew and I hit a huge stone."

"Stephanie, that is what caused your car accident outside the cemetery?" asked Wylder.

Stephanie continued, "When I got to the entrance of St. David's I heard the tire blow, I saw the boulder, and I was headed straight for it. I thought I would crash into it, but instead, the car flipped over, and I was trapped in the driver's seat. I smelled gas and thought the car might blow up. Then, I saw this woman climb under the car to help me. I was so torn; I didn't know if I wanted her to help me and get hurt herself. She and her dog stayed with me and got me out of the car before it blew up. The paramedics kept me alive, despite the burns, until we got to the hospital, but I died a short time later. I hope the woman will be ok. I never meant to hurt her. She has a special spirit, jumping in to save me like she did."

"Stephanie," said Wylder, "Wade is not lost."

"How do you know? You can't know for sure. He was just a child. I told him that all children go to heaven, but I didn't know for sure. I was just telling him what everyone was telling me," said Stephanie, looking desperately into Wylder's eyes.

"I know because I took him to Heaven myself," said Wylder, "I was there when you buried him.

I was sitting on the wall watching the funeral. I saw you there."

"You are just trying to make me feel better, but I really need to find him," said Stephanie, her eyes filled with sadness, "I have to see for myself".

"I am telling you the truth. I took Wade through the Portal to Heaven. He is there now with my friend Michael and two other children, Max, and Isabelle," said Wylder.

"I don't believe you," said Stephanie, "I want to, but I can't."

"I would not lie to you," said Wylder, looking straight into Stephanie's eyes, "I saw you put a silver charm bracelet on the cross headstone at his grave."

Stephanie's eyes softened, "How could you know that?"

Wylder shrugged her shoulders, smiled, and said, "I told you, I was there."

Greg spoke up next, "I met him too," he said. "Wylder brought him to meet me before going through the portal. I was waiting for Jan, so Wylder was going to take Wade. He is a beautiful boy."

"I can't believe this," said Stephanie, with excitement, "I need to go see him! Please take me to him."

"Wade is in Heaven," said Wylder, "but you are not."

"What do you mean?" asked Stephanie, with panic in her voice.

"You have to cross over into Heaven by going through the portal," said Wylder, "That is what Greg was explaining. You must go into the Beyond, the place where you are faced with your life choices, and once you come to terms with the pain you have caused others, you will be granted access to Heaven."

"Alright, I'll go," said Stephanie, "Just walk towards that little blue light?"

"Yes," said Wylder, "Take your time and really face what's in there. It seems that time passes much faster in the Beyond than it does out here."

Stephanie straightened her hospital gown, faced the blue light, and walked towards it. She hesitated when it began to pull her in, but she stopped resisting and the group watched as she stepped into the Beyond, and then vanished from the bright lights of St. David's Hospital.

"I didn't have the heart to tell her," said Wylder, still looking at where Stephanie once stood, "that once she gets back from the Beyond, I am still not sure how to find Wade."

WHERE'S NOAH

Wylder looked at Greg and Jan, "While Stephanie is away, let's figure out the plan."

"OK," said Greg, "Everyone, gather 'round'"

Jessica, Steve, Brian, and Jim joined Greg, Jan, and Wylder.

"Where's Noah?" asked Jan.

Everyone looked around, but he was nowhere in sight.

"Maybe he went back to check on Summer," said Greg, "I'll go."

Greg started towards the hall to Summer's room, leaving the rest of the group in the waiting room.

"I'll look around the rest of the hospital and see if I can find him," said Wylder.

"I'll go with you," said Jessica.

"We'll wait here in case he comes back," said Steve.

"I'll keep an eye out for Stephanie," said Jan.

Wylder looked at Jim, "I'll stay with Steve and

Brian," he said.

"OK," said Wylder, "We'll all meet back here in the lobby. Nobody leaves the hospital," she ordered, "We all stay together."

Everyone nodded in agreement, Wylder and Jessica headed down a different hall than the one that led to Summer.

"Do you know where you are going?" asked Jessica.

"Not really," replied Wylder, "I'm just following my gut. The signs say Intensive Care Unit, I thought we'd start here."

"I'll go down this hall, and meet you in the ICU," said Jessica.

Wylder continued down the main hall, that led to the circular ICU nurse's station with monitors beeping and lights flashing. The large space was a square with three hospital rooms on each side, all with a direct line of sight to the nurse's station. An urgent alarm went off at the station and the nurse rushed to room E2, Wylder followed. The nurse entered the room and Wylder had to pass the police officer standing guard at the door to follow the nurse into the room.

Inside was a man, unconscious, head wrapped in gauze, and handcuffed to the rail of the hospital bed. There was another officer seated next to the patient's bed.

"Step aside," said the nurse.

"I have to stay next to him, ma'am," said the officer, not moving from his chair.

"Well, I have to do my job," said the nurse, "Move," the alarms echoing in the small room.

The officer did not budge.

"My nurse asked you to move, officer," said Sage, walking in, stopping to clean her hands with the disinfectant at the door. "You can still do your job from the other side of the bed where you are not in the way."

The officer looked at Sage, "Please," she said with a smile, "Don't make an old lady get feisty."

The officer stood and walked around the bed, keeping his hand in contact with the bedrail the whole time.

The nurse stepped closer and pulled out her penlight, lifting the patient's eyelids and flashing the light back and forth across the pupils. "No response," said the nurse, looking at Sage.

The patient started to seize, and Sage looked at the nurse and said, "Call the doctor, he's going to need to get back into surgery." Anticipating the doctor's orders, "Let's head to the O.R.!" yelled Sage as the other nurse unplugged the monitors and got behind the bed to start pushing it out of the room.

"I'm going too," said the officer.

"You are not allowed in the operating room, but you can wait outside," said the nurse, pushing the bed out the door.

Both officers and Wylder followed the nurse to the O.R. where they prepped the unconscious man for surgery. As they pushed the bed into the operating room, the two officers took a seat in the chairs placed on either side of the door.

Wylder followed the nurses into the room and watched as they moved the patient from the hospital bed to the operating table, exposing multiple wounds that had healed over time. Stab wounds, road rash scars, and a round scar that looked like a spider web.

"I wonder what that's from," said Noah, from behind Wylder, "Maybe a gunshot wound?"

Wylder turned around, startled, "Where have you been?" she asked.

"Looking for the Swarm," said Noah, "So far I have not found it."

"It doesn't stick around long," said Wylder, "once it has what it came for."

The doctors began the surgery and Wylder stared at the process unfolding in front of her. "Have you ever seen a surgery before?" she asked.

"Only the ones on the battlefield, messy and

without anesthesia," replied Noah.

The heart monitor alarm sounded, and the doctor said, "We're losing him!"

The sound of the Swarm drowned out the voices of the doctors and nurses, and the feeling of death filled the room, even the nurses felt it as they looked back and forth at each other with an expression of fear in their eyes, visible even behind a medical mask.

Noah stepped forward and laid on the table over the unconscious man, his spirit sinking into the body.

"What are you doing!" yelled Wylder.

"I'm going with the…"

But Wylder did not hear the rest of Noah's sentence. The Swarm filled the room, Wylder could hear the sounds of moans and screams, and smelled burning flesh like she remembered from the ranch as a child.

Wylder squatted down and covered her eyes as the Swarm filled the space above her. The doctors and nurses, oblivious to the presence of death, rushed around the room calling out instructions and following the orders of the attending until finally, the surgeon turned off the monitor.

"Time of Death, 11:07 pm," she said.

The Swarm started to dissipate, and the feeling of dread and fear lifted.

Wylder stood up and looked at the body on the table, "Noah, are you in there?"

There was no response.

"Notify the next of kin," said the doctor.

"Yes, doctor," said the nurse.

As the medical staff followed the protocol for a death on the operating table, Wylder stood over the body looking for any sign of Noah. When 15 minutes had passed, Jessica appeared in the doorway of the O.R.

"There you are," said Jessica, "I was waiting for you in the hallway. Did you find Noah?"

Wylder continued to look at the body on the table. Without looking at Jessica she said, "Yes, I found Noah."

"Great," said Jessica, looking around, "Where is he? Let's get out of here. This place is creepy."

"The Swarm came for this guy," said Wylder.

"Yeah," Jessica said, "I felt it. It was a bad one!"

"Noah went with the Swarm," said Wylder, quietly.

THE CHOICES WE MAKE

Stephanie grabbed her keys and headed to the door and said to herself, "Today I will do it, today I will go visit my Wade".

She stopped at the door, purse on her shoulder, keys in her hand, sweat on her forehead. She had not been to the cemetery since the funeral.

"You can do this, go!" she told herself, "If you can't do it for yourself, do it for Wade."

Stephanie took a deep breath and stepped outside the door.

Stephanie's spirit watched herself walk out the door and followed her younger self to the car.

I remember this emotional moment in my life, thought Stephanie, *torn between the need to speak to my son, if only from above his grave, and the need to stay far away from the memory of his death. When he died, it sent me into a tailspin of depression, anxiety, and suicidal impulses. It had taken years to get to the place I am on this day, emotionally – not drowning in intrusive thoughts, and able to reasonably function.*

Stephanie sat in the driver's seat and started the engine, then rested her forehead on her hands which gripped the steering wheel with such force her knuckles turned yellow.

Stephanie watched herself pull it together, shift into reverse, and back out of the driveway.

The younger Stephanie drove down the quiet street towards St. David's cemetery and Stephanie's spirit watched her from the passenger seat.

"The world has gotten darker," she said to her younger self, "Good, is harder to find. It's no wonder you were afraid for Wade. Where is God in all of this?"

When they had driven the short distance out of town, they took the winding road through the countryside. Stephanie stared out the window at the beautiful scenery. It seemed like no time had passed when they pulled onto the road that led to St. David's.

Stephanie's spirit remembered this mental transition when she was alive, and she saw it on the face of her younger self now. Her hands gripped the steering wheel tightly, her face lost all its color, and her breathing became erratic. *I remember that something about seeing the cemetery brought back the weight of the loss*, thought

Stephanie, *the permanence of the situation. I could not bear the thought of a life without Wade. I could not see the other blessings in my life. I could not feel the love I had for others, or the love others had for me. I felt only the pain of grief, but I had to face it.*

She saw herself crying, wailing, the anger was visible in the vein on her forehead, and the tears that fell from her chin and dripped into her lap. Stephanie felt the stab of grief, that gripped her younger self. She wanted to comfort her younger self, to stop her pain. She knew it was more than she could handle.

Just then, Stephanie saw the boulder on the road and remembered the thought that crossed through her mind at that moment – *Make it stop*. Half the size of the car, but still unremarkable in the beauty of the countryside. Stephanie felt the car lurch as the tire blew, watched the car veer towards the huge stone, and the impact of the explosion made her foot hit the gas pedal. Stephanie knew what came next.

***

Stephanie was now outside the car, standing on the dirt road watching the event unfold before her eyes. She saw herself aim the car at the boulder, then the front end launched in the air. The car smashed down on the driver-side tires, flipped onto its roof, and skidded down the dirt road sideways to a stop. The boulder had punctured the gas tank and drips of gasoline could be seen from the 30 feet between the boulder and the car. Steam escaped from the engine and rose into the air. Stephanie looked over and saw a little Honda Civic driving from the opposite direction, heading to St. David's.

Stephanie watched as the young woman pulled to the side of the road and ran from the vehicle, her dog following, and an older woman remained in the car.

She watched the woman climb under the car and yell, "Ma'am!" When there was no response, the young woman tried again, "Ma'am, can you hear me?"

Stephanie heard her own voice reply to the woman who had crawled under the car, "My back," said her younger self in a weak voice, "I can't feel my legs."

"You're going to be ok," replied the young woman, "I have to get you out, I smell gas. I'm Summer and this is my dog, Ruby."

Stephanie could see the gravity of the situation from outside the vehicle. She saw the smoke start to rise from the back of the car, and little sparks flared from an exposed wire.

Stephanie looked at the woman trying to save her, and her dog that fetched a dropped tool. She saw the older woman no more than 25 feet from the car.

What have I done? I could have killed them.

She looked at herself, trapped in the car, suspended by the seatbelt. She was bleeding and drifting in and out of consciousness.

She watched Summer risk her own life to save a stranger, with no regard for her own safety. *There is still good in the world,* thought Stephanie, *I see it right here in front of me.*

Stephanie looked down, "Summer," said Stephanie, to the woman who could not hear her, "thank you. You are truly a good person. You could have kept driving; you could have just called 911. You did not stand by and watch but instead, because you had the skills to help, you stepped in and acted. You put me first, a total stranger, because you were uniquely qualified for the situation. Maybe that is what God is, humans using their gifts for good."

Stephanie looked at the boulder on the side of the road, the one that launched her into the air, but this time there was a blue spark near it. Stephanie took one last look at Summer and Ruby and headed towards the spark.

Now I can find Wade.

***

Stephanie expected to be back in Saint David's hospital lobby; instead, she was in her bedroom, the one she shared with her husband. He was lying in bed facing the wall. The clothes were stacked up in the laundry basket and on the floor and on the bed. Old pizza boxes filled with uneaten pizza we're on the nightstand. The light on the answering machine flashed showing that there were 11 voicemails that had not been answered. His cell phone rang. He did not reach for it. Stephanie walked over and looked at the screen which read "Mom". After six rings the screen went blank and a few moments later she heard the sound indicating that a voicemail was waiting.

She noticed that her husband was not asleep, he was just lying in the middle of the bed staring at the wall. The lights were off, and the windows were closed, even though at this time of year he liked to have the fresh breeze through the house. Stephanie heard voices coming from the other room. She walked through the closed bedroom door and into the living room. The curtains were drawn, and the entire house was dark except for the television which was tuned to an old western movie channel. She walked down the hallway and into the nursery which was exactly the same as it was the day Wade died.

She walked through the closed front door and stepped onto the porch where there were bundles of flowers, home-baked goods, and what looked to be a pan of lasagna that had been sitting there for quite some time. There were cards on the step along with a stack of unopened mail. Their cat Sparkle stood at Stephanie's feet and meowed once.

Stephanie sat on the steps of the house taking it all in. *It's like a chain reaction. Something took Wade from me, and an accident took me from my husband. Now he has suffered two devastating losses. His grief is double and now he is all alone; I am not able to help him like he tried to help me. How will he handle this second death?*

She stood and Sparkle looked up at her again, she turned and walked back through the closed door of the house, and then into the bedroom. She sat on the bed, though she made no impression on the messy comforter. She looked at her husband, lost in his thoughts.

"Jack, I am so sorry," she said, *"I wish I could still be here with you. I don't want to leave you to handle this all alone."*

Jack did not move, he barely blinked.

"I wish I could tell you I am OK, so you do not worry about me like I worried about Wade," said Stephanie.

Then she remembered the hospital of St. David's and what happened when Noah whistled.

Stephanie let out a whistle, but nothing happened.

Stephanie looked around the room, saw her husband, and heard Sparkle meow loudly outside. She looked at the place on the blank wall he was staring at, "this is not about making things right," she said aloud, "I can never fix this."

Stephanie looked at her husband, then looked back at her hand that still wore her wedding ring, "you will have to live life with the impact of the decisions I have made. My part here is about taking responsibility for the pain I caused you, and others in my life, with my actions. I feel it, Jack. I feel the sadness and the pain and the finality that is crushing you. I am so sorry that I left you with all this to handle on your own. You are a strong man, a good husband, and a kind person. I was lucky to have you in my life, you were a blessing. I love you, and I hope you can forgive me for leaving you with this burden to handle alone," said Stephanie.

Stephanie stood from the bed and tried to kiss him on the forehead though her lips went through him. She walked through the bedroom door and back through the front door onto the porch where Sparkle was now looking right at her.

"Sparkle, I owe you an apology too," said Stephanie, sitting down on the steps. "I am sorry there is no one here to feed you. I'm glad you are outside where you can find food on your own. Stay with Jack, will you? He is going to need some love when he is able to face the day again. He is strong, he will get through this, but you can help each other."

Stephanie stood and looked at the house that she shared with her husband for over a decade. The paint was peeling, the grass needed to be mowed, the garage door still had the dent from the first week after they moved in, when she forgot to put the car in park, and it rolled right into the closed door.

"I thought you'd be mad at me, Jack," said Stephanie, smiling, "But you just laughed and laughed. You laughed so hard I thought you might fall to the ground."

"Jack," said Stephanie, "I remember how you wanted everything to be perfect before we started a family: money in the bank, a house, and good jobs. I remembered how you told me you were ready to have a child. We had decided to paint the inside of the house, and even though we stayed up until 2 AM listening to Guns and Roses to stay awake, we still could not finish the last room before we collapsed from exhaustion. The next morning was a Sunday, and I woke up before you. I went into the guest room to start taping the walls and when I opened the door, in huge block letters it said: Want to make a baby? It was the best surprise ever. I still don't know when you did that. We went to bed at the same time the night before. I wonder if that was why you wanted to keep painting, so I would open the door and see your message."

This was such a good life, and I just walked away, thought Stephanie. *I should have gotten help, but I thought I could deal with it on my own. How could anyone deal with the loss of a child on their own? It's unnatural to bury a child, it is not the way things are supposed to be. Maybe if I had gotten help, as Jack did, I could have handled it.*

"You said it diluted the pain, when you shared it with someone else," said Stephanie.

If I had shared it, let someone help carry the burden, maybe I would not have been crushed by the weight of it. Maybe I could have helped Jack. We could have helped each other.

A spark appeared and Stephanie walked towards it. Before she walked through, she turned back towards her house, her cat, and her husband.

"I wish you peace, Jack. I wish you happiness and that you find love again. I wish you children, and grandchildren, because you are a wonderful father. I wish you good health, and prosperity, and a long life of joy."

Stephanie turned back to the light, blew Jack a kiss, and walked through the portal.

POWER OF THE AFTERLIFE

Stephanie stepped back through the portal, walking intentionally through the pull of that which surrounded her. Like being underwater, she could not hear those around her. After only taking a few steps away from the portal, the sounds became clearer, and the grip released her.

Jan was waiting for her, "Are you okay?" she asked Stephanie.

"I forgot the pain I was in, it blinded me. I put others at risk, and I hurt Summer. I'd like to go see her, to say thank you, and then I want to go see my Wade," said Stephanie.

"I'll take you to Summer," said Jan.

"I know the way," said Stephanie, "I'd like to go by myself. Will you all wait for me?"

"Yes," replied Jan, "I will let the others know you are back."

"Thank you," said Stephanie, "I won't be long."

Stephanie turned and walked down the

hallway to Summer's room. When she arrived, Summer was awake, and Dane was holding her hand.

"I'm so glad you are okay," said Dane, kissing her scratched knuckles, "Why did you do that?"

Summer gently pulled her hand away, "I was right there, Dane. You would have done the same thing," said Summer, "We were trained for that."

"Yes," said Dane, "in the military... where we had equipment... and protective gear!"

"I had to do something," said Summer, "I will not stand by and do nothing, ever again." Summer looked away and Dane gently turned her face back towards him.

"That was not your fault," said Dane, "No one could have changed things, except Major Miller."

"We survived, but we lost one of our own," said Summer.

"Major Miller was in command, he chose not to pull back," said Dane, "That is the burden of leadership, the call was his to make, not yours."

"He didn't have the view that I had, I should have said something," said Summer.

"The decision was his, Summer," said Dane, "right or wrong."

"Regardless of whose decision it was, I have to make things right. While I am alive, I will always step in and help if I can. That is how I will make amends," said Summer.

"I understand," said Dane, "That is one of the things I respect about you most."

"I'm really tired, Dane. I think I'll rest a little. Will you come back later?" asked Summer.

"Try to stop me," said Dane, smiling. He stood to go, then walked right through Stephanie as he left.

Stephanie took the seat where Dane had been sitting.

"Hi Summer, I am Stephanie, the driver of the car," she said.

Summer looked back towards the window, closed her eyes, and fell asleep.

"I wanted to thank you for putting yourself at risk to save me," said Stephanie, "I never meant to hurt you, or anyone. I only wanted to see my son. My decision affected you and will leave scars that you will carry for the rest of your life. I am sorry, I hope you can forgive me."

Summer smiled in her sleep, and in a dreamy voice said, "We're good."

Stephanie looked shocked, and said, "Summer, can you hear me?"

Summer put her bruised hand under her pillow and as she drifted into sleep she said, "Yeah".

Stephanie stood and smiled at Summer. Just

as she headed out of the room, she heard a soft sleepy voice finish the sentence, "I can hear you, Stephanie".

***

When she got to the lobby the group was gathering. As she walked up she asked Wylder, "Did anyone find Noah?"

Wylder looked at Stephanie, "I was just about to tell everyone what happened," she said.

All eyes were on Wylder as she started to speak, "Noah was taken by the Swarm," said Wylder.

"How is that possible?" asked Greg, "He has already been through the Beyond; he was in Heaven."

"He chose to go," said Wylder," He went intentionally."

"What do you mean, 'intentionally'?" asked Steve.

"There was a prisoner in surgery. I know he had done something wrong because he was handcuffed to the hospital bed. When he died, the largest Swarm I have ever seen came for him. Noah laid over his body and when the Swarm took the prisoner, it took Noah too. There was no sign of either of them. I waited 15 minutes, that is what took Jessica and me so long to get back," said Wylder.

"Does anyone else have something to report?" asked Greg.

Stephanie raised her hand and all eyes turned to her. "I talked to Summer, and she answered me," said Stephanie, "She was asleep, but I think sometimes, we can talk to the living."

The group all started to ask questions at the same time, speaking over one another, until Greg lifted one hand in the air and then whistled. His attempt had the expected result; the sliding glass doors of the hospital opened and closed repeatedly; the room shook.

"A whistle," said Wylder, loudly, "It pierces right through me."

"I wanted to see if I could do it, or if it was only Noah. It seems a whistle will reach all of us. I wonder how far away it can be felt," said Greg.

"I wonder how Stephanie talked to Summer," Said Wylder, sarcastically.

"You win," said Greg, "The floor is yours, Stephanie."

Stephanie looked around at the new faces, and began, "I went to say thank you to Summer. When her boyfriend left, she fell asleep, and I started talking to her. When I said, 'I hope you can forgive me, she responded with 'we're good.' When I asked her if she could hear me, she answered, 'yeah'."

"Was she asleep?" asked Jan.

"Yes. And on some strong medicine I assume," said Stephanie.

"Maybe she was not talking to you at all," said Brian, "She could have been talking in her sleep and it just seemed like she was talking to you."

"I think she was talking to me," said Stephanie, with confidence, "I know she was."

"How do you know?" asked Brian.

"Because she called me by name," replied Stephanie.

"Awesome," said Jessica, "We can talk to the living. Do you think you could talk to her because she was heavily medicated, or because she was connected to you somehow since she tried to save your life?"

"That, or because she was asleep," replied Stephanie, "I'm not sure."

Wylder interrupted, and said, "What about Noah? He might need our help."

Greg asked the group, "Has anyone been able to connect to Noah, telepathically?"

All eyes looked around, but no one answered.

Greg continued, "How can we reach him if he is with the Swarm?"

Jessica spoke up, "I have an idea."

"Go ahead," said Wylder, "Out with it."

"I can reach Jason and he is in the Elsewhere. If Noah is also in the Elsewhere, maybe Jason can find him," said Jessica.

"Reasonable," said Wylder, "Let's try it."

"I like the idea too," said Greg, "But I suggest we have a plan. What will we do when we reach Jason?"

"I don't see how I can help find Noah and I really want to go find Wade," said Stephanie, "Wylder, you said you would bring me to him."

"We need to help Noah and we need to bring Stephanie to Wade," said Greg, "We can divide and conquer. I also think we can find my sister Maddie," said Greg.

Jan looked up at Greg, "Of course!" she said, "We need to find her!"

"Well, I'm going after Jason," said Jessica.

"I'm going to find Wade," said Stephanie, "And Wylder is going with me."

"I think I should go with Jessica to find Noah," Wylder said to Stephanie.

"But you know where Wade is!" Said Stephanie, panicked.

"I do too," said Jan, "Greg and I will go with you. We can find Wade and Maddie."

Jim spoke up next, "I'll go with Wylder and Jessica. I want to rescue Will if I can."

Greg looked at Steve and Brian, "Where do you want to go?"

"We want to help rescue the people from the Elsewhere," said Steve.

"Everyone deserves a second chance," said Brian.

"OK, let's meet back at New St. David's in 3 days at the next full moon," said Wylder, "Even if we have not accomplished our goal. We can check in."

Everyone nodded in agreement and then looked back to Wylder.

"Well, what are we waiting for, let's get going," said Wylder and started the procession to the door.

WHEN YOU WANT SOMETHING DONE RIGHT, SEND A HORSE

Blaine stood a few yards from the portal.

Don't just stand there like a big stupid muffin!

Walk to the portal, he told himself.

You're a horse, not a chicken!

Blaine took a few steps forward.

Feel the pull, beautiful.

Blaine stopped and resisted the tug.

Don't be a French pig! Get a move on.

Blaine lifted his head and walked forward with confidence.

Think "Wade".

HOLD ON, WE'RE COMING!

"Where do we start?" Jessica asked Wylder, "At the quarry?"

"Could you connect with Jason anywhere?" Wylder asked.

"Yes, the location didn't seem to matter," replied Jessica.

"What else do we know?" asked Wylder, walking in the direction of St. David's.

"Will said it was dark and hot, that he could hear other voices," said Jim, "and it feels angry."

"Why are they there?" asked Steve, "It's like a holding tank for Hell."

Jessica shot Steve a look of irritation.

"Jessica," said Steve, "Jason is your friend, right? You must know him pretty well."

"I think I do," Jessica answered, "Why?"

"He is there for a reason, and you are not. We need to figure out the rule. What lands you in the Elsewhere instead of in the cemetery?" asked Steve.

"We talked a little about this before you arrived. We think you have to take a life, you have to kill someone," said Jessica.

"Jason killed someone?" asked Brian.

"Yes, me," said Jessica. Seeing the look on their faces, she added, "Because I asked him to. Long story."

"It's not just killing someone," added Wylder, "Because Noah and Greg have killed someone, and they didn't end up in the Elsewhere. In fact, they both eventually got to Heaven."

"Jessica, you are the key. Would you tell me more about your death?" asked Steve.

Jessica recounted the story of the quarry to the others as they walked the rest of the way to St. David's. They all walked in silence for the last few minutes.

"Here we are," said Wylder, who led them all to the stone benches at old St. David's.

"This is where I died," said Jimmy, "and Will too. Someone must have cleaned up the mess."

"You and Will both died right here?" asked Steve.

"Yes, we died on the same night," said Jim.

"Just like Jessica and Jason," said Steve.

"Maybe when two people die together, one gets

the path to Heaven and one gets the path to Hell," said Brian. "All the people we know who died at the same time have been split up – one being taken by the swarm."

"I don't think so," said Wylder, "When I was in Old St. David's, Elizabeth and her daughter Nala were both killed on the same day and they both ended up on the path to Heaven."

"Was the daughter a child?" asked Brian.

"Yes," said Wylder, "She was twelve."

"Then that might not count," said Brian.

"True, but why would that be fair?" asked Wylder, "How would it be decided who would get the path to Heaven?"

"Life is not fair," said Brian, "Death may not be fair either."

"I choose to believe that there is a balance to things in the afterlife, not a random assignment of heaven or hell," said Wylder, "What else do we know?"

"We know that Will intentionally killed me," said Jim, "He was drunk and misguided, but he did it on purpose."

"Jason intentionally killed me too," added Jessica, "I asked him too, and I told him I took full responsibility, but he did it on purpose."

"A soldier would kill on purpose too, but he is following orders," said Brian.

"The intention seems to matter," said Steve, "We only have two examples to go by. We know that in both cases, the person taken by the Swarm killed someone intentionally because they wanted the person dead. That seems like a pretty good reason to be taken to Hell, if you ask me."

"I disagree," insisted Jessica, "Jason was only doing what I asked him to do!"

"But he pulled the trigger," said Wylder, in a soft voice, "He had a choice."

"I can't bear the thought of him being in hell for eternity because of something I asked him to do," said Jessica, "There has to be a way to get him out. Jason is a good person, the world was a better place because of him."

"In a weird way, the world was better because of Will too," added Jim. "When we were just little kids, and my dad would come at me, Will would create a diversion and direct my dad's anger towards him so I wouldn't take another beating. I finished high school, he dropped out. I graduated college and started a career, he jumped from job to job. Kate saw something in him, and when he proposed, she said yes. Will always said she saved him. He thought she could bring back the person he was when he was saving his little brother, but he couldn't shake the anger. It was a generational curse. Do you think we can get them out?"

"I am hoping Noah can figure that out," said Wylder, "He went there of his own free will. The problem is that no one can reach him telepathically. We all just met. We have not developed the trust necessary to communicate."

"But I can reach Jason," said Jessica.

"And I can reach Will," said Jim, "What if one of them can find Noah?"

Wylder looked at Jim and said, "It's worth a try. Is there any risk in this that I am not thinking about?" Wylder looked from face to face, and each one shook their head.

"Ok. Jessica, Jim, let's see if you can reach them," said Wylder.

"I'll go first," said Jessica.

Jessica closed her eyes and spoke aloud so the others could hear, "Jason, it's Jessica. Can you hear me?"

Yes, I can hear you. Where are you? Replied Jason, **Are you coming?**

"We don't know how to get there," said Jessica, "but we think that our friend Noah found a way. Do you know if there is someone there named Noah?"

Wylder exchanged surprised glances with Jim, Steve, and Brian.

I don't know, Jessica. I can hear voices but none of them are near me. I don't recognize any

of them.

"Can you speak to them?" asked Jessica.

"What's he saying?" asked Brian.

"Shhh, quiet," said Jessica.

Why are you telling me to be quiet? Asked Jason, **I thought you wanted me to try to find another person here.**

"Not you, Jason," said Jessica, "I was telling the others here to be quiet so I could hear you."

There are others there? Asked Jason.

"Yes," replied Jessica, "A lot of people."

Are you in Heaven? Asked Jason

"Jason, let's focus on getting you out of there," said Jessica.

You are in Heaven, oh God, that means I am in Hell, cried Jason.

"Find someone named Noah," said Jessica.

I'll try, Jessica, but I don't think I can, said Jason, **I hear voices, but I think I am alone.**

"Just try, Jason, OK?" said Jessica.

OK, Jessica, I'll try, said Jason.

Jessica opened her eyes and looked at the others waiting to hear the story.

"He thinks he is alone there," said Jessica, "but he is going to try to find Noah."

"Let me try connecting with Will," said Jim,

"Maybe he will have different results."

Jim closed his eyes like he saw Jessica do. After a moment he spoke. "Will, can you hear me? It's Jimmy."

Where the fuck have you been? asked Will.

"I've been trying to find a way to get you out of there," said Jim.

Well, you are taking your damn sweet time. I'm not sure you want me out of here, bro, said Will.

"I do," said Jim, "I found out that there are others that went where you are. Do you see anyone?" asked Jimmy.

No, I hear people, but I don't see anyone, replied Will.

"Do you recognize any of the voices?" asked Jim.

No, said Will, **mostly they just say that I was right to have killed you. Am I in Hell Jimmy?**

"I don't think so, Will," said Jim, "but I am trying to find a way to get you out."

Hurry, Bro, It's pretty bad in here, said Will.

"I'm trying, Will, I really am," said Jim.

Hurry the fuck up! said Will.

Jim opened his eyes, "He can't see anyone either. How are we going to get them out?"

Wylder was looking off in the distance.

"Wylder?" said Jessica.

"I was just thinking," started Wylder, "We have not seen anyone get out of the Elsewhere, but we have seen people go into it. I saw Noah go with that guy on the operating table."

"But we have not heard from him since," added Steve.

"I think that is because no one has a telepathic connection with him," said Wylder.

"What are you saying?" asked Jessica.

"I'm wondering," said Wylder, pausing for effect, "if someone who has a telepathic connection with someone in the Elsewhere, goes in to get them, if they can find each other while they are both there."

"You mean go into the Elsewhere?" asked Brian.

"I mean, try to save them from the inside," said Wylder, "and bring back Noah too."

"Going into the Elsewhere seems pretty risky," said Steve.

"I'll go," said Jessica, "I want to save Jason."

"I'll go too," said Jim, "I want to save Will."

"What if you get stuck there, like Noah?" asked Brian.

"I have to try," said Jessica, "I owe it to him."

"Me too," said Jim.

"Now, you just need to hitch a ride with someone who is going there," said Wylder, "As the great Noah once said, 'Where better to find a soul right after death, than in a hospital?'"

REUNITED

"How will we find Wade?" asked Stephanie.

"I am not exactly sure," said Jan, as they sat in the lobby of St. David's Hospital.

"I thought you said you knew the way!" insisted Stephanie.

"I have a few ideas," said Jan, "and one of them is bound to work."

"It's all you, Jan," said Greg, "I have not been there."

"When we came back to get you," said Jan to Greg, "we took Blaine and went through the portal. Wylder focused on a place she knew that was not geographically far from the real St. David's cemetery. When we came out the other side, we were in the place that Wylder was thinking of. If we go through the portal and I focus on where we were the last time we saw Wade, we should be able to get back there."

"How do we know that the three of us will end up in the same place?" asked Stephanie.

"I can answer that one," said Greg, "We hold

hands and Jan leads the way. Where she goes, we go. It's more accurate to say that the one who knows the way, can take others with them by holding their hand."

"Jan, I am willing to try anything. Can we go?" asked Stephanie.

Jan looked to Greg, and said, "Let's go find Wade, and then we will look for Maddie. At least we have some idea where Wade could be."

"Good plan," agreed Greg.

Jan smiled and put her hand on Greg's knee, "It's strange for me to be in the lead," said Jan, "On Earth, you were always the one in front."

"Different times," said Greg, "You are the one qualified to lead us in this situation. You have been to the place where Wade is. Where you go, my Love, I will follow."

"Me too," said Stephanie, standing, "Let's go."

Jan and Greg stood and followed Stephanie, who had already started walking to the portal. When she felt the gentle pull of the gateway she stopped and waited for Jan, reaching out her hand.

When Jan reached Stephanie, she took her hand and then reached for Greg. When Jan had a hold of both of her passengers, she closed her eyes and let the gateway pull her in. There was a flash, and all three of them were gone.

Only a moment later, Wylder, Steve, Brian, Jim, and Jessica walked through the doors of St. David's hospital, looking for someone who was on their way to Hell.

MOM

Jan stepped out the other side of the portal, still holding hands with Stephanie and Greg. She looked around to see the same lush field, smell the sycamore trees, and feel the soft breeze.

Stephanie let go of Jan, looking up at the blue sky and feeling the sun on her face, "Is this Heaven?" she asked.

Greg, still holding Jan's hand, said "This is what I saw through the portal when it was destroyed. It's beautiful."

"This is where I last saw Wade," said Jan. "He was walking down that hill with Michael, Wylder's friend, and two other children."

"Where is he now?" asked Stephanie, with an urgency in her voice, "How do we find him?"

Jan made eye contact with Stephanie, looking at her with an expression reserved for mothers looking for a lost child, "I don't know."

"Jan," asked Greg, "you said they were walking down that mountain. What is on the mountain?"

"Wylder said that they climbed the hill every

night to watch the sunset," said Jan.

Greg looked at Stephanie, "Let's wait here until sunset. Maybe they will come to us."

Stephanie looked down at the ground, "It doesn't feel like heaven."

Jan looked around and saw the things Wylder had described in conversation, the shaded trail through the trees, the huge rock where Bo had first seen Nala.

"Would you like to hear the story of Mama and Nala?" Greg asked, looking at Stephanie, "We have some time before the sun sets."

"Sure," said Stephanie, not sounding interested at all.

Greg started walking over to the large flat rock at the edge of the field. Jan and Stephanie followed. When he reached the rock, he sat down and smiled. "Jan, you would have loved Nala," he said, "She was a brave little girl, and so was her mother, Elizabeth."

Jan took a seat next to Greg, "Elizabeth's nickname was Mama, right?" she said, for Stephanie's benefit.

"Yes," said Greg.

"From what I gather, Mama and Nala were some of the first people buried in St. David's. They arrived about 200 years before I did. They came from a time in our history that I am not proud of, a time of slavery and oppression for black people. Mama and Nala were both a victim of that period."

Stephanie joined Jan and Greg on the rock, "How old was Mama?" she asked.

"I'd guess she was no more than 30," said Greg, "She was described by Nala as a healer. In life, she knew the medicinal properties of flowers, tree bark, and dirt. She worked in the main house and would help in the stables with the horses. That is where she met Bo, another slave on the plantation."

"She was a slave?" asked Stephanie, sadness in her voice.

"Yes, and there were others buried at St. David's too. There is a historical marker outside the slave portion of the cemetery, and the place where Wade is buried is a garden of reflection that looks over the whole cemetery. It was designed to allow visitors the opportunity to see how far society has come regarding segregation and to see that humanity all ends up in the same place in the end, but then, you already know that. Wasn't it you who put the garden in?"

"No," said Stephanie, "The garden had been in St. David's for a while. It was placed by a member of the community who wanted to bring people together. Multiple generations of families, representing several faiths and various races, are buried in St. David's. It's really a beautiful representation of diversity. We asked that Wade be buried in St. David's but there was no open gravesite. The next closest cemetery was very far away. The Mayor helped us to get our son into St. David's. What does the historical marker say?"

Greg closed his eyes and tried to recall the wording from the marker. As he did, a transparent image of the marker began to take shape, and it materialized right in front of Greg.

This one-half-acre site of old St. David's cemetery was reserved for slave burials. Marked by oak posts and hand-barbed wire, graves are marked head and foot with bricks made of mud and rock by hand. Some bricks are marked with names and dates, although most of them are no longer legible. The oldest legible marker indicated the gravesite of a twelve-year-old girl named Nala Jones whose cause of death is not recorded. Although the main cemetery is still in use, no former slaves were buried here after 1900.

"Greg, do you see that?" asked Jan. Greg opened his eyes, and the historical marker again became transparent and then disappeared altogether.

"I did!" said Greg, "Now it's gone."

"Try again," said Jan.

Greg closed his eyes and concentrated on the

words of the marker; the steel sign again took shape in front of Greg.

"Keep focusing, Greg," said Jan, "It's here."

Stephanie stood and touched the cool steel of the marker, "Amazing," she said.

Greg opened his eyes and the steel marker again faded and disappeared.

"Well, we learn something new every day, even in Heaven," said Greg.

"Did you bring the actual historical marker here?" asked Stephanie, "Meaning, did it disappear in the real world?"

"I don't think so," replied Greg, "because it faded and then disappeared. Maybe it was just a manifestation that can only stay as long as I concentrate on it."

"Does it work with people?" asked Stephanie.

Greg and Jan exchanged glances, and then Greg replied to the question, "I don't know, but we can try it. Are you thinking you can find Wade that way?"

"It's worth a try," said Stephanie.

"I don't think that is a good idea," said Jan. "Greg manifested something from the real world. You want to see Wade's soul, not his body."

"I had not thought of that," said Stephanie.

"What if I focus on his soul? His beautiful spirit?" said Stephanie, "That is the part I held onto all these years."

"That feels right," said Stephanie, "I want to try."

"I've met Wade," said Greg. "You close your eyes and focus on him. I will tell you what I see. When I opened my eyes, the manifestation disappeared so if you want to stop, just open your eyes."

"OK," said Stephanie, "I'm ready."

Stephanie closed her eyes and said, "I have been waiting for this for so long, my sweet boy. I can't wait to see you."

Jan and Greg waited, but there was nothing.

"Do you see anything?" asked Stephanie, her eyes still closed.

"Not yet," said Jan, "Keep trying."

Stephanie began to speak aloud, "Hi Wade, it's mommy. Are you here?"

"Keep talking," said Jan.

Stephanie continued, "I'm here Wade. I came to be with you. Can you hear me?"

Jan tapped Greg on the shoulder and pointed to the sky, which was changing colors from blue to purple to green.

Stephanie smiled and relaxed.

"Do you see him?" asked Stephanie, keeping her eyes closed.

"No, I don't see him," said Greg, "but I see the sky changing color."

Stephanie opened her eyes to see the colors and they faded away returning the sky to the beautiful blue it had been.

"What did you see?" asked Stephanie, "Maybe it was him!"

"Do you remember when we went to Alaska?" Jan asked Greg.

"Yes," replied Greg, then a smile of recognition crossed his face.

"Stephanie, have you ever heard of the Arora Borealis?" asked Greg.

"No, what is that?" asked Stephanie.

"It's also called the Northern Lights," said Jan.

"Yes!" said Stephanie, "I've seen it on TV. They are so pretty."

"Beautiful natural phenomenon," said Greg, "It's sort of like a storm in space that we can see on Earth. It's the result of interactions between the Sun and Earth's outer atmosphere."

"It's in Alaska, right?" asked Stephanie.

"Yes, and there is also one in the south, called the Aurora Australis, but it's lesser known because it occurs in the oceans around Antarctica and few people can see it," said Greg.

"When you were concentrating on Wade, it

was kind of like that," said Jan.

"The physics of the phenomenon are fascinating. The energy of certain types of auroras are thought to be derived from a dynamo effect of the solar winds which collide against the Earth's magnetic field to make the night sky light up with sheets of color," said Greg.

Jan looked at Greg, "Perhaps we can give the science behind it later," said Jan smiling.

"OK, later then," smiled Greg, "Let's try it again, Stephanie."

Stephanie closed her eyes, and the sky began to change colors again, but this time the sky became dark, and the vibrant colors danced all around them.

"It's stunning," said Jan, "It's the most beautiful thing I have ever seen."

Stephanie kept her eyes closed, with a soft Mona Lisa smile on her face. When she opened her eyes, she said, "I think I saw him. He's with a horse."

STOWAWAY

Wylder led the way into St. David's Hospital and headed to Summer's room. As they approached the nurse's station, she saw Sage walking down the hall with a brown paper bag.

"I'll be back, you guys go see what you can find," said Wylder, "Jessica, I'll be out back if you need me."

"Where are you going?" asked Jessica.

"I'm going to see my mom," said Wylder.

Jessica nodded, and led the others in the opposite direction, leaving Wylder to follow her mom.

Wylder picked up the pace and caught up with Sage just as she was walking to the parking lot.

Sage opened the paper bag and took out an apple, taking a bite as she walked.

"Hi mom," said Wylder, "How are you?"

Sage continued to walk and eat the apple.

"I miss you," said Wylder, "and dad. How is everyone?"

Sage stopped when she got far away from the

lights of the hospital and looked at the stars in the sky. She put the apple core in the bag and took out a sandwich and kept walking. She reached a dirt path behind the hospital and walked under the tall trees and out into a clearing. The trees blocked the light of the parking lot, and it was pitch dark.

"Where are you going, mom?" said Wylder, "It's dangerous out here; you might fall, you're old you know."

Wylder looked at her mom, "Sorry," she said, "You're not old, but you shouldn't be walking when it's this dark out."

Sage continued to navigate the dirt path like she had memorized the terrain. Finally, she reached a bench, in the middle of the open field. Wylder recognized it right away.

"Did dad build this?" asked Wylder, "There is one just like it by my gravesite."

Sage sat down and put the crust of the sandwich in the baggie and put the baggie in the paper bag with the apple core and rolled down the top of the bag.

"Hi Wylder," said Sage.

"Mom, you can hear me?" said Wylder, "Oh mom, I have missed you so much, I can't even tell you."

Sage continued, "Your brother and his wife had their third child last weekend. You should see him as a daddy, he's a pro."

"That's so nice to hear," said Wylder, "How is Dad?"

"Your dad would have been so happy, he always did get excited at the birth of a baby," said Sage.

"Mom," Wylder paused. "Where's Dad?"

Sage continued to look at the stars.

"I bet you two are ice fishing right now," said Sage, "probably with Grandma."

Wylder stood in front of Sage and saw her mother in the moonlight, with all the beauty that age brings.

For the second time since Wylder had passed away, her mom stood from a bench that her father had made and walked right through her.

***

Wylder followed her mom back into the bright hospital. When Sage went to the nurse's station Wylder continued down the hall to the ER.

Wylder saw Jim running towards her, and she picked up her pace to meet him in the middle.

"What's wrong?" asked Wylder.

"It took her, Wylder," said Jim, "The Swarm took Jessica."

He turned around and led Wylder back to the ER where Steve and Brian were standing near a tiny woman lying on a gurney with an oxygen mask covering her mouth and nose.

"Did she come back?" asked Jim.

"No," said Steve, "Jessica is gone."

"What happened?" asked Wylder.

Jim spoke up, "The four of us had split up, but we were all here in the ER. When the ambulance pulled in and brought this woman through the doors," pointing to the woman on the gurney, "we all heard the Swarm coming. Jessica was the closest. I think she wanted to see what happened when the Swarm took someone; she must have thought she was safe. The Swarm was bigger and darker than it was last time. It surrounded Jessica and the woman. It was so dense that we couldn't see through it. When it dissipated, Jessica was gone. Wylder, it took them both."

***

"Jason!?" yelled Jessica.

I'm here, said Jason.

"Where? I can't see you! I can't see anything!" replied Jessica, with panic in her voice.

Listen to my voice, said Jason, **we will find each other**.

"I hear you in my head Jason, not with my ears," Jessica said. "I don't know which direction to go."

Your eyes will adjust, and you will see a little,

but it is still dark, said Jason, **you are okay. Don't panic, I am here with you.**

"I feel claustrophobic like I am on a crowded city bus with no lights. It smells like body odor and fear," said Jessica.

Do you see a tiny red light? asked Jason.

"Yes," replied Jessica.

Let's both walk towards the light, and we will meet there, said Jason.

Jessica began to walk towards the light and felt the pull, like the one that took her to the Beyond, but this one was desperate like someone drowning and grabbing for a life preserver. The pull got strong and aggressive.

"Jason, I don't think this is a good idea," said Jessica.

A red shockwave went over her and for a brief second, she saw Jason, then it all went dark again.

Is this your little burden?

Jessica, did you hear that?

"Hear what?" asked Jessica.

She doesn't look like she is in pain anymore
You did the right thing by killing her

Shut up! Do you hear me? Shut up!

"Jason?" asked Jessica, "Is everything ok?"

Can't you hear that, Jessica?

There is a way out of here Jason
She can take your place
No one has to know

AGAINST
THEIR WILL

"The Swarm took Jessica?" asked Wylder, "As in, took her against her will?"

"Maybe she wanted to go save Jason, but we never talked about that," said Steve, "We would have made a plan, don't you think?"

"We need to talk to Greg," said Wylder, "Can anyone here reach him telepathically?"

"Only Jan," said Jim, "and she is with him."

"We did not think this through," hissed Wylder, "We should have made the groups so that one of us could have reached them. Instead, we let everyone choose where they wanted to go and now we can't talk to each other. That's just great."

Wylder paced back and forth in front of the nurse's station in the ER.

"What would Guy do?" asked Wylder, aloud.

"Who is Guy again?" asked Jim.

"Guy is our friend," said Brian, "He was buried

in St. David's with us. He and his wife Patty passed over to Heaven. We have not seen them since we got back."

"Guy would list the facts," said Steve.

"Then let's list the facts," said Wylder, "One, Jason is in the Elsewhere."

"Two," said Jim, "Will is in the Elsewhere too, but they are not in the Elsewhere together."

Brian added, "They are all in their own 'Elsewhere'", adding air quotes for effect, "but they can hear voices. At least Jessica said Jason heard voices."

"Three, Noah is probably in the Elsewhere, but he went intentionally," Wylder said.

"Four, Stephanie made it through the Beyond," said Steve.

"So did Greg," said Brian.

"Five, Jessica is probably in the Elsewhere," said Steve, "but she may not have intended to go."

"She may, or may not, be with Jason," said Wylder.

"Heaven got two new players, Greg and Stephanie," said Jim.

"Three, right?" said Brian, "Jessica made it through the Beyond."

"But now she's in the Elsewhere," said Jim, "I'm not sure she counts if she can't help."

"Hell is holding four new souls in the Elsewhere, that we know of, Noah, Will, Jessica, and Jason."

Heaven, 2

Hell, 4

Hell's winning thought Wylder.

The lights began to flicker, "Do you see that?" asked Steve, "The last time that happened…" But he did not get to finish his sentence before the sound of the Swarm and the feeling of death overcame them. The size of the Swarm had doubled, and when it went through the halls, there was no way to see through its density. As it passed through the ER, people began crying loudly in the rooms that it passed through. Alarms went off at the Nurse's station and the staff scattered in different directions attending to patients who had all suddenly worsened to the point of pressing call buttons or setting off emergency alarms in the center of the station.

When the lights stabilized, and the Swarm dissipated, Wylder was still watching the nurses scramble in and out of rooms. "Is that Dane?" she asked, looking at a man in scrubs, running to the station.

"Where is Sage?" he asked loudly, looking at all the nurses, "Summer is not responding."

One of the Nurses replied, "Dane, we just had a wave of emergencies come through the ER. She is tending to patients."

"Let's go," said Wylder, "We need to be there if Summer dies."

"Wylder?" said Steve, "Where's Jim?"

Wylder looked back to where Jim had been standing, with nothing but a blank wall there now.

"Fuck," said Wylder, "What the actual fuck is happening?"

AURORA BOREALIS

Stephanie looked at Greg and Jan, "I'm sure I saw him," she said.

"We can walk up the mountain and wait to see if he comes," said Jan.

"Or we could explore around here while we wait," added Greg, "Jan and I didn't get the chance to look around. I only have the stories that Wylder told me."

"How did you find this place?" asked Stephanie.

"Wylder found it," said Greg. "Actually, Nala took Wylder here, and they rode horses."

"I saw a horse when I saw Wade," said Stephanie, "Are there a lot of horses in Heaven?"

"I know of two," said Greg, "Cinder, Nala's horse, and Blaine, Wylder's horse. Wylder and Blaine knew each other from their life on Earth, but I believe Cinder and Nala met here in the Beyond."

"Are we in the Beyond or are we in Heaven?" asked Stephanie.

"That is a complicated question," replied Greg, "When I put the pieces together, it seems to me that the Beyond is a test to see if you can come to terms with the mistakes you made on Earth. If you pass, you go on to Heaven which simply means you can move around unrestricted and use the heavenly communication system and the transportation system."

"And if you don't come to terms?" asked Stephanie.

"Then you go back to the place where you died until you want to try again," said Greg.

"Is there a limit to the number of times you can try?" asked Stephanie.

"It does not seem like there is a limit," said Jan, "When Greg and I were helping all those from the Dark Side of St. David's to cross over, some of them tried many times before they had successfully made it through."

"It seems to be at your own pace, and you have eternity to make it," said Greg.

"How does the Swarm play into this?" asked Stephanie.

"That seems to be the other option after death," said Greg.

"Except it's not a warm, welcoming pull that

brings you to a place where you can face your choices on your own terms," said Jan, "The Swarm takes you by force, and we don't exactly know what happens to those who are taken."

"So, at death, there are two paths," said Stephanie, "one to Heaven and one to Hell. What about the children? Do all children go to Heaven?"

"As far as we know, yes," said Jan, "The only children we know are Nala and Wade. When I got to Heaven, I learned that Michael had found two other children, Max and Isabelle."

Jan looked at Greg, "Maddie was a child too!" said Jan.

Greg smiled, "I realized that when I was in the Beyond. I think we can find her once we find Wade."

"The sun is setting," said Jan, "Let's walk up the mountain."

The three of them started up the mountain in silence, watching the sky change colors. Halfway up the mountain, Greg said, "It's amazing to be climbing up a mountain without fatigue."

"A benefit of Heaven I guess," said Stephanie.

Greg reached for Jan's hand, and they continued to walk and look at the beauty that surrounded them. When they reached the top of the mountain, they could see an endless view.

"I can see why Michael comes here each night," said Jan.

The colors of the night seemed to surround them.

"Do you mind me asking what happened to Wade?" asked Jan, "I cannot imagine losing a child. I am sorry for your loss."

"I don't mind you asking," replied Stephanie, looking at Jan, "I like to talk about him. Wade was our first child. He was a happy baby from the minute he was born. He seemed to have a joy about him that would radiate to anyone who held him. He was like most young children, spoiled by his grandparents, loved by animals," laughed Stephanie. "We had no children before Wade, but we did have a cat, Sparkle, who thought she was our child. She was a bit needy and demanded attention. When Wade was born, Sparkle got a little competition. It was not long before they were best friends. Later, they were inseparable. Sparkle followed Wade everywhere."

"A boy and his pet are not soon parted," smiled Greg.

"When Wade was three, on a random Tuesday, after a bath and bedtime story we put him to bed like we always did. The next morning, I got up and went to his room. I talked to him as I picked out his clothes for the day. When he didn't respond, I called him a sleepyhead and kissed his forehead."

Stephanie stopped talking, closed her eyes, and said, "he had died in the night. We had no explanation. No one prepares you for the death of a child. It goes against nature. The police did an investigation. They treated us like criminals at first; our home was a crime scene, but they found nothing. The Coroner did a complete autopsy and found no cause of death. The investigators dug into our medical history to see if there was a hereditary explanation, but again, there was nothing. In the end, they ruled it was SUDC – Sudden Unexplained Death in Childhood."

"I have heard of SIDS," said Jan, "but not SUDC."

"It is only called SUDC when all possible causes of death have been ruled out," said Stephanie, "It gives parents a name to call it when there is no rational reason for it. It has to be one of the most tragic deaths because there is never closure for the parents."

The colors of the night sky began to take form and swirl around them, blues and purples, greens and a silver sparkling ribbon weaved in and out of the small group.

"Do you feel that?" asked Stephanie.

"It's like a warmth and a happiness," said Jan.

"It's like the opposite of the Swarm, it's pure joy," said Greg.

"Stephanie, close your eyes and think of Wade," said Jan.

Stephanie closed her eyes and Wade appeared before her.

"Open your eyes," said Jan, with both hands over her mouth and a genuine smile from ear to ear.

Stephanie opened her eyes and saw Wade, standing right in front of her. She couldn't move, she just stared at him.

"Wade?" asked Stephanie, kneeling down to be at his height, "Is that really you?"

Wade did not say a word, he just stepped forward and put his tiny arms around Stephanie's neck. Stephanie hesitated, and then closed her eyes and returned the hug.

"Oh, how I have missed you, my sweet boy," said Stephanie.

SUMMER LOVE

Wylder ran into the patient room and her mom was standing over Summer hooking up a fresh I.V. and talking to her.

"Summer, not to worry. It's not your time, do you hear me?" Said Sage. "I know these things, always have, and you're going to be just fine, you have a special spirit."

Sage sat in the chair next to the bed and whispered to Summer. "Now I don't like to meddle and it's probably none of my business, but Dane really likes you. He's a good boy, got a big heart, and does a good job. You can't ask for more than that. Of course, there has to be a spark and whatnot, but if you needed someone to put in a good word for him, I'm doin' it now. Well, I've said my piece," said Sage, "now it's up to you."

"Too bad he's not my type," whispered Summer, with a scratchy voice and closed eyes.

"You're awake," said Sage, "good, because someone is here to see you."

Sage stood up and turned to go. Dane was just walking in the door to the room. Sage walked by and had to reach up to put her hand on his shoulder as she passed. "I told you, she is going to be fine. You don't need to come running every time she is in a deep sleep," laughed Sage. She patted his shoulder and then turned back to Summer.

"Summer," said Sage, "what type is that?"

"Asshole," said Summer, weakly.

"Ahh," said Sage, understanding her meaning, and walked past Wylder as she went out of the room.

Wylder watched her mom go as Dane went to the empty chair and sat next to Summer, taking her hand.

"So, just a deep sleep, huh?" said Dane, "Don't scare me like that, Private Stevens. I am a nurse, mind you, I am supposed to know these things. But Sage has a way of knowing when it's a person's time to go. I wanted her to be here with you if it was your time."

Summer didn't open her eyes but said, "That shows a huge lack of confidence in my ability as a fighter; you know me better than that."

"Summer?" said Dane with a big smile, "There's my bad bitch,"

"I am not," Summer cleared her throat, "YOUR, bad bitch. But I am a bad bitch."

"I stand corrected Private," said Dane with the

same big smile, "I'm glad you're back."

"I need to sleep," said Summer.

"I'll check on you in a little while," said Dane, releasing her hand and standing.

As he turned to go he pumped his fist in the air. Wylder laughed and shook her head, "Dude, you're going to get your heart broken."

"Dane," said Summer weakly, "where is Ruby?"

"She's with Mrs. Miller," said Dane.

"Don't let her give Ruby too much people food," she said, then she fell back asleep.

"No promises," said Dane, as he walked out the door.

Wylder looked at Steve and Brian, who were walking in the room and said, "Summer is going to be fine. My mom knows these things. Let's go find the others, and then stick together," said Wylder.

"We should head back to St. David's," said Brian, "We were going to meet them there at the next full moon."

"That's in about two days," added Steve, "If we don't find them before that, we'll be there when they arrive."

"I don't want to leave the others for days," said Wylder.

"Got a better idea?" asked Steve. "I'd like to get out of this hospital. Seems to me like all of them were taken from here."

"Alright," agreed Wylder, "let's go."

As they walked down the hall, Steve asked, "Where is Blaine? Is he still at St. David's?"

"I wish I knew," said Wylder.

"What do you mean?" asked Brian, "Didn't we leave him there?"

"A lot has happened since we left the cemetery," replied Wylder.

"Where else would he be?" asked Steve.

"Let's just go and see," said Wylder, "He's probably there."

Please be there Blaine, thought Wylder.

I am back, said Blaine.

Blaine? It's so good to hear your voice, thought Wylder, *where did you go*?

I went to help Wade, said Blaine.

Did you find him? asked Wylder.

I did, indeed, and he has been reunited with his mum, said Blaine.

His Mum? Mocked Wylder, *do you mean his Mom*?

No, I mean his mum, has death made you hard of hearing? said Blaine.

Very funny, said Wylder, *I see that death has given you a sense of humor.*

Yes, you may think we horses are dumb as a donut, but we have quite a way of dealing with mundane moments, with a good joke, said Blaine.

"It's going to take some getting used to," said Wylder, aloud.

"What is?" replied Steve.

"Oh nothing, I was just talking to myself," said Wylder, with a smirk.

I see I am still your dirty little secret, said Blaine, **you cheeky monkey. But seriously, there is one thing I should tell you**.

Go on, thought Wylder.

What would you say if I told you I saw your dad? asked Blaine.

THE JOURNEY
OF A SOUL

Stephanie released Wade from the hug and put her hands on his small face. "You look just like I remember," said Stephanie, "I wondered if I would recognize you."

Wade looked at her and said, "You decided how I look."

"I don't understand," said Stephanie.

"This is how you remember me, so this is how you chose to see me," said Wade, "but this is not my actual form."

"What is your actual form?" asked Stephanie.

"I am a sound, most souls are," replied Wade, "but we take the form of our body on Earth when we first meet people here in Heaven. That is only necessary once," smiled Wade, "Did you notice the purple, blue, and green colors a few minutes ago?"

"Yes, they were beautiful," replied Stephanie, "They looked like the Northern Lights from

Earth."

"The Aurora Borealis is a phenomenon that happens when two souls find each other in Heaven for the first time," said Wade.

"Amazing," said Greg.

"It is a pleasure to see you again," Wade said to Greg.

"You sound so grown up," said Greg, smiling.

"I am quite old," said Wade, with a laugh that still sounded like a three-year-old, "However this trip to Earth was quick."

A light swirled around Wade and became brighter as it surrounded him, spinning, and expanding until there was a flash and he was gone.

"Wade?" said Stephanie.

I am here, said Wade.

"I can hear you, but I cannot see you," said Stephanie.

Jan looked at Greg, "Can you hear him?"

"No," said Greg, "Can you?"

"No," replied Jan.

"Stephanie, you can hear Wade in your head?" asked Greg.

"Yes, I can," said Stephanie."

"I could hear him when he was here with us," said Greg, "that's so strange."

The warm feeling of love and puppies surrounded them and then Wade reappeared before them.

"When you take a physical form, anyone close by can hear you," said Wade, "When you are in your natural form, only those bonded to you can hear you."

"Bonded?" asked Greg.

"Yes, as your soul ages, you bond with a few other souls, and you stay connected to them. You can reach out to them anytime you are both in Heaven, and they will hear you."

"What if they are in Hell?" asked Greg.

Wade looked at Greg with a stoic look and said, "that is a very different thing altogether. Why do you ask?"

"Because we have friends who seem to be hearing from people who are in Hell, and they want to rescue them," said Greg.

"They are not in Hell," said Greg, "they are in the doorway to Hell, not in but not out. They will be tested. If they pass the test, they will be released back to the last place they were alive, to wander the Earth. I still have only limited experience to share on the subject, and I could be mistaken in my belief, but that is my understanding."

"What about souls that are not in the doorway,

but are in actual Hell?" asked Greg, "Can they be reached?"

"No, or, not for a long time," replied Wade.

"Is it what we were told on Earth?" asked Jan, "Fire and brimstone for eternity?"

"Not exactly," said Wade, "in some ways it's worse."

"Worse than the pit of fire I heard about in Sunday School?" asked Stephanie.

"You must relive the pain you caused others, but through their eyes," said Wade. "I don't know if it works like this only when you kill someone, or if it is applied for emotional pain as well."

Greg looked at Jan, and then look down, "I have killed someone," he said, "and I did not go through that."

"You did not kill anyone intentionally," said Wade, "and you did not get satisfaction out of the death that you caused."

"So how does it work?" asked Stephanie.

"When you murder someone, it is recorded in your soul," said Wade, "when you pass away, if you have not made amends for your actions, the swarm will take you and put you to the test. Those that pass the test are released and those who do not pass, are cast into Hell."

"Forever?" asked Greg.

"No, not forever," said Wade. "For each murder,

311

the soul must relive the pain it caused through the eyes of its victim, and not only the victim, but also the soul must relive the life of the spouse, the children, and the parents; anyone who deeply loved the victim. For a soul to cleanse itself of the murder, it may have to relive many lives. The more people a soul has murdered, the more lives it must relive. When a soul has completed this penance, it is given the chance to go back to Earth and try again. All the memories are wiped and the soul is reborn, with the chance to make new choices. For some serial killers, it can take centuries. Eternity is a long time."

"You're saying the soul can be reincarnated?" asked Jan.

"After a time, yes," replied Wade.

"What is the test?" asked Greg.

"It seems different for everyone, but it usually involves someone you deeply love," said Wade, "someone you are bonded to."

"Like Greg and I?" asked Jan.

"Yes," said Wade.

"Can someone be bonded to more than one person?" asked Greg.

"Yes, the older your soul is, the more bonds the soul can have. However, these bonds are still very uncommon since they transcend lives on Earth. It is unusual to have even one from a previous lifetime."

"Wade, if it is possible to be connected to more than one person, I think I might be bonded to my sister. Can I reach out to Maddy?" asked Greg, cautiously.

"If you are bonded to Jan, it is very unlikely that you would also be bonded to another person from the same life on Earth," said Wade, "Bonding is a process that takes immense trust on both parts. It is a willingness to sacrifice anything for the other soul, even at your own suffering."

"So, you and I are bonded, right?" asked Stephanie, "Is it common for parents and children to be bonded?"

"We were parent and child on Earth, but we are not any relation here in Heaven. We have been bonded for a very long time," said Wade.

"I don't understand," said Stephanie, "Then why don't I remember you as anyone but my son?"

"It will take time for the memories to come back," said Wade, "You just arrived."

"So, if I gave you the name Wade, that is not your real name?" asked Stephanie.

"No," said Wade, "Here I do not have an Earthly name. My name is a feeling. When I am in a place you can feel my presence with a mixture of my soul's personality, like a signature."

"Love and puppies," said Jan with a laugh.

"Yes, that is me," said Wade, "Others might be a color, or a sound, or a smell, but you will recognize their presence by their 'signature."

"I taste pancakes," said Greg.

A GOOD RESCUE MISSION

Wylder, Steve, and Brian arrived at Old St. David's Cemetery and saw Blaine at the Stone benches.

"Blaine!" said Wylder, "I am so glad to see you. I wasn't sure you'd be here."

Don't be daft, darling, I told you I was here, said Blaine.

Wylder laughed and put her arms up around Blaine's neck. He nuzzled her head and snorted.

"Where is everyone else?" Wylder asked Blaine, but Steve responded, "I don't know, but we may have a couple of days to wait."

"They don't have days," said Wylder, "We need to go get them."

"How do we do that Wylder?" asked Brian, "The only way we know to get there is to go with someone being taken by the Swarm. That could be many days."

"I think I know how to get in," said Noah,

walking up behind them.

"Noah!" said Wylder, running up to hug him, "How did you get back? Did you get into the Elsewhere?"

"I did," said Noah, "and I did a little investigation work before I was spat out back at St. David's Hospital."

"Investigation?" asked Steve, "What did you find out?"

"I found there is a way to rescue them," said Noah, "By the way, this is Joe," said Noah, stepping out of the way to show a tattooed man about twenty years old, bald, with his hands in the pockets of his dirty jeans, and looking at the ground.

THE ELSEWHERE

What do we have here?
Joseph, you brought a friend

"He's not my friend, I don't know him," replied Joe.

But he will do, he will do nicely

"Where am I?" demanded Joe.

"I don't know, exactly," replied Noah, "but we affectionately refer to it as The Elsewhere. What's your name, son?"

"Joe," said Joe, "I don't think you want to be here. You should go."

Don't be silly Joseph
Today is your lucky day

"I am trying to find a way out of here, for both of us," said Noah, "Can you find your way to me?"

"You should stay far away from me," said Joe.

Don't you see, Joseph?

You have been given a unique opportunity

"Go Mister, you need to leave but I have a feeling I deserve to be here."

He deserves to be here Joseph

"I have killed people," said Joe, "I have done bad things."

"We have all done bad things," said Noah.

He has done very bad things, Joseph

He has also killed innocent people

That is why he is a good trade

"What do you mean?" asked Joe.

He can take your place

He can stay here, and you can go free

"I mean that we all have done things we are not proud of," replied Noah, "It's how you come to terms with those decisions that matter."

"You better go, mister," said Joe, "I'm not good

at doing the right thing, please go away," said Joe.

He is your ticket out of this place
Do you feel that, Joseph?
The weight of your choices?
It only gets worse, the longer you are here
Take the offer, Joseph

"I can tell you are a good kid," said Noah, "I'm going to figure a way out of here."

"No!" said Joseph, "I deserve this."

Are you sure?
One of you can leave, but only one of you

"I'm sure," said Joseph.

Have it your way

A red shockwave ripped past and for a moment, they could see each other, then it all went dark.

The red light flickered, then faded, and both Noah and Joe were back in the O.R. of St. David's hospital, where the Swarm had taken them not that long ago.

"How did you do that?" asked Noah.

"It gave me a choice," said Joe, "I guess I made the

right one."

TRADING PLACES

"Will?" said Jim.

Yes, Jimmy, where the hell are you? said Will, **Glad you're here brother.**

"Where are we Will, I don't like it here," said Jim, "It feels dark and angry."

That's because it is, said Will, **Do you know how to get out of here?**

"We were working on a plan," said Jim, "but we hadn't figured it out yet."

Who's 'we'? asked Will, **you were going to leave me in this shit hole, weren't you?**

"Will, we were trying to work out a plan; you are not the only one in here we wanted to help," said Jim, "there are others."

Look Bro, I could give a rat's ass about the others. Get me out of here! Demanded Will.

"I don't know how, Will," said Jim, "and now we are both stuck here."

It doesn't have to be this way, Will

"What do you mean?" asked Will.

"When I left, people were being taken by the Swarm, the people who were trying to get you out of the Elsewhere. What if we all get trapped in here and there is no one to rescue us?"

He deserves to be here

He slept with your wife

You deserve another chance, you were always taking the heat for him

You'd be living the good life right now if you had not confronted Jimmy's infidelity

"Go on," said Will.

"There weren't that many of us, Will," said Jim, "We were planning to rescue our loved ones. Noah figured out how to get in here, we were waiting to see if he could get back out. If not, we were going to try to find another way."

You can trade places with him

He stays here with us, and you go free

He deserves to be here, not you

"**Let's do it**," said Will, "**I want out of here**."

"That's just it, Will," said Jim, "Apparently we can get in, but we don't know how to get out."

Are you sure?

There is no changing your mind later

You will trade places with your brother, do we have a deal?

"**Yes, I'm sure**," said Will.

"Sure about what?" asked Jim.

Just go to the red light and you're out

You get what you deserve, and so does he

"Will, do you see that red spark?" asked Jim, "It's like the blue spark I saw at St. David's Cemetery. It had pulled me towards it, and…"

A red shockwave ripped past and for a moment, Jim saw Will, then it all went dark.

The red light flickered, then faded, and Jim was back in St. David's hospital.

"Why do the lights keep flickering," said Dane, "Someone call the electrician!"

Jim looked around; he was back where he had been when the Swarm took him.

"Where is Will?" asked Jim, but no one was around to hear him.

HELL

Welcome, Will

I've been expecting you

It's time to pay the price

What price? asked Will

GINGER

I think it's almost time, my babies. I can hardly wait to meet you. The pain is getting worse now, is that you knocking at the door?

The contractions started in the afternoon; first a twinge and then it felt like ripping flesh. Ginger's water broke and she slowly crawled under the bed, dripping water as she went.

The moment has come, my littles, I am so excited to meet all of you.

Ginger made a low grunting sound and Kate walked quickly into the room. Ginger tried to bark but the sharp pain took her breath away.

Kate looked around, "Ginger?" she called, "where are you girl?" she asked, concerned.

She heard a soft groan. Kate got down on the floor and looked under the bed.

She reached for Ginger and pet her head, "Is it time little lady?" she asked.

Yes! I can feel my babies making their way here.

Ginger looked at her and then another ripping pain hit and Ginger cried out in pain. She came a little closer to Kate, rolled on her side and whimpered quietly.

"Ok, mama," Kate said sweetly, gently pulling Ginger from under the bed. She picked her up and brought her to a soft place she had made on the floor.

"This is for you," said Kate, "I hope you are comfortable. I can hardly wait to see your beautiful puppies."

Hours passed with Kate on the floor near Ginger. The bright sunlight outside faded and darkness took over the room. The bedroom door opened, and Will stood in the doorframe.

"What are you doing?" Will asked.

"She's in labor," said Kate, petting Ginger's head, which was resting in her lap.

"Don't just sit there with the dog all night, Kate. Get up and make dinner!" he yelled.

"I'll make dinner in a little while, she's having her puppies," said Kate.

"I don't give a rat's ass if she is having puppies," snapped Will, "Now, get up and make something to eat before I put that dog out of her misery."

"I'll order pizza," said Kate as she gently placed Ginger's head on the blanket and walked out of the room.

When Kate returned to the room, she brought a bowl of water. "Are you thirsty?" she said softly, sitting on the floor near Ginger. But the dog just laid on the blanket, unable to move and waves of pain took over her tiny body.

The unfamiliar pain brought an awareness to Will that he was seeing this memory through Ginger's eyes, feeling her sharp pains of labor, helpless to stop them.

Please babies, please come to meet me, Will heard Ginger thinking.

Holy Shit, I'm Ginger?

It was then Will realized, this was just the beginning of a very bad day for Ginger.

The pain was coming faster and faster, and Ginger began to pant.

Kate looked worried as she added more blankets to the bed she had made on the floor. "Okay, little lady, ready to have some puppies?"

Are you fucking kidding me right now?

Ginger did not move, and her breathing became shallow. "I know it hurts," said Kate, rubbing the firm belly, "but you will feel better when you have your babies."

Kate, I am not a fucking dog*!* What the hell is happening right now*?*

"Will?!" yelled Kate, through an open bedroom door, "I think something is wrong. We should take her to the vet."

Will walked into the room, shaking his head.

"I told you," Will said, "I am not taking her to the vet. She's a dog, having puppies. She will be fine, stop overreacting."

Oh my God, the pain is unbearable

It's okay my littles, you can come out now. Don't be afraid.

Ginger's heart started to pound and the puppies inside her were growing hot, and still.

"It's okay, Ginger," said Kate, "you are doing great. Soon you'll have some sweet little puppies to make you feel better."

The sharp tearing feeling was getting worse, Ginger started to bleed. Kate looked at Ginger and then stood to look at Will, "We have to take her to the vet," she said, "Please, Will."

"She doesn't need to go to the vet, Kate. Dogs have been having puppies since the beginning of time," Will scowled.

"She's been in labor for almost a day now, she has not had a single puppy. She's panting and she won't drink. Her water broke hours ago and now there is blood coming out. Will, please, can I take her to the vet?" asked Kate.

"Hell no, Kate," Will said, "You know how much that is going to cost?"

"I don't care how much it cost; she is in distress Will, we have to go," said Kate.

"Are you paying for it?" Will asked, "Last time I

checked, you were not employed. You stay home and take care of the kids, watching TV all day. If you had a real job, you might get a say in some of these decisions, but you don't. That means I make the decisions in this house, and we are not going to the vet."

Kate's phone rang, and she answered it.

I know how this will end.

At the vet, the darkness closed in, and Ginger's pain was registered in Will's soul, as it began again.

***

The tiny body shivered, but Kate held her close to her chest and wrapped her coat around the puppy.

It's f,f,freezing

Kate walked into the warm house with Jim following behind her. Will was sitting on the couch and Kate walked past him and into the kitchen, ignoring him.

She opened the drawer and got a dish towel out and wrapped the puppy in the towel. She walked to the bedroom and gently placed the tiny puppy in the center of the bed. In the closet, she found her heating pad and one of Will's shoe boxes and dumped the new shoes on the floor, taking the box to the bed where the puppy lay sleeping. She took the pillowcase off her pillow and arranged it inside the box over the heating pad.

Kate held the sleeping newborn puppy on her chest and cried.

"Your mama was Ginger," she whispered through tears. "She was my friend."

The puppy squirmed and yawned a big yawn, nuzzling back down in place.

"I'll take good care of you," said Kate. "You look a little like your mama. I think I'll call you Cinnamon."

Kate fell asleep with the puppy and when she woke up, Will was still in the other room. Not willing to talk to him yet, she placed the puppy in the warm box and got ready for bed. Before she climbed in, she looked at the sleeping puppy, "goodnight Cinnamon," said Kate, "I'll see you in the morning."

No, you won't

Later that night, when Kate was fast asleep, Will got up and found the puppy sleeping in the box at the foot of the bed, warmed with a heating pad and wrapped in a dish towel.

"Come on little thing," he said, and he gently picked up the pup. He quietly walked out of the bedroom, and into the living room. He opened the front door and felt the cold rain on his face. He set the puppy outside on the porch, closed the door, and went back to bed.

No, come back! Don't do this!

The puppy began to shiver violently, and Will knew that this was going to be a long painful night.

What have I done?

***

With the fear and pain still fresh in his soul, he felt the shift in his perspective from the puppy to a man. A feeling of love passed over him, but also a deep frustration.

Will, I love you man but sometimes you are a handful, he heard.

This time I will be Jimmy. Oh God, not Jimmy.

"Why did you do it, Jimmy?" Will asked Jimmy, slurring his words and unsteady on his feet.

"Put the bottle down," said Jimmy, seated on the stone bench.

"I thought you were a good person, but a good person doesn't sleep with my wife, Jimmy."

"You're my brother Will, and I would never sleep with your wife," said Jimmy, pausing, "anyone's wife!" Jimmy finished. "Why did we come here Will? Why are we in a cemetery, in the dark, miles from home?"

"I wanted to talk to you in private, where no one would hear," Will said, stumbling.

"You're drunk Will," Jimmy said, "Let me drive you home."

Will, come on man, we're brothers. I love you.

He is really worried about me, and I'm going to stab him with a bottle. Oh God, what was I thinking?

Will tried to close his eyes but he was seeing this memory through the soul of his brother, an observer, witnessing the death he caused and feeling it from the other side.

"I don't want anything from you, except an explanation and an apology," Will said.

"I have nothing to apologize for Will, I did not sleep with Kate," Jim said calmly.

Will lunged at Jimmy, plunging the broken beer bottle into his neck.

What? Will, what are you doing?

A feeling of shock crossed Jimmy's face as the glass ripped open the flesh of his neck. Blood sprayed from the wound and Will felt the strength drain from his brother instantly. Will felt Jimmy instinctively put his hand to his neck and then pulled his hand away to see the blood before falling to the ground.

Will looked at his brother, "Jimmy? Oh, Jimmy!" then he reached for him, and stumbled, his skull cracked loudly when it hit the stone bench.

Will stared up at the starry sky through the open eyes of his brother, shallow breaths, and the taste of blood.

He heard Jimmy thinking, *Why? Will. I love you still.* Then the darkness closed around him, and he felt the shift in his perspective from the man on the ground to a spirit looking at his dead body, and the body of his brother.

The sound of the Swarm started almost immediately and grew louder as it got closer.

WE NEED SAM

Wylder stepped around Noah and walked to Joe, who did not look up.

"Hi Joe, I'm Wylder," she said.

Noah brought Steve and Brian over to Joe.

"I'm Steve," said Steve, "and this is my partner, Brian. It's nice to meet you. I bet you have quite a story to tell."

Without a word, Joe turned around and walked away, Wylder followed him to the stone benches. When Noah and Brian started after them, Steve stepped in front of them, "Give them some space," he said.

Wylder walked ahead of Joe and sat down on the cold stone, "Do you want to sit with me? I'm sure you have a ton of questions."

Joe looked at Wylder, sitting on the bench, and took a seat on the same bench, facing the other way.

"This is my favorite spot in the cemetery," said Wylder, "I come here to think."

She waited for Joe to say something, but after

a moment of silence, she continued. "I saw you in the O.R. at St. David's hospital. You were handcuffed to the bed, so I am guessing you had a rough day."

"I shouldn't be here," said Joe, "It's not fair."

"When I first arrived, I was angry too. I was about your age I'd guess. I died in a car accident, and it all seemed so unfair," said Wylder, "But we have an expiration date. It was just my time."

"That is not what I mean," said Joe, "It's unfair to all the people I hurt on Earth. I should be in Hell, not here in some cushy cemetery."

"Well, I wouldn't call it cushy," laughed Wylder.

"You were not where I was," said Joe, "This is cushy."

"Can you tell me how you got out?" asked Wylder.

"There was this voice, talking to me," said Joe. "It told me that Noah could take my place and I could go free. I know what I have done, I know that I deserve hell, so I said no. Next thing I know, we are both back in the ER where I died."

"So, you could have left Noah there, and gone free, but you chose not to sacrifice him so you both got out?"

"It's temporary. When they know what I did, they will come back for me," said Joe.

Wylder waved at Noah to come over. The three men joined them, pretending they had not been listening.

"Did you know that Joe was offered a trade?" Wylder asked Noah.

"What kind of trade?" asked Noah.

"He could have let you take his place, and he could have gone free," said Wylder.

"But we were both freed," said Noah.

"I think that Joe was faced with another chance, and he made the right decision, so they let him go," said Wylder.

"Like the devil didn't know if he was good or bad so he was given a choice to let an innocent person take his place," said Steve.

"I am not an innocent person," clarified Noah.

"Joe didn't know that," said Brian, "He could have left you there. He chose to let you go. The result was that you both got out."

"Got out of where?" asked Jim, walking up to the stone benches from the dirt road that led to St. David's.

"Jim!" called Steve, "You're okay. We were worried about you when you disappeared. Did you go to the Elsewhere, did you see Will?"

When Jim arrived at the stone benches, he sat down. "The last time I sat here, was the day I died, killed by my brother," said Jim "When the

Swarm took me from the hospital, I could hear Will, but I could not see him. He was talking to me, but it seemed like he was talking to someone else too."

Jim noticed Joe, "Who is this?" asked Jim, pointing to Joe who was seated on the bench but facing away from the group.

"That is Joe," said Noah, "I met him in the Elsewhere."

"Is Will your brother?" asked Joe, still looking away, "And he killed you?"

"Yes," said Jim.

"Where is he now?" asked Joe.

"I don't know," said Jim, "There was a flash of red light and I saw him for a second, then he was gone, and I was back in the hospital where they took me."

"Will was not with you when you got back?" asked Joe.

"No," said Jim, "It was just me."

"Then he tried to trade you," said Joe.

"What do you mean?" asked Jim, offended.

"I was offered a choice. I could let Noah take my place and I could go free, or I could stay, and they would let Noah leave. I deserved to be there so I would not trade places. They asked me if I was sure and when I told them that I was, we both ended up back in St. David's Hospital, in the O.R. right where I was when they took me. He must have accepted their offer to take you instead of him."

"That's not possible, he is my brother," said Jim, defensively, "We have been through hell together! Well, maybe not hell in the 'fire and damnation' sense but hell as in abuse and neglect. He was always the one to protect me, he took a beating many times for me when we were kids."

"That can change a person," said Joe, "It changed me."

"It doesn't have to change a person," said Noah. "I wish you could meet Sam. He was my friend or as much of a friendship you can have with someone trapped in a POW camp with you. He saw atrocities that you could not imagine, yet somehow, he kept his honor and sense of humor. I wish he was here; he could tell you that it's always a choice. You can't choose your circumstances, but you can choose how you respond to them."

Did someone call my name?

"Did any of you hear that?" asked Noah.

"I didn't hear anything," said Wylder, "What did you hear?"

"I heard someone ask me if I called his name," said Noah.

Well, did you?

"Sam?" said Noah.

I have not been called that in a very long time. This must be Mother Trucker!

Noah looked around at the faces staring at him, even Joe had turned around, "I think I just reached Sam," he said.

You sure as hell did! How the hell are you man?

MADDIE MY MADDIE

"Do you taste pancakes?" Greg asked Jan, with a little-kid smile on his face.

"No, I don't taste anything," replied Jan, laughing.

"What does the taste of pancakes remind you of?" asked Wade.

"My little sister Maddie," said Greg.

"I don't taste pancakes, but I have this image of a tiara in my head," said Wade.

"She was obsessed with Princess Grace," laughed Greg.

In the distance blue and purple and yellow swirled in the night sky.

"Look, Wade, it's the Aurora Borealis! Isn't it beautiful?" said Stephanie, pointing. "I'm sorry, Wade, you are no longer a little kid who needs things pointed out."

"It is beautiful," Wade said to Stephanie, "and it's a good sign for Greg."

"Greg," said Wade, "when that happens it is two souls reunited in Heaven for the first time. If I were a betting man, I'd say you are about to meet your sister."

Greg closed his eyes and thought of the last day he and Maddie had breakfast together, eggs and pancakes.

"Oh my God," said Jan, "Open your eyes."

In front of Greg stood his twelve-year-old sister, with a strawberry jam stain on her pink t-shirt.

"Greggie!" said Maddie, and wrapped her arms around his neck, "I have waited so long to see you again."

Greg returned the hug and looked at Jan over Maddie's shoulder, "This is the first time since I left life on Earth, that I thought there was a God."

BACK TO ST. DAVID'S

After all the hugs and introductions, Stephanie spoke up, "I told Wylder that I would help her after I found Wade. I have to go back; can you show me the way?"

"We should all go back," said Jan.

"But I just found Maddie," said Greg, "I have so much to ask her."

"You stay," said Jan, "I'll take Stephanie back and you can join us later."

Maddie smiled a big smile, "I'll go," said Maddie, "I love a good adventure. Greg and I can catch up on the way,"

"You are speaking so clearly, so articulate; I didn't expect that," said Greg.

"During our life together, I chose to have Down Syndrome. It was a way to build my soul's ability for compassion and grace," said Maddie.

"You 'chose' to have Down Syndrome?" asked Greg.

"Yes, once we come home, we can stay here or we can go back to Earth to build our character," said Maddie, "Some go only once, and others go many times to become the best version of themselves. We call them an old soul."

"You also made a choice Greg," said Maddie, "Do you remember yet?"

"No," replied Greg, "What did I choose?"

"You chose to be my brother, knowing the event in the car would take place," said Maddie.

"But why?" asked Greg, "Don't we have free will? Wasn't the car accident, just that, an accident?"

"When we go back, we choose a life lesson," said Maddie, "You and I both chose compassion. The best way to develop concern for the sufferings or misfortunes of others is to experience suffering and misfortune yourself."

"How do we know that we will succeed in our life goal?" asked Greg, "What happens if we don't?"

"We are not guaranteed success," said Maddie, "We are trying to develop an old soul, to be strong and resilient. Heaven needs these skills to face the battle that is coming."

"What battle?" asked Greg.

"The battle between good and evil," replied Maddie. "We do not know when it will happen, but we have to be ready. It's already becoming evident down on Earth. The scales must stay tipped in the favor of Good; if the scales tip the other way, we will have to fight to rebalance the universe."

"Or?" asked Greg.

"Or" Maddie looked him in the eye, "humanity will fall into a state of violence and death until the scales can be brought back into balance. Those of us willing to protect humanity, go back to develop our skills for the army of Good."

"How many times have you gone?" asked Greg.

"Our life was my seventh time around," said Maddie, "I want to go back, but I waited for you, so we could decide together what the next goal would be based on what was needed to ensure the balance of Good over Evil."

"Does everyone go back to build their skills?" asked Greg.

"No," said Maddie, "Although everyone knows the situation and can choose to go back to Earth, some stay in the bliss of the Beyond or choose Heaven on Earth with their loved ones."

"So, they just stand by and do nothing?" asked Greg, unbelieving.

"It is a very difficult choice," said Maddie, "You go back with no memories, no plan. You forget those you love and face your life all alone. You must figure it all out on your own. You will be faced with challenges you are not equipped to handle; this is how you develop the soul."

"Do only the good souls go back?" asked Greg, "The ones preparing themselves for the battle?"

"There are fewer and fewer souls going back to Earth, it means leaving this place of comfort and love to experience cold and discomfort. It is getting more difficult on Earth. Souls who are trapped in Hell are always given a chance to go back to try again. Some go back because they do not want to stay in hell. They want to try again. With no memory of their past mistakes, their soul is given a life lesson. If they accomplish that goal, they get a chance to go to Heaven when they pass on. The situation is that many old souls are choosing to stay in Heaven, so it is tipping the scales of good and evil on Earth."

"So," Jan interrupted, "we need to recruit souls to go back and help increase the mass of good on Earth while developing the skills necessary to win the ultimate fight of good vs. evil?"

"Yes," said Maddie, "The more souls that go back, to grow and learn, the bigger the presence of Good. Those people who are on the fence, equally good and evil, can be persuaded by acts of kindness. Good souls can recruit the neutral souls by setting the example, by taking action instead of standing by and doing nothing in the presence of evil."

"If they can be persuaded by an act of kindness, could they not also be influenced by an act of violence or greed?" asked Jan.

"Yes," replied Maddie, "Those who are not committed to one side, or the other, are vulnerable to persuasion."

"What if we stay here?" asked Greg, "Is there a role here in Heaven we can play to help?"

"Yes," said Maddie, "We need souls to guide those who are stuck in a cemetery. Someone to let them know that it's not too late. They can go to the place of repentance and forgiveness; only then can they make it to Heaven and choose to fight."

"Fight?" asked Jan, "in Heaven?"

"Yes," said Maddie, "If Heaven does not maintain the advantage, the next life could be the last, as we know it."

"We need to go tell Wylder," said Greg.

***

Back in St David's cemetery, Wylder saw the sky light up with beautiful blue and green streamers. Staring at the beauty, she was aware that this was a new phenomenon that she had not ever noticed before. When the colors faded, she looked over and saw Stephanie and Wade walking toward her and shrieked with excitement.

"You found him!" said Wylder, running to meet them. She knelt down to Wade's height and said, "Hi Wade, do you remember me?"

"I do," said Wade, "You are Wylder, and you carried me over the threshold to Heaven when I arrived here in St. David's. Thank you, Wylder, that was very kind of you."

Wylder looked at Stephanie and back to Wade, "You sound so grown up for just three years old; heaven has made you very talkative."

"Thank you, Wylder," said Wade, "I am actually much older than three. You chose this form because this is how you remember me."

"I did?" smiled Wylder, "It is the only way I have ever known you."

"It is not my true form, but you can choose to see me however you want," said Wade, "and I rather like this form."

"I don't understand. How old are you in Heaven years?" asked Wylder, "I didn't realize you could age after you die."

"Your soul has no age in years," explained Wade, "It ages in experience. You chose to take the form of Wylder at eighteen years old. You must like that form."

"Wait a minute," said Steve, "I can choose what form I take? ANY form?"

"Yes," said Wade, "You can take a form that you

had on Earth or make up any form you'd like. But if the person you are talking with chooses a different form for you, that is what they will see. If you are speaking with five souls, each of the five souls may see a different form of you."

"What if you speak a different language?" asked Brian.

"Great question," said Jim.

"What language am I speaking right now?" Wade asked Brian.

"English," said Brian.

"I am speaking French," said Wade, "You are only hearing me in English. As with my form, you will hear me speak the language that is most comfortable for you. Each of you may hear me in a different language, even though I have chosen to speak French."

"Amazing," said Wylder, standing, "Since I know everyone here, let me introduce all of you."

Wylder began, pointing to each soul until she got to the last person whom she did not recognize, "Oh my God, are you Maddie?"

"I am," smiled Maddie.

"It is so nice to meet you," said Wylder.

"Wylder," said Greg, "we have a lot to tell you."

"I'm sorry to interrupt you Greg, but Wylder, where is Jessica?" asked Jan.

"Right here!" said Jessica, walking up behind

Jan.

"Jessica!" said Wylder.

Everyone turned and saw Jessica walking from the road, with a new face following behind her.

Noah walked over and extended his hand, "You must be Jason," said Noah, "It's good to finally meet you."

"You don't know how good it is to be here," said Jason.

Greg spoke up, "We need to tell you what Wade and Maddie explained to us. There is a battle coming and we need to be ready for it. Wade, Maddie, can you start from the beginning and explain the situation?"

"A battle? That's my specialty. If we only had Sam," said Noah, "we'd have quite a squad."

"Whoever Sam is," said Wade, "why don't you go get him?"

"I would like that, but I am not sure where he is," said Noah.

"Whistle to him," said Wade.

"Whistle?" asked Noah,

"Yes," said Wade, "If you whistle, and he whistles back, he will come to you. If you know where he is and you want to go there, you just Whistle and point your mind in that direction- you'll be there in no time."

"You don't have to use the portals?" asked Noah.

"You can if you want to, but why take the bus when you can take a jet?" asked Wade, using Earthly terms.

"I can't argue with that," said Noah.

Noah let out a quick whistle and waited. Nothing.

"You need to hold the whistle for a while. Think of it as opening a door for someone. When the whistle stops, the door closes. You may have just slammed a Heavenly door in Sam's face," laughed Wade.

Noah let out a long strong whistle, looking around while he held the sound. When he saw a man with only one arm walking up to him, he stopped his whistle.

"You learn to control it more over time. The more lives you live, the better you get at it," said Wade.

Noah smiled and walked to meet Sam. When he reached him, he slapped him on his good shoulder and pulled him into a strong embrace. "Thank you, Sam, I never got to say thank you."

Sam returned the embrace and said over Noah's shoulder, "I knew, man, I knew."

Wylder looked at Sam in disbelief, then at Wade, "Are you saying that reincarnation is real?"

Blaine walked up behind Wylder and nuzzled her hair.

Hi Wylder, said Blaine.

Hi, said Wylder.

Are you ready to tell them about me? Asked Blaine.

Not yet, said Wylder.

Sweet Fanny Adams, when then? asked Blaine.

Soon, said Wylder, *soon. I just don't want to interrupt this moment between Noah and Sam.*

That is rubbish, said Blaine, **let's get on with it already,** in a flash of light Blaine was gone and a man stood in his place.

Every eye turned to see the new man standing behind Wylder.

I wonder how long it will take her to notice her dad, thought Jessica.

EPILOGUE

"I can walk myself to the door," said Summer.

"Hospital rules," said Dane, "All patients take a wheelchair to the exit and are loaded in the waiting car by hospital staff. Safety first."

They passed through the lobby and the sliding doors opened and closed, opened and closed, then the lights flickered on and off.

"What's going on?" asked Summer.

"I don't know," said Dane, "It looks like maintenance is working on the doors, again."

Dane walked up to the young man working on the electrical panel, "Excuse me," said Dane, "can we go through?"

"Yes, but first, let me lock them in place," said the man working on the doors, "Ok, you're good to go."

"Thanks, man," said Dane as he pushed Summer through the threshold.

A little Honda Civic was running in the patient pick-up loop and Mrs. Miller was waiting in the back seat with Ruby. Mrs. Miller opened the door and the dog jumped out and ran to Summer.

"Hi, Ruby! I missed you girl," said Summer, "Are you eating too much people food?"

Ruby barked once then rested her chin on Summer's leg, "Hold on girl, let me stand up."

Ruby sat down on the blacktop and Dane helped Summer stand when another car pulled into the loop and jammed the car into Park.

A man got out of the car and ran to the passenger side and opened the door to show a pregnant woman in the seat, panting.

"Someone help!" yelled the man, "My wife is in labor!"

Sage came running out pushing a wheelchair, "Dane, help me get her in the chair," she said as she put the wheel locks on.

Dane went over and helped the puffing woman out of the car and into the chair that Sage held still. Sage removed the wheel locks and turned the chair to the double sliding doors still locked in the open position by the maintenance worker.

"You should go help Sage," Summer said to Dane.

"Mrs. Miller can't drive," said Dane. He looked over at Sage pushing the pregnant woman into the hospital.

"I can drive," said Summer.

"No, Summer, you just got out of the hospital,"

said Dane, but Summer had already headed to the driver's side of the car and opened the door with her bandaged hand and Ruby jumped in.

"Safety third!" yelled Summer, as she sat in the driver's seat, put the car in Drive, and drove away from the bright lights of the hospital, leaving Dane standing in the circular drive.

"That's my bad bitch," said Dane, and he jogged back into St. David's Hospital to help Sage.

***

"What do I have to do to get out of here?" asked Mason, "I'll do anything."

> *Unfortunately, there is no one*
> *here to speak for you*
> *No one here to take your place*
> *Do you know of anyone, Mason?*

"Summer, she knows me," said the Major, desperate.

> *Summer is still alive Mason*

"I know she will vouch for me," said Mason.

> *You have a long time to wait*

***

Did you see?

"See what?" Will asked.

The pain you caused others
You took a life, with intention
When faced with a choice, you were willing
to sacrifice your brother to save yourself

"I'm sorry, I shouldn't have said I would let Jimmy trade places with me," Will said.

That was your choice
Your future is always your choice

"I'm sorry, I made the wrong decision. I take it back," Said Will.

You cannot take it back
But you can start over
Do you want to start over?

"How do I start over?" asked Will, "I want to get out of this hell hole."

You will not remember anything
You may make the same mistakes, Will
Your next life will be even harder,
you will have to prove yourself

"I'll be better," said Will, "I swear."

Very well

***

"Push," said the Doctor, "I can see the crown."

Sadie's husband stood behind her supporting her head and holding her hand.

Sadie grunted in pain as she pushed as hard as she could.

"Here he comes," said the doctor.

"Look Sadie," said her husband, "there is little William!"

"Can I hold him?" asked Sadie.

Sage brought the newborn to his mother and laid him in her arms. As she did, Sage's heart jumped, and she clutched her chest.

"Are you okay?" Sadie asked Sage.

"Can someone get the nurse some water?" asked Sadie's husband.

"I'm ok," said Sage, "I just had a pain in my chest, but I am fine."

"Good," said the doctor, "because I need you."

"What's wrong doctor?" asked Sage.

"Nothing is wrong," said the doctor, "but Sadie, you are having twins!"

***

The service at New St. David's Cemetery began with a Mariachi band. Friends, family, co-workers, and neighbors took a seat under the pavilion.

"We are gathered here today to celebrate the life of Keith Cortez, beloved husband, father, and grandfather," said the pastor. "Although his life could have been extended by medical science, Keith said he lived a long and happy life and now wanted to be with his wife Brenda who he lost many years ago. I had the honor of speaking with Keith many times before his passing to ensure he understood the finality of death and that I understood his wishes for this service. I consider it my job to help people through these times, to consider their choices in life, and come to terms with their mistakes. Keith was not afraid of this transition. He had spent years making amends to anyone he had hurt intentionally or unintentionally. He apologized where necessary and gave forgiveness where it was asked for. Keith was a man who saw the good in people.

When they did not deserve compassion, by the standards of society, Keith was there to give it. Even though he was ready to pass on, we are left here without him and will feel the void he has left behind."

A small blue spark appeared in the trees just beyond the pavilion, barely noticeable in the bright light of the day. Although no one saw her, Brenda quietly took a seat in the back row, listening to the stories, laughing at the memories, and waiting for Keith to arrive.

Hurry love, we have work to do.

THE END

RELATIONSHIP MAP

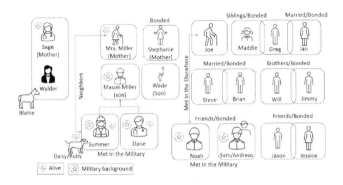

ACKNOWLEDGMENTS

To Lauren Michael, who edited the book until it was right. Thanks for sticking with me on this journey.

To Melissa Tieszen and Amy Onest who listened to countless ideas, offered thoughtful input, read the book countless times, and kept me on my toes.

To Cal Schlotzhauer, my dad, who had the best description of Hell I have ever heard, to relive your mistakes from the other side of them, through the eyes of those you hurt in life.

To my daughter Katie Albers, who let me read the book to her. She pointed out inconsistencies, unanswered questions, and added cool interesting military facts.

To Shane Anthony, 1st Lt, USAF who helped me communicate military rank, formal procedures, and accurate descriptions so it would be comfortable for readers with a connection to the US Military.

To John Denver, who wrote Country Road, and the lyrics are in the book because it is my dad's favorite song.

To Brandy, the United Airlines First class flight attendant from SFO to Austin on 3-3-22 who said the Wi-Fi isn't working so I must have something very important to do.

As always, to my sweet husband Paul Albers, who supports me in all that I do, challenges me to be my best, and loves me no matter what. 1434!

RESOURCES

988 Suicide and Crisis Lifeline | Federal Communications Commission (fcc.gov)

From the website:

Today, "988" is the three-digit, nationwide phone number to connect directly to the 988 Suicide and Crisis Lifeline. By calling or texting 988, you'll connect with mental health professionals with the 988 Suicide and Crisis Lifeline, formerly known as the National Suicide Prevention Lifeline. Veterans can press "1" after dialing 988 to connect directly to the Veterans Crisis Lifeline which serves our nation's Veterans, service members, National Guard and Reserve members, and those who support them. For texts, Veterans should continue to text the Veterans Crisis Lifeline short code: 838255.

Rabbi Sharon Kleinbaum Sermon at BCC Feb. 22, 2019 - YouTube

Military Funeral Honors Ceremony & Requests · Military OneSource

Jewish Funerals and Burial | Shiva, Jewish Mourning

Sudden Unexplained Death in Childhood | SUDC Foundation

https://sudc.org/

National Domestic Violence Hotline, PO Box 90249, Austin, TX 78709 800-799-7233

www.thehotline.org

Hours: 24/7. Languages: English, Spanish and 200+ through interpretation service

ABOUT THE AUTHOR

Deborah Albers

Deborah Albers is a social responsibility expert and has traveled the world teaching and speaking. Deborah is a member of the Society of Children's Book  Writers and Illustrators (SCBWI). Through the Paul and Deborah Albers Foundation, she and her husband have supported many charities that served as an inspiration for her books. She lives with her husband in Austin Texas. Her two daughters, and three grandchildren are never far away.

BOOKS IN THIS SERIES

St. David's

St. David's Wylder is an 18-year-old girl whose life is interrupted by death. In the afterlife she realizes that there is a much bigger battle raging than what she was aware of. She must find a way to unite people of all ages, races, genders, and walks of life, to fight the ultimate battle: Good vs. Evil. Before she can do that, she must first unite the residents of St. David's to conquer the hate in her own cemetery.

Escape From St. David's

Escape from St. David's - Book1 Wylder is an 18-year-old girl who finds herself in St. David's, the local cemetery in her small country town. When she meets a young girl who's been at St. David's for 200 years, she is shown a secret passage to another world. Wylder longs for the life that was taken from her, but each time she tries to leave St. David's without her new friend, she finds herself in a terrifying place.

Wylder does not know she is just one of the

warriors who will be needed in the ultimate battle of good vs. evil. Will she acquire the skills necessary to unlock the secrets to the afterlife before it's too late?

The Devil's Playground

The Devil's Playground - Book 2 When the secret passageway to heaven in St. David's collapses, Wylder sees her friend Greg is trapped on the wrong side. As she plans to rescue her friend, Greg discovers a plot from the devil to take over heaven. Together they must recruit souls to help fight for an eternity of love and peace. They will need an army of GOOD to win the battle against EVIL, a battle to the death. But first, they must find a way to get Greg out of St. David's.

Good Vs. Evil

When it comes to the End Times, no one knows if religion has it right, or what will admit a soul into heaven. Wylder discovers that the ticket into heaven may not be the religion of a soul, but the character of that soul.

Every soul is given a choice, in life and in death. Some will choose to do good and risk everything to save humanity. Some will stand by and do nothing in the face of evil.

Everyone must choose a side, winner take all.

Made in the USA
Middletown, DE
15 August 2022

71454661R00210